ESCAPE TO SEAHAVEN BAY

NICOLA MAY

Storm

ALSO BY NICOLA MAY

Seahaven Bay

How Do I Tell You?

How to Fix a Broken Heart

Cockleberry Bay

The Corner Shop in Cockleberry Bay

Meet Me in Cockleberry Bay

The Gift of Cockleberry Bay

Christmas in Cockleberry Bay

Ferry Lane Market

Welcome to Ferry Lane Market

Starry Skies in Ferry Lane Market

Rainbows End in Ferry Lane Market

A Holiday Romance in Ferry Lane Market

Ruby Matthews

Working it Out

Let Love Win

Star Fish

The School Gates

Better Together

Love Me Tinder

Christmas Evie

Escape to Futtingbrook Farm

haven (noun) a place of safety or refuge: *a haven for wildlife. A haven in times of trouble: a haven of peace and tranquillity*

'There is a voice that doesn't use words. Listen.'
— Rumi

For Harry and Jeff – my safe haven

<h1 style="text-align:center">ONE</h1>

Rita Jory sat at her desk in the study surrounded by curling receipts, unopened bank statements, and a growing sense of dread. She was sorting through bills she couldn't afford to pay, juggling minimum payments on credit cards that had long since lost their shine. Living on credit and dust, she thought as tears sprang to her eyes. The five thousand pounds she'd squirrelled away, her 'just-in-case' safety net, had all but vanished.

With her head in her hands, she let out a long, tired breath. Something had to give.

She couldn't keep pretending this was sustainable. The farmhouse, beautiful as it was, was too big, too quiet and too expensive for one. The idea of selling up flickered at the edge of her mind, unwelcome and frightening. She looked around at the familiar, worn furniture in the study that had once been the farm office, the framed family photos on the shelves, the view of the fields from the window by the desk. This place held everything, memories, love, mistakes. Letting it go would feel like losing the last thread connecting her to a life that once made sense. It would feel like letting Archie down.

She stood abruptly. She had to get out, clear her head, breathe in some sea air, talk to someone with two legs. Anything to stop the rising panic from settling in.

The blue Suzuki Jimny coughed into life with a familiar judder, the engine giving its usual unnerving shake before settling into a throaty purr. Twenty years old and proud of it, the car was squat, boxy, and slightly battered. One wing mirror was held on with duct tape, the paint had faded to the colour of a stormy sky, and the interior smelled faintly of wet dog. Archie had always said he'd buy her a new car, but Rita didn't want one, saw no point. Plus, she loved the quirkiness of Jimmy the Jimny. She checked the petrol gauge, relieved to see she wouldn't need to fill up just yet – another expense she could ill afford right now.

Archie's much newer Land Rover still sat parked behind the hay barn. Despite everything, she couldn't bring herself to sell it. It still smelled of him inside and besides, as Archie always used to say, 'It's always good to have a back-up.'

He had always been a sensible husband in so many ways. Practical, measured, a man who rarely acted on impulse. That steady nature had rubbed off on her over the years, quietly taming her spontaneity. Was that a good thing? She wasn't sure anymore.

Which was why the convertible he'd bought himself had taken her by surprise. A shiny, impractical flash of mid-life madness that didn't fit the man she knew. She couldn't understand how it figured into all his carefully laid plans, but, as always, he'd schmoozed her into it with that easy charm. He'd promised moonlit drives along the cliff path, the roof down, the wind in their hair, and a bottle of something fizzy waiting in the boot.

She turned the radio up loud to drown out the familiar, exhausting whirl of *what ifs* circling her mind like greedy gulls. What if she'd been firmer, forbidden him from buying it altogether? What if she'd chased after him that day instead of letting the door slam shut on his obvious anger? What if he'd just stayed five more minutes, long enough to cool off, long enough to come back? What if he'd taken a different route? What if she'd made him a coffee, distracted him, delayed him, anything? He might still be here now.

As Rita's old jeep rolled out of the gravel drive of Seahaven Farm, tyres crunching over the potholes, and turned left onto the lane that wound its way the ten-minute journey to the harbour, she tried to push her muddled thoughts out of her mind. It was ridiculous to live somewhere so beautiful, in a place she loved, and not be able to appreciate it, nor make ends meet. She had to find a way. The road snaked steeply downhill, flanked by hedgerows, bright green and heavy with springtime, and fields that sloped lazily toward the glinting sea. With the windows down, she turned the music up and breathed deeply, inhaling the salty air whipping through the car. For the first time in a while, Rita felt a moment of much-needed peace.

The harbour at Seahaven Bay really was picture-postcard beautiful. A horseshoe of weathered stone wrapped protectively around a jumble of fishing boats, yachts, and a couple of old trawlers which, when on fishing downtime, served as a favourite perch for the odd cormorant. Tangled ropes and salt-stained buoys lined the quay, where lobster pots were stacked beside coils of sun-bleached rope. Gulls wheeled overhead, crying out as if they owned the place. Which, in a way, Rita thought, they did.

On the corner where the cobbled quay met the narrow, winding road up through the town stood the Winking Pilchard, Seahaven Bay's oldest pub. Despite its peeling teal paint, tile-slipped roof, and empty hanging baskets waiting for their summer injection of colour, it still remained a firm favourite with locals and tourists alike.

From the first time she had holidayed here as child, Rita had loved the hustle and bustle of Seahaven Bay, with its harbour the centre point, flanked by narrow, winding, and sloping streets and even steeper stone stairways. A plethora of businesses new and old, including the Pasty Palace, Batter Days and Fiona's Fudge endlessly flogged their wares.

Dotted amid the shops and eateries were street-facing houses and short, pebbled alleyways leading to secret low doorways.

Betty's Tearoom had been a regular haunt for Rita and her children through the years. Painted a cheerful buttercup yellow, the harbourside café's awning fluttered like a gingham flag in the wind.

Betty Bloom, with her white hair, now dyed a bright pink, ran the place like a flour-dusted general. She'd been baking in Seahaven Bay longer than Rita had been alive and swore she could judge a person's character by how they prepared and devoured a cream tea. Woe betide anyone who put cream on a scone first on her shift!

As Rita walked by, Betty waved frantically from the large bay window to usher her inside.

'All right, my lover.' Betty's soft Cornish accent soothed Rita's frayed nerves as she stepped into the café. 'I was thinking of you just yesterday and wondered how you were getting on. Even said to my Derek, "I haven't seen that Rita Jory for a while," and here you are.'

Rita made her way to the counter. 'Aw, that's nice to hear and wow, it smells extra good in here today.'

Betty, standing behind the counter, expertly slid a tray of plump and golden scones into the display case, then wiped her hands down her apron, smiling gently. 'How are you coping, darling? I bet you miss the big fella, like we all do.'

'I'm all right.' Rita sighed. 'Grief's a funny thing. I'll be OK for days then something, a song, or an expression Archie might have used, will just trigger me and I'll start howling like a banshee. Last time it was "Fields of Gold", would you believe. Sting was on the radio. And suddenly I could picture Archie, laughing in the field behind the barn, grass in his teeth, pretending to be a scarecrow. And there I was, sobbing like Robbie had left Take That again.'

Betty shook her head in sympathy. 'I can't even imagine. Derek grinds me down most of the time, and – husband number four or not – I'd miss the old bugger if he weren't here.' She blew out a huge, exaggerated breath. 'Well, the good news, young Rita, is that you're just in time for a hot cuppa and one of these.' The pink-haired woman pointed to a fresh batch of cinnamon buns. 'On me. And I insist.'

Rita smiled. 'And I will gladly take you up on that offer, thank you.'

Rita sat whilst the affable baker served a giggly young couple who were clasping hands across their table as if they couldn't bear to let go. Rita watched them with a quiet smile, and a touch of heartache.

Betty, tea towel over her shoulder, brought over the tea and tasty pastry and with a massive 'oof' sat her ample frame down opposite Rita. She lowered her voice. 'Look at those two, either having an affair or just met. No normal couple would be that close once they realise men and women shouldn't really share a bath-room, let alone a whole life together.'

Thinking that maybe Betty and her mother-in-law should do a comedy double act, Rita shoved a bit of pastry in her mouth and shut her eyes at the deliciousness of it.

Betty smiled at the sight of her enjoying her fresh bakes.

'I see a Reformer Pilates studio has opened on Fore Street,' Rita said, taking a tentative sip of her tea ready for the full rundown.

'Ooh yes.' Betty's expression became animated. 'Very plush. Not sure why they had to show off with all those balloons outside, though. Caught a glimpse of the woman who runs it – has eyebrows on her hairline and dressed head to toe in pink Lycra. She's come down from Liverpool, evidently.'

Rita couldn't help but laugh.

Betty lowered her voice again. 'So, forgive me for being so ancient, but what exactly is it? I've heard of Pilates, of course, but the "Reformer" bit makes it sound even posher. I was going to say I'd better get with the lingo if they are going to be coming in here, but the people who go there will probably only eat tofu and drink milk straight from the teat of a donkey like those Egyptians used to do.'

'Machines.' Rita shook her head at Betty's bluntness and grinned. 'Apparently, it's all about strengthening your core and stretching muscles, but with a bit of fancy equipment.'

Betty raised an eyebrow. 'Oh, I tried one of those wobbly plates once. My tits went so berserk I had to get off for fear of giving myself two black eyes.'

Rita laughed again. 'What are you like! It's meant to be brilliant exercise. I might try it when I get some time.' Rita didn't dare add 'and money' for fear of the Seahaven Bay Facebook Gossip Group getting hold of that news flash.

'Fortunes to be made in this fitness lark now, aren't there?' Betty said as she stood up slowly. 'Maybe it's time *I* got into Lycra and started flogging glutes instead of gluten.'

Rita's shoulders shook. 'Please don't do that.'

Betty was undeterred. 'Evidently, charging twenty-eight quid a session, they are. I could use something to straighten this old back of mine. Do you think they'd let me come along for a trial?'

Rita nodded. 'I expect they'll be keen to get locals through the door.'

Betty's eyes shone playfully. 'I'd be better off getting my Derek to strap one of those physio resistance bands to the clothesline and shout encouragement at me from the patio.'

And with that, both women burst into fits of laughter – even the doe-eyed couple looked up to wonder at what was so funny.

TWO

Rita had told herself the trip into Seahaven was for a bit of human contact and some basic supplies: eggs, butter and teabags, for her, and apple cider vinegar for the chickens. But deep down, she knew the real reason for her visit: she needed a book.

Lately, her mind had been so jumpy. She'd started to read three novels and finished none, each one abandoned for a worry or dark thought and left dog-eared beside the bed. Reading used to soothe her, help her feel like herself. It was the quietest kind of healing, the kind that asked nothing, expected nothing, just let her rest inside someone else's world for a while.

The bell above the door of Sail Away chimed as she stepped inside, the hush of the little bookshop soothing her as it always did.

Jude Finch looked up from behind the counter, his half-moon glasses sliding down his nose in a way that somehow felt intentional. His hair, already silvering, gave him a gravitas beyond his thirty plus years. Today, he wore cropped navy trousers, vintage trainers, and a Breton jumper, making Rita's indigo jeans, black hoodie, light rain jacket and muddy trainers look especially scruffy by comparison.

He'd arrived in the village six months ago, and as quite often happened in Seahaven Bay, his story quietly passed around the locals. Big London job, big flat, big break-up with a long-term boyfriend. Burned-out and broken-hearted, he'd packed up his curated coffee table books and swapped Soho for the sea.

And now he ran Sail Away, a bookshop stroke literary hideaway, with handwritten recommendations, a back corner that perfectly fitted two immaculate Lloyd Loom chairs, and a fancy coffee machine.

The locals had taken to him with curious affection. He was clearly not a local, but there was something about Jude's presence that made people instinctively soften. Maybe it was the way he listened. Or maybe it was the quiet sadness he carried, the kind worn by people who'd left their old lives hoping to outrun their feelings, only to find they'd packed them too.

'Long time, no see, Rita. I can't even guess what you'd want to be disappearing into at the moment,' he offered gently.

Brushing a crumb off her jacket, she smiled weakly. 'Something not too heavy, as yes, I'm finding it hard to concentrate for long on anything at the moment.'

He tilted his head. 'Leave it with me.'

He disappeared into his neat shelves, returning a moment later with a copy of *Wild* by Cheryl Strayed.

'It's not a recent release. It's about walking.' He handed it to her. 'But really, it's about grief and losing your way, and then clawing it back through nature, solitude, and sheer bloody determination.'

'I've heard of it.' Rita turned it over in her hands. 'Reese Witherspoon was in the film adaption wasn't she? It's been on my virtual list of must-get-round-to-reading for years.'

'Then take this as a sign.' Jude smiled.

Mrs Munroe, Rita's former cleaner and Queen of the Seahaven Bay Facebook Gossip Group, had said in her thick Cornish accent, 'There's a smell of a past unknown about that lad.' But Rita, not one for gossip herself, always took Jude as she had found him. Past or no past he was polite and an incredible bookseller. It was the personal touch that always got to her. It was the way she believed all bookshops ought to be.

She was just heading back up the hill to the car park when her eyes and ears were drawn to a bunch of neon pink balloons and the thumping music being piped from the external speakers of the Seahaven Bay Reformer Studio.

Curiosity getting the better of her, Rita pushed the door open to be immediately hit by two things: Britney Spears' 'Toxic' blaring from hidden speakers, and the gleam of a fully mirrored studio. One wall was boldly branded with a LONG SPINE, STRONG MIND slogan, scrawled like it had been written in pink lipstick. Inside, four red-faced Pilates devotees lay on their backs on Reformer machines, looking one shaky exhale away from total collapse as they finished their session.

'Engage your cores, you floppy tarts! You'll thank me when your arse looks like Margot Robbie's!' a Liverpudlian accent instructed.

Rita tried to disguise her grin as the teacher spotted her in the mirror, swung round and ushered her to sit on one of two balance balls by the reception desk.

Once the sweaty ladies had left, the woman approached Rita in a waft of delicious grapefruit-scented perfume. Betty had been spot on with the woman's description, for she was in head-to-toe lilac Lycra, her bleach-blonde hair scraped into a high ponytail. Her lips were like plump cushions and her eyebrows so sharp they could slice through ham. Her perfectly fake-tanned body was firm and toned.

'Jesus, babe, you look knackered. Fancy a cuppa?'

Rita found herself nodding at the instant friendliness of the woman, who returned swiftly with two pink mugs of builders' tea. She pulled up another balance ball and perched next to her.

'So, this is me. Jilly Cooper. Not as talented or as loaded as the great Dame, God rest her gloriously filthy soul, but probably just as raucous. So, I take it you're interested in having a little go at one of my torture sessions?'

Rita smiled. 'Rita Jory, I live up at Seahaven Farm and I'm not sure yet. Was just being nosy, to be honest.'

'Oh, Rita, that's right, it was your al fella that went over the cliff in a sports car.'

Rita recoiled in horror, then took a breath. 'Mrs Munroe's been in, I'm guessing.'

Jilly took a sip of tea. 'Her daughter.'

Rita nodded knowingly.

'Good and bad, this gossip lark, for me, anyway. Spreads the word of the new business at least, but I'm not one for airing my dirty laundry in public and there's been plenty of that in the past.' Jilly's laugh was a humorous cackle. She stood up and put her mug on the reception desk. 'I'm so sorry for your loss and totally with you on the grief bit. My old man, stupid, useless bastard, only went and offed himself, didn't he?'

Rita shifted more uncomfortably on the ball. 'As in...'

'They found him hanging in his cell.'

Rita's eyes widened. 'Shit, Jilly. I'm...'

'Don't say sorry.' She waved her manicured hand. 'He made his bed. Or didn't, as usual. Lazy sod. Got put inside and left me with a half-finished extension and some really scary-looking men knocking at my door asking if I knew where *it* was hidden. Anyway.' Jilly sniffed. 'I didn't, or I'd be in the Costa del Caribbean rather than the Costa del Cornwall by now. So...' she wiped her brow with her pink sweatband, 'health is where it's at now. Wellness, babe. Bodies. Only good energy allowed.'

Rita smiled. 'Well, you're a fabulous advert for this place; you look amazing.'

'Thanks, Reets! Those jabs, you know, the ones half the planet seem to be on. Well, turns out they're a miracle. Three stone, I've done. I can see my knees again.' Jilly jiggled her arms. 'Still got the bingo wings, mind you. But I'm on a mission. Pilates saved me, I swear. Something about all that breathing and stretching... it sort of pulls your soul back into place.'

'Seahaven Bay has a habit of doing that, anyway.' Rita stood up and smiled.

'Don't you be telling everyone that, girl; I've got a business to run.' Jilly grinned. 'And sorry I didn't even ask how you're doing. Like 'em or not, we loved them once.'

'I miss him, you know.' Rita sniffed. 'He was a pain in the arse sometimes, my Archie, but he was my pain in the arse.'

'Tough, innit? But I'm not done. We may be widows but looks at us, girl. Still hot to trot. I'm after a man with huge wealth and no emotional baggage. Or, failing that, one with a huge cock and a Louis Vuitton luggage set.'

Rita laughed aloud.

'Laughing suits you, girl.' Jilly winked.

The music changed to Madonna. Jilly drained her tea.

'Come on. Hop on one of the machines; I'll show you how it works.'

THREE

Seahaven Farm was a traditional farmhouse, standing proud against the rolling landscape of the rugged north coast of Cornwall. Its huge arched wooden front door had been pushed open by generations of families and time. Weathered grey stone walls were softened by a vibrant passionflower, planted by Archie for their tenth anniversary, its inquisitive tendrils having since crept their way right across the façade. Beyond the circular courtyard, there were low stone outbuildings: the former tack room now an animal food store, and the stables – not used since their daughter Sennen became a teenager and got bored of mucking out – had become Archie's work room. A vegetable patch, once Rita's pride and joy, had also gone slightly to the worms and the greenhouse needed at least one glass panel replacing. Trees in the fertile-soiled orchard needed pruning and further on from the high-grassed pen where her beloved goats grazed like eccentric lawnmowers was the now-uninhabited High Meadow. It was, however, the huge, empty, former cow barn that remained the family's elephant in the room.

Back from her harbour visit, Rita stood at the edge of the overgrown orchard, cradling a cup of tea, and surveying the place. A light breeze whispered through the blossoming fruit trees. Birds chattered their delight at the warm early spring evening. To the west, the sky showed off its glory in hues of oranges, reds and pinks.

Gazing way beyond the perimeter of the crumbling grey stone wall, she tuned in to the slow, rhythmic sigh of waves against the cliffs below. A direct contrast to her thoughts of late, which often swirled around her head like a whirling dervish.

It was funny, Rita thought, how nothing else had changed. That the world still spun. The cockerel still crowed, and the chickens still clucked. The goats, amusing, stubborn creatures that they were, still knocked their feed buckets over at precisely 7 a.m.

Unexpected things got to her. The absence of the radio humming in Archie's workshop or the familiar groan as he tugged on his boots. Even his maddening habit of leaving mugs in the greenhouse. No more. All gone. Gone forever.

The farm had always been *his* dream. *She* had married into it.

And now, standing here with forty-five years on the life clock, what was she left with? Twenty-five acres of half-wild land, four goats, four chickens, a dilapidated farmhouse, twins (who'd already fled the nest), an eccentric mother-in-law (who would *never* flee the nest), more sympathy cards in a drawer than money in the bank, a dog called Henry and Nigel the cockerel.

She took a sip of tea. Cold. Of course it was.

Rita's dad had always believed that their lives had already been written. The night she met Archie Jory seemed to prove that. *She*, an impressionable young Londoner on a girls' surfing holiday. *He*, the handsome, tall, broad-shouldered Cornish farmer, ten years her senior, out on the town with his mates.

Rita and her pals had originally planned to go to a live comedy night at the local cinema-cum-theatre that night, but when they arrived, there weren't enough seats for all of them. The only appealing alternative was a fiddler playing sea shanties in the Winking Pilchard.

It had been lust at first sight and the rest, as they say, was history.

The honeymoon period had been dreamy. Due to Archie's farm commitments, every other weekend, Rita had religiously commuted down to Seahaven Farm from her family home in Bethnal Green. But the travelling became too much to sustain, so on Archie's insistence and without any regret, it hadn't taken her long to throw her manic city marketing manager job to the wind and move down to the peace and beauty of Seahaven Bay. There, with love as her guide, she had easily adjusted to the smell of manure, the early mornings, and the endless small talk about milk and crop prices, because looking after the farm was his passion and *he* was hers.

Oh, how she had adored big Archie Jory and his even larger infectious personality.

With a huge sigh, wishing she could get the big man out of her head, Rita tipped her cold tea onto the grass and looked out over the ever-changing vista which never once bored her.

Seahaven Bay truly was an idyllic setting, where countless visitors flocked for the wild beauty of the landscape, the crashing surf, and the kind of stillness that made you breathe a little deeper.

With its breathtaking view overlooking the bay, one of her daughter's mates had described the farm's High Meadow as 'heaven on earth'. Rita had quietly agreed with Morag. This place always had been that. And now, more than ever, the meadow was her sanctuary for peaceful contemplation.

Many a night when Rita and Archie first got together, they had taken a picnic up there, occasionally even making love under the stars. Yes, this farm was an idyll, a safe haven that she had been lucky enough to live in for the past twenty-five years. The thought of imagining her life anywhere else was just too hard to bear. She'd never expected to have to imagine it – until Archie's death she'd had no idea that the farm's finances were in such a mess, and despite the hours she'd spent trawling through paperwork, she still couldn't work out how Archie had managed to get them into quite so much debt.

Henry the labrador gently nudged at her knee. At eight years old, his once jet-black coat had softened to a gentle charcoal, with a distinguished smattering of grey around his muzzle. He followed Rita everywhere, his heavy paws padding softly behind her, dependable as the tide.

Leaning down, she gently scratched behind his soft ears. 'What are we going to do, old boy? Just what are we going to do?'

The ageing canine let out a low and familiar reassuring sigh.

That evening, Rita set down a bowl of steaming vegetable soup onto the heavy wooden coffee table, its surface crowded with a stack of well-loved books, the one she had purchased earlier placed on top of the pile, waiting for when she was ready to pick it up and start reading again. She loved this little room. It had always been her sanctuary. *The Den. Mum's Den.* A single round window looked out over the sea, framing the shifting colours and moods of the Cornish countryside and coast below. From the cushioned seat beneath it, she would sometimes sit for hours, reading or watching the weather roll in, wild and beautiful.

The house felt different, though, since Archie's passing. The air stiller somehow, the quiet deafening. The marital bed still felt like a safe place to snuggle down in, but since the accident, she hadn't been able to bring herself to sit in the big lounge, with its low-slung beams and vast inglenook fireplace. There were too many memories, not just in the many photographs of the family but also in her mind, of her and Archie spending cosy evenings in there, cuddled into the sofa side by side.

Shifting the lopsided pottery vase that her daughter had made in primary school out of the way of the television, Rita sank herself into the familiar, worn two-seater sofa and was just beginning to tuck into her soup when her mobile rang.

She groaned softly, set the bowl on the coffee table, and fumbled for the phone.

'Hello, darling.' Her voice was scratchy with tiredness.

'Mum?'

'Sennen, darling?' Rita gave a weary laugh. 'Not sure who else you thought might be picking up my phone at this hour.'

'You sounded different.' Her daughter's voice lifted. 'Are you OK? Just checking in as usual.'

'Knackered, that's all. But I'm fine, everything's fine. Animals fed. Henry is asleep next to me.' Rita gently played with the labrador's soft ears. 'He's been noticeably quiet this evening.'

Sennen's voice lowered. 'Maybe he's missing Dad, too.'

'I'm sure he is, but we can't change that, can we, Sen?' Rita replied tightly.

'Mum. Listen to me. The lady from the grief charity says that it will do us all good as a family to talk about it. We need to.'

Rita sighed. 'Need, want, should, could. Not tonight, eh, love.'

On hearing her second-born take a deep intake of breath at the end of the phone, Rita twitched uncomfortably.

'I miss him so much, Mum.'

'I know, darling.' Rita ineffectively rubbed dog hairs off the sofa arm. 'Have you heard from that brother of yours lately?'

'No. You know what Thom's like now. Only calls when he wants something.' Sennen paused. 'I miss him too, Mum.'

Rita's heart squeezed. Of the twins, Thom had always been the strong, silent one. Tall, handsome and forthright, the absolute image of his father. When he was younger, he and Archie had been inseparable on the farm. From feeding lambs at dawn to fixing fences at dusk, he had trailed after his dad like a small apprentice. Archie's accident had carved a hole straight through him. Rita still believed it was grief, not ambition, that had driven him to London straight afterwards to work as a salesman for a large IT company. Despite her selfish attempts at soft persuasion, he'd had no interest in staying and getting his hands dirty on the land without his father beside him. And since then, he'd rarely looked back; calls had become practical, sporadic, and always on his terms.

Sennen, beautiful and flighty, had always dreamed of being in event management. She had flown the nest at eighteen to study it at university and was now living in Reading with her partner, running her own wedding-planning business.

'I miss him too, darling,' Rita murmured. 'Maybe when things are less raw for us all, we'll get our Thom back.' Rita reached for the remote control. 'Are you and Alex OK, darling?'

Sennen sighed. 'It's leading up to silly season, so I'm manic, but I think we're fine.'

'Look at us Jory girls and our flagrant use of the word "fine".' Rita dipped her finger into her soup and put it to her lips. 'Come down for Easter, Alex included, of course. It's a couple of weekends away, I think, isn't it?'

'I'd love that. I'm actually working on a wedding in Dorset on the Good Friday, so I'll be halfway down to you anyway.'

'I'd love that too.' Rita smiled. 'OK, I'm going. I don't want my soup to get cold. Talk to you soon, darling.'

'Mum, before you go, have you watched the new *White Lotus* series? This one's set in a health retreat somewhere exotic. Maybe I should find out if it's a real place and we could go together.'

Rita, still not daring to confess to her daughter that she was in such dire straits she couldn't even afford her favourite shower gel, replied brightly, 'Brilliant. Yes, we watched the ones with Jennifer Coolidge in. Hilarious! Had me and your dad in hysterics.' Rita coughed to rid the lump that had formed in the back of her throat. 'Haven't seen the new series, though.'

Sennen's voice wobbled. 'That's you sorted for tonight, then.'

'Sennen... Please don't worry about me. The locals have been nothing short of wonderful. I've got enough fish pies in the freezer to keep me going for at least a year. And your granny and Henry are company of sorts. Although we know how much my dear mother-in-law likes to hide herself away in that annexe of hers.'

Sennen laughed. 'Dear Granny Hilda, she does make me laugh. Love you, Mum.'

'Love you too.'

FOUR

The next morning Rita headed out to a grey March sky which suddenly gave out rain in thick, unyielding sheets. Even Henry wasn't moving from his bed by the Aga. With a heavy sigh, she headed back inside, pulled on her trusty old raincoat, the one with the frayed hood, swapped trainers for wellies, grabbed her wicker egg basket and set off into the downpour to tackle her early morning chores. Noticing the light on in Hilda's annexe reminded her that she still needed to drop off the laundry she'd recently done for her.

With a sack of dried food over her shoulder, she scurried across the courtyard towards the goat field, where she could hear them kicking their cans for food. Whinnies of protest drifted on the wind from the horses at neighbouring Hawthorn Acre, displeased by the sudden precipitation.

On seeing Rita approaching, the goats' comforting, soft *maa*s soon changed to high-pitched, demanding bleats that filled the rain-fresh air with energy. In a hopeless attempt to shield her face from the rain, Rita tugged her hood down until it nearly met her nose. 'Morning, your majesties,' she trilled, squinting through the torrent. 'Breakfast is served.'

The goats stared at her, unblinking, their rectangular pupils giving an unsettling, almost alien expression. No matter how many times she'd fed, herded, or wrestled them out of the vegetable patch, and as much as she'd grown a fondness for them, she still couldn't get used to that eerie, side-glancing stare.

The four, Elizabeth, Camilla, Mary and Anne – were all does of a similar age.

Now climbing over each other in hungry anticipation, the drenched quartet snuffled eagerly at the goat pellets in their tins, their beady eyes already fixed on the apple pieces Rita had begun scattering around their enormous grassy pen. She had never known animals so greedy, but their ridiculous antics and constant humour more than made up for their mischievous traits. Not having the head space, time, or money at the moment to breed them, they had become expensive pets – pets that Rita could barely afford but just couldn't bear to part with.

Rita held up the pellet bag and shook its final contents into the pen. As she was folding it up ready to dispose of, her eyes were suddenly drawn to a sharp streak of red, a fresh-looking cut, just above one of her girls' ankles. 'Aw. Camilla, what have you done now, sweetheart?'

Realising she'd have to go in and investigate, Rita hoisted herself onto the top of the splintered wooden fence and with a whispered, 'You can do it,' she swung one leg awkwardly over. As she tried to balance, she felt herself wobble. Arms flailing for dignity, she let out a sharp cry and half fell into the pen. Ignoring both her antics and the worsening weather, the goats continued chewing lazily.

She managed to steady herself, just as her boots touched the earth, when a sudden flash of lightning split the sky, followed instantly by a deafening crack of thunder. The goats scattered in all directions, bleating in alarm as they tore around the pen.

In the chaos, Mary clipped the back of Rita's ankle, sending her sprawling backwards with a spectacular squelch. She landed hard on her bum, instantly drenched in a cocktail of mud, manure and rain. Her fingers went instinctively to her neck, searching, panicked, as though her necklace might simply have slipped to the side. But Archie's sapphire and diamond gift – the thirtieth birthday talisman she had clung to like a tether – was gone. Maybe she'd misplaced it before. She frantically tried to find it. But deep down she knew. Another loss. Another piece of him slipping from her grasp.

She sat there stunned, before the tears came: hot, snotty, unrelenting – born not of pain, but of bone-deep frustration and the long, raw ache of grief.

The storm vanished as swiftly as it had arrived. With a gust of sea-damp air at her back, Rita stepped into the coat-filled hallway, slammed the front door, and pulled off her filthy wellies.

The farmhouse was quiet, but as with all old homes never truly silent. Floorboards creaked. The Aga ticked. Somewhere above, a gull cried out as it wheeled past the chimney.

With a deep sigh, she headed through to the warm and welcoming heart of the farmhouse. The flagstone floor, smoothed by decades of footsteps, stretched beneath a much-scrubbed pine table scarred with knife marks and ringed by mismatched chairs. Copper pans hung from a rack above the Aga, which radiated a steady, dependable heat. A vase of bright daffodils added a splash of much-needed spring sunshine to the windowsill.

Stripping off her muddy clothes, she put them and her old raincoat straight into the washing machine and pushed the hot cycle button. As she flicked on the kettle, she stood naked for a moment, staring out of the back window over the orchard, where a post-storm mist eerily clung low to the ground.

Trying to push down the familiar wavering panic she had felt since Archie's death, she took a deep exaggerated breath. There was so much to do! The orchard was going to ruin; the goat field fence needed repairing. The vegetable garden was growing weeds on weeds. The house needed decorating. A complete sadness washed over her. It was a lot. It had been a lot. This place. This house. It had seen her through everything. Her magical courtship in her early twenties, a not-long-enough marriage, the raising of her now twenty-three-year-old twins, the premature death of her father-in-law from a sudden heart attack. Her parents' deaths. The laughter of summer guests, and the tears from terrible crop years. Beloved pets and livestock had come and gone. Life had come and gone as if in an instant. Then, six months previously. The accident. Followed by the insurmountable grief and anger that she hadn't quite learned how to let go of.

She fed a hungry Henry then made her way slowly upstairs to the bathroom. As the bath filled, Rita studied her reflection in the full-length mirror. At five foot six, she was a reasonably toned size twelve. Her finger traced the faint line of her caesarean scar – a quiet reminder of an exceedingly difficult birth. Grey roots peeked through her wavy, light brown hair, which just skimmed her shoulders. Her eyebrows were out of shape. The skin on her cheeks dry. Oh, to be able to book herself a regular facial like she used to.

She leaned in closer to examine her face and, without warning, thought of Archie behind her. His strong arms wrapped tightly around her. His tall, six-foot frame leaning down to kiss the back of her neck, an unspoken invitation that always led to something more. He had been so handsome, and he knew it, but never in a showy way. He had got his quiet confidence from his mother, a woman who taught him to stand tall, speak kindly, and never need to boast. That lopsided smile of his always hinted at some private joke, but he was never a flirt. His dark hair had stayed thick and strong, not a grey in sight, as if ageing had politely passed him by. And those green eyes, always watching. They'd shared a great sex life: intimate and attentive. Even when the kids were young, they carved out time for each other. Their monthly 'date night' was a constant. Even if they couldn't get a babysitter, they would cosy up in the big lounge, with a bottle of wine and a takeaway.

They had a long-running joke between them: Archie had nursed a not-so-secret crush on Keeley Hawes as Louisa Durrell in

The Durrells, and insisted Rita was her spitting image. Rita would just laugh and say it was a pity he didn't look like Spiros, Louisa's ruggedly handsome love interest in the show. Ironic that, just like Louisa, she was now managing her own dilapidated farmhouse and menagerie, only without the kids at home.

She sighed at her reflection. She hadn't had her hair cut or coloured once since Archie had passed. As for the facials she used to enjoy, these days her only luxuries were a dab of cheap face cream and a smudge of Vaseline on her lips.

Despite the chaos of farm life, she had always made an effort with her appearance. People often said she looked young for her age. She and Archie, without ever trying, had been a *beautiful* couple. She'd put it down to fresh air, constant movement, and a life that had once been filled, mostly with happiness.

But today, with her coccyx twinging from the earlier fall and the weight of the world pressing down on her, she felt she looked more like Eddy from *Absolutely Fabulous* after a three-day champagne bender than the elegant Keeley Hawes.

Turning slightly, she lifted her still perky breasts with both hands and gave a small, approving nod. She then homed in on the dried mud smeared across her face, hands, and somehow even up her arms, and her thoughts turned to the tranquillity of the health retreat on the *White Lotus* programme she had watched the night before. Clearly in need of an escape, she had also recently watched a series about luxurious hotels around the world and how at one of them in the Caribbean, mud wraps were a huge part of their offering as well as pampering their guests with lavender-scented towels, monogrammed slippers, and breakfasts delivered on floating trays in private infinity pools. Oh, how she could do with a holiday. Or maybe it wasn't a holiday she was after; she just wanted to run away from this mess.

But running away wasn't the answer. If she wanted to stay at Seahaven Farm she needed to act, and soon. Finding an office job of some sort had crossed her mind, but after twenty-five years away she wasn't sure she had the technical skills, or that it would even pay enough to drag her out of the mire. She'd also considered sprucing up a few farmhouse bedrooms to offer B&B, renting out the top field... or even opening a children's petting farm.

But in the midst of grief, nothing had stuck.

She was stuck.

FIVE

There was something about a Sunday, even on a farm where animals still needed feeding and chores never truly stopped, that felt different. Softer somehow. The air seemed quieter, the light gentler, as if the day itself were asking for a pause. Rita called it her 'Sunday feeling'. It wasn't about rest, especially when there were chickens squawking for their breakfast and the goats were kicking their tins. But there was a slowness to it, a rhythm that invited reflection.

The sunshine that had drenched the farm all week had been replaced by a dull grey sky. The hens clucked and rustled like gossiping aunties the moment Rita unlatched the gate. Nigel, the resident cockerel, strutted forward like he owned the place. With his glossy feathers, ridiculous swagger, and a comb that flopped to one side like a drunken hat, he gave her the usual once-over before letting out a proud, unnecessary crow.

Archie always said that, since they were only after eggs and not chicks, Nigel wasn't strictly needed. 'He's only really there to keep the ladies company and protect them a bit,' he'd argue, threatening to get rid of him. 'They're perfectly safe in the covered pen from foxes and the like, and as long as you keep collecting the eggs, you won't end up with chicks.' But Rita liked Nigel's unpredictable presence on the farm, strutting about like a feathered lunatic and picking fights with his own reflection. She also liked using him as a free, albeit noisy alarm *cock*.

The Barred Rock hens were a striking bunch, their plumage patterned in smart, tidy stripes of black and white, like they'd been dressed in old-fashioned pinstripe suits. From a distance, they looked almost grey, but as they clucked and scratched through the straw, the detail in their feathers caught the light, crisp, orderly bars running from neck to tail. Their bright red combs bobbed cheerfully as they moved, a splash of colour, and their yellow legs stamped with purpose. Their eyes, sharp and knowing, missed nothing.

Rita had initially worried she wouldn't be able to name them as they looked so similar to one another, but as she got to know them, their characters soon emerged. Vera was the boss, a no-nonsense hen with a stare that could put anyone in their place. She was the one who wasted no time strutting forward to claim the first handful of feed, pecking with confident authority. Mavis was quieter but steady, the dependable type who liked to keep an eye on everyone else's business. Deirdre was the dramatic one, her feathers a little ruffled and her eyes wide as if every meal was a performance demanding attention. And then there was Blanche, sharp-tongued and cheeky, always ready to steal a morsel from the others when they weren't looking.

Rita scattered grain across the ground, smiling at their familiar chaos. She topped up a water bowl, added apple cider vinegar to a water bottle that poked through the steel wire fence, gently retrieved four warm brown eggs, then cleaned out their coop, laying down fresh, soft hay.

Rita smiled as Nigel picked, poked and strutted between his ladies. 'I should have called you Mick Jagger with that swagger.' Rita had a sudden sad pang that her beloved rooster was probably around the same age as Mick in human years. Nigel crowed again, loudly as if denouncing the absurdity of taking the moniker of a legendary rock icon.

She was just about to head back to the farmhouse when she noticed out of the corner of her eye a white streak darting up the High Meadow. Her heart lurched – it was Camilla with no sign of a cut leg now, running fast and wild toward the cliff's edge. Knowing how senseless her favourite goat could be, a cold knot of panic rose within her.

'Shit! Shit!' Rita shouted, the urgency sharp in her voice.

She set off in hot pursuit as Camilla raced ahead, little hooves skittering dangerously close to the drop.

By the time Rita had reached the top of the meadow and rounded the thick hedge of gorse, bristling with needle-like thorns and bright yellow blossoms, the goat had slowed, exhausted, and was peacefully grazing.

Relief flooded through Rita, quickly replaced by curiosity as her eyes caught sight of a faded two-man tent nestled half in the tall grass at the field's edge. A camping stove sat in front of it, a black cauldron-like pan bubbling gently on it. Archie would bellow at random campers to get off his land, but now Rita had so much on her plate, if they weren't getting in her way, she tended to just ignore them. They rarely stayed for more than a couple of nights anyway.

Then a woman appeared, crawling out of the tent as if she'd been expecting company. No make-up, no shoes, a wild tangle of blonde hair. And jeans and a sweatshirt that looked like they hadn't seen a washing machine for weeks. Despite the rough edges, her face was striking, pretty, but with sharp, sculpted angles that gave her a fierce beauty. She looked straight at Rita with dark, unreadable eyes that seemed to see through things, past the clothes, past the weather, past pretence.

'You've got a restless energy,' she said quietly, her Mancunian accent soft but steady. 'The earth feels it. I can feel it. People's pain leaves a scent on the wind. Do you understand?'

Rita blinked, caught between disbelief and an aching resonance deep inside her.

'I'm Zenya, by the way,' the woman added.

'Rita. Rita Jory. And your new landlady, it seems.' She smiled faintly.

Zenya's eyes flicked to the bubbling pot. 'The nettles up here are perfect for tea. Best picked before the sun's too high. Clears the blood, lightens the heart. Would you like a cup?'

Rita hesitated, then laughed nervously. 'No thanks.'

Her gaze wandered to a battered rucksack just inside the tent, where a deck of tarot cards peeked out from a side pocket. The top card was face up, The Tower, depicting lightning splitting a crumbling building in two.

Rita looked away quickly, a chill creeping up her spine at the image.

Zenya caught her glance and smiled faintly, not moving to hide the cards. 'I read for people sometimes,' she said quietly. 'Not to tell them their future, but to help them hear themselves. Most people already know what they need to do, but the noise of life drowns it out.'

She gestured towards the ocean below, which currently mirrored the dull and uninviting drab sky above. 'The air cleans you. The salt in the wind... it blows the grit out of your soul if you let it. The land holds you. If you listen long enough, it will tell you things.'

Rita's eyes dipped towards the tarot card on show. 'What does that one mean?'

Zenya leaned in. 'The Tower is the card of upheaval. Sudden change. Destruction of what's no longer true. Like lightning tearing down old, shaky foundations so something new can grow. It's raw, it's chaotic, but necessary. Sometimes, things need to fall apart before they can get better.'

Rita swallowed hard, the weight of those words settling deep inside her.

Zenya watched her for a long moment. The silence stretched between them, until the wild woman broke it. 'Sorry for pitching up on your land like this. I never mean to be a nuisance. And I honestly didn't think anyone would find me up here.'

'Camilla does have her uses, then.' Rita smirked, wondering if she should be more concerned about this particular trespasser, but equally feeling an unexpected pull toward the bohemian woman. 'It's OK. Come down for a real cup of my tea and a shower if you ever need one.' Rita realised her mistake and backtracked, 'Not saying that nettle tea isn't... or that... you do need one, I mean, of course.'

Zenya's smile deepened. 'Maybe, thank you.'

Rita looked to Camilla, who was still happily grazing away. 'I'd better get Houdini here back down to the herd and hope none of the others have followed her lead. They don't usually, thankfully.'

Zenya lifted her metal cup of tea aloft. 'Until our starry paths cross again, Rita Jory. This place has a way of healing, of making things right. It's going to be OK, you know. I can feel it.'

With the goat pen fixed after a fashion, chores complete and a jacket potato cooking in the Aga, Rita sat with knees curled in her window seat in the Den, a steaming cup of Earl Grey next to her. Henry was snoring on the sofa. She was knackered from her unexpected sprint earlier but also weirdly felt a sense of calm after meeting Zenya.

Her thoughts then drifted back to livelier days. She remembered the kitchen bustling with life on a Sunday, Archie carving their favourite beef joint. Yorkshire puddings the size of plates and crispy roasties, with thick gravy and fresh vegetables picked from the garden. A perfect meal amidst the comforting chaos of family chatter around the table.

And then the kids had flown the nest, leaving just her and Archie. After the initial wrench of change, they'd slipped back into the rhythm of being just the two of them, almost like a second honeymoon. They could walk around naked again, have noisy sex without worrying who might hear. Dinner could be nothing but snacks if that's what they fancied, and they could argue freely, without needing to keep their voices down.

Now she had to work out how to be alone. Solitude could be beautiful but she was too gregarious for it to sustain her. As if trying to wash away these memories, she physically shook herself and sat tall. She was only forty-five and a young forty-five at that and despite waves of grief still engulfing her, there was a spark in her eyes that refused to dim, a restless energy humming just beneath the surface. She wasn't ready to hang up her dreams or settle into quiet routines. Age was just a number; it was the spirit that counted, and hers was far from ready to fade.

Outside, gulls shrieked across the grey March sky, as if offering their approval of her thoughts. And down in his pen, a crowing Nigel was trying to fight the wind.

She opened the book Jude had pressed into her hands a few days previously with that knowing smile of his. *It's about walking,* she remembered him saying... *about grief and losing your way, and then clawing it back through nature, solitude, and sheer bloody determination.* She'd meant to just dip into it. Just a few pages. Instead, she read for an hour. And if it weren't for suddenly remembering with a jump her lunch in the Aga, she could have read for much longer.

Maybe, she thought, slipping the book onto the coffee table, it was time to start clawing things back herself.

SIX

After lunch, the skies had brightened and, craving a bit of fresh air, Rita, with book and fold-up chair in hand, made her way towards the aptly named Singing Tree. The ancient sycamore stood alone above the cliffs, its broad green canopy forever whispering and murmuring in the sea breeze. On gustier days, the branches didn't just rustle, they *sang*, a high, haunting note that carried across the fields like a hymn. Its silver-grey trunk, mottled and peeling in papery patches, looked as though it were slowly shedding the decades it had spent standing sentinel over the bay.

She noticed how the meadow could do with a mow, but that had been Stan's job and the trouble was, she couldn't exactly ask Stan. Not now that she'd let him go as a farm hand as she couldn't afford him and *especially* not now that she had heard he was working for Jago Jenken over at Hawthorn Acre.

The feud between the Jorys and the neighbouring Jenkens had been simmering for as long as Rita could remember, though she'd never been involved herself. She'd quickly learned that even uttering the Jenken name was enough to make Hilda, her mother-in-law's face harden and her voice turn to a growl. Archie, meanwhile, if she ever asked him, would just grow cagey, offer a stiff smile, and murmur, 'It's nothing to be worrying yourself about.' Which, of course, made Rita want to know about it all the more.

But she didn't have time to be worrying about any of that now. With her home on the line and not wanting to leave it, it was time to swim, or she would most certainly sink. Troubling thoughts of how she was going to pay the next wave of credit card bills engulfed her.

A sudden flutter of wings pulled her from her thoughts. A robin landed on a low branch, its russet chest puffed out as if it had something important to say. The sight of it brought an unexpected wave of calm, as though the little bird had been sent on a quiet mission to reassure her.

From where she stood, she could see a faint ribbon of smoke curling up from Zenya's cauldron in the distance, drifting lazily into the brightening afternoon sky. Oh, to be that free, Rita thought, suddenly wondering how the Mancunian had ended up in a field in Cornwall as she clearly wasn't just on holiday.

She sighed and opened her book, read a few pages, then, not able to concentrate, closed it again and stared out at the sea beyond. As her gaze moved between the horizon and Zenya's camp, the little robin returned and began hopping around near her feet, and the sentiment between the pages of *Wild* began to stir wild thoughts within her. The courage it had taken the woman to walk the Pacific Crest Trail alone, hauling her grief and her pack over mile after mile until she'd shed more than just the weight on her back was incredible. And with her mind feeling suddenly clearer, her dad's words drifted in: 'Everything is written, Reety; you just need to sometimes look for the direction signs.' What if she could create that space for herself... and, even better, for others too?

Images tumbled into her head: *The White Lotus* and that glossy hotel show she loved. The new Pilates studio in town. Sennen's tales of digital detox weekends and yoga retreats for hen parties. Morag, describing the High Meadow as 'heaven on earth'.

Betty had even told her about a woman in Polheron who

charged eighty pounds a head to lead 'transformational hikes' to Seahaven Point. The finale involved screaming into a pillow in the back of a converted camper van to 'release years of buried emotion'. People cried, journalled, then paid extra for herbal tea and a grounding crystal.

Rita had thought it was ridiculous when she'd heard about it. And yet... not. The mud, the screaming, the overpriced tea, it all pointed towards something. Not just wellness, but purpose. A softer kind of hope. And in a world spinning faster with war, wildfires and fakery, there was a real hunger for stillness, for healing. Maybe she could offer it, right here, in a setting that was already perfect.

Her thoughts picked up speed. A place for people whose lives no longer made sense. Who'd lost something, or everything, or themselves. Not five-star, swans made out of folded towels... just quiet. Kindness. Healing in mind and body, cradled by nature.

Seahaven Bay had the cliffs, the peace, the surf, the views. And when the weather played fair, Cornwall could pass for anywhere in the world. She had bedding, plenty of it. And, certainly, space for screaming.

Mad? Possibly. Reckless? Definitely. But so was surviving without Archie, but six months on, she'd managed that.

Her pulse quickened. A retreat needed a name. A website. Social media. Start-up cash... she'd cross that bridge later.

Names began swirling.

'Salty Haven,' she tried aloud – too sharp.

'Seagull's Rest' – too tired, like a postcard.

'The Sea Sanctuary' – no, sterile, like a clinic.

She rubbed her temples, trying to catch the balance between coastal calm and new beginnings. Then, almost without thinking, the words slipped out softly: *The Seahaven Bay Retreat.*

'Yes!' Rita shouted. That was it.

It felt right.

SEVEN

'A retreat? At the farm? Reet, it's only ten o'clock, don't tell me you've been on the sherry already!'

Rita smiled at the familiarity of her best mate's Cockney accent.

'One sec, Kel.' Pushing in her earbuds, she continued to scrape burnt soup from the bottom of a pan. She'd meant to soak it last night. She'd meant to do a lot of things.

'I'm serious, Kelly.' Rita sighed, throwing the pan back in the soapy water and wiping her hands with a tea towel. 'I've got the peace, I've got the quiet, the sea air, two beautiful beaches down the road, mud, plenty of mud. You can't move online without being lured to survive on just fruit juice in some fancy resort for the joylessly thin, or someone sobbing into a mug of cacao saying it's the best thing that's ever happened to them.'

'But you hate yoga, and the one and only time you did Pilates, you couldn't walk for a week.'

'I don't *hate* it,' Rita replied, defensively. 'I'm just suspicious of any activity that makes me fart involuntarily.'

They both laughed heartily.

'Rita Jory, née Brown' – Kelly reverted to the tone she reserved for both her husband and her particularly maddening beauty clients – 'I've known you since we were eleven years old. You're grieving. You're lonely. You can't just have a load of random strangers sleeping under your roof.'

'I'm not talking about random strangers. I would be selective. Hopefully, the sort not to steal the towels. Maybe even a bit... woo-woo. Saying that, they can bring their own towels. And they won't be under my roof. I was thinking more of yurts in the High Meadow than a deluxe double with a courtyard view.'

'Oh God, yes.' Kel sounded excited now too. 'That would mean having to clean. And you don't want to be doing too much of that. And I guess if they are a bit woo-woo, as you say, they won't care about luxury.'

Rita put on an affected voice. 'The natural world can become their temporary home.'

Kelly giggled. 'Look at you with your yurt talk. And what the deuces do you mean by woo-woo?'

'You know. Crystals. Meditation. Ecstatic dance.'

'Ecstatic dance? That sounds a bit pervy, if you ask me.'

Rita sat down on one of the mismatched wooden chairs at the kitchen table. Henry had been on one of his regular wanders around the farm, and barked at the window to be let in. She got up to open the door for the old labrador, while continuing to think out loud. 'Maybe I can invent some new activities. How about a bit of naked star and moon watching out in the fields? And I'm sure that there was a programme on the other Sunday showing goat yoga too? YES! That would be free to run as well! I just need to gen up on the universe and teach the girls how to balance on the back of a downward dog and we're sorted. No one ever need know they are coming to the Fawlty Towers of fitness.'

Kelly guffawed. 'If any of it involves getting naked with Jago Jenken from Hawthorn Acre then I'm in.'

'Kel! Who's being pervy now! You only met him the once, when his tractor careered through the back field, didn't you?'

Kelly laughed. 'Once met, never forgotten, that stud.'

Despite the long-standing Jory–Jenken tension, Rita had to

admit that the few times their paths had crossed, there had been something about the neighbouring farmer: a wicked sort of charm she used to ogle from afar without it ever feeling like she was misbehaving.

Rita laughed back. 'Don't let your Ron hear you say that.'

'He wouldn't even notice. He's getting on my wick at the moment. In fact, I was thinking I may come down for Easter if you don't mind. On my tod.'

'Sennen and Alex may be coming then, too, so yes, the more the merrier.'

'Perfect. My Dylan is on manoeuvres. He's not even allowed to tell me where at the moment. So, I'd love to get out of London for a break.'

'And Kel, I know it might sound mad to you, but I need to try something. The farm's not going to run itself, and the finances are... well, they're a bit of a mess. I don't want to sell it. I can't.'

'So, what are you waiting for, Gwyneth Paltrow?' Kelly laughed. 'You'd better get down that work shed and start whittling a new sign for this retreat of yours.'

Rita ended the call and slowly shook her head. Dear Kelly was practical, sharp, and allergic to nonsense. That was why she loved her. But it had been a long time since she had felt even a tiny flicker of enthusiasm about anything. The retreat idea had planted itself in her like a seed, and for the first time since the funeral, she wasn't just surviving the day. She was imagining something beyond it.

EIGHT

The next morning, Rita woke with purpose. Goats and chickens fed and Henry snoring at her feet, by 8 a.m. she'd made a strong coffee, flipped open her laptop, and sat at the kitchen table ready to start drafting a business plan. It was time to stop drifting. Time to make something of Seahaven Farm before it slipped through her fingers.

With a grimace she checked the balances of the various outstanding credit cards, took a huge slug of coffee and had barely written the words WELLNESS RETREAT – DRAFT IDEAS when there was a light tap at the door.

Zenya stood on the step, smiling politely, as though this were the most ordinary thing in the world. 'Morning, Rita. Would it be terribly rude to ask for a shower and a proper cup of tea right now?'

Rita nodded her inside. 'Come on in. I'll pop the kettle back on.'

Zenya followed her into the kitchen, glancing at the laptop. 'You're at it early.'

Rita hesitated, suddenly self-conscious. 'I've had an idea. A sort of wellness retreat. Using the barn and the High Meadow where you are. Obviously the barn will need a good scrub and clear-out and I'll have to buy stuff. Yoga mats, cushions et cetera.

Maybe a gong. Plus get in staff for all the, you know, woo-woo stuff.'

Zenya's mouth curved into a slow smile. 'Woo-woo stuff, eh.' She sat down at the table.

'Well...' Zenya tucked a loose strand of hair behind her ear. 'I major in all kinds of weirdness, so would of course be up for an interview.'

Rita laughed before she could stop herself. 'Well, how about now? I guess it doesn't hurt to get things moving!'

Zenya shrugged lightly. 'I like helping people find their way back to themselves. And this place...' She glanced towards the window, where morning sunlight spilled across the fields. 'You already know what I think of it here.'

Rita folded her arms, pretending to think it over, though her heart had already jumped ahead of her. 'All right, then. What can you offer, Ms... er...'

'Just Zenya. And energy work. Herbals. Meditation. Bit of sound healing,' she replied matter-of-factly, taking the mug Rita offered. 'I also make an excellent lemon balm tea and for the record, I'm actually a pretty good cook.'

Rita raised an eyebrow. 'Do you have a gong?'

'Not yet.' Zenya's eyes gleamed. 'But I know exactly where we can get you one.'

'Right. Let's do this properly. First question. What does the word "retreat" conjure up for you?'

Zenya's expression softened. 'A soft place to land. And maybe a gentle shove in the right direction when you're ready to learn about yourself.'

Rita stuck her bottom lip out. 'That's lovely. I may have to use that for my website, if you don't mind.'

'It'll cost ya.' Zenya grinned.

Rita laughed. 'OK, next question. Why would you want to work for the Seahaven Bay Retreat?'

Zenya's smile widened. 'Because I think it's exactly where I'm meant to be.'

Rita nodded slowly. 'Big statement, that. Care to elaborate?'

Zenya took a sip of her tea and let out a little groan of pleasure. 'Because it wouldn't feel like working. This place has got heart.' She paused. 'I can already tell that you've got heart. And I suppose...' She let out a small, self-conscious laugh. 'I could do with a bit of that myself.'

Rita felt emotion welling. 'You realise it may not always be zen and candlelit, right? I'm new to this, but I can imagine it may also be cleaning out compost loos and guests complaining.'

'That's fine.' Zenya smiled. 'People are messy. Life's messy. Doesn't mean it isn't worth pouring yourself into. And I'm more than happy to muck in from the start and help you get up and running.'

Outside, a gull screeched. Rita took another sip of coffee to disguise the sting behind her eyes. 'Bloody hell,' she murmured. 'You're good.'

Zenya laughed. 'Is that a job offer, then?'

Rita lifted her mug in cheers fashion. 'Zenya, *just* Zenya. Welcome to the team.'

NINE

A few days later, Rita pushed open the farmhouse annexe door with her hip, arms full of folded laundry, and was immediately hit by the familiar, heady mix of Chanel No. 5, cigarette smoke, and Fisherman's Friend lozenges.

'Oh, there you are,' croaked a voice from the depths of a maroon velvet recliner. 'Close the door, will you, dear. You're letting in all that optimism.'

Hilda Jory was neatly tucked beneath a crocheted rug, legs crossed at the ankle in satin slippers, a cigarette burning with casual menace in one hand and a champagne glass full of neat gin in the other. Her silver bob was, as usual, perfectly in place as she read the obituary section of the local newspaper.

'Sorry it's taken me so long to get this back to you. You all right?' Rita said as brightly as she could muster, dropping a mix of clothes and bedding on a side table.

'Still breathing, so yes, I guess so.' The old woman let out a rattling cough.

'Eleven a.m. and on the sauce already; that's even early for you, isn't it?' Rita started to clear glasses from the high table next to her mother-in-law's reclinable armchair.

'Darling girl. At eighty-six years young, I've earned the right to care not what anybody thinks about what I do and when I do it. Or for any of your madcap schemes, for that matter.'

'What do you mean? Madcap scheme.' Rita looked at her mother-in-law in shock – was she a mind-reader?

'I haven't seen that glint in your eye or that brightness in your voice since I told you I was moving out of the farmhouse and into here.' Granny Jory blew a perfect smoke ring toward the ceiling and gestured towards a stack of packages on the sofa. 'The Amazon man went to the wrong door. Three meditation cushions, some sort of gong, and an incense burner? Why don't you see if you can get hold of Charles Manson? Or how about you pop out and daub the chickens with chakra symbols whilst you're at it?'

'Hilda, I'm not starting a cult! I'm thinking more of a retreat. And how come you know so much about that kind of stuff?'

Rita moved the packages near the door so that she didn't forget them.

Hilda coughed again. 'I've always had a secret fascination for old Charlie boy, dead now but aside from him being terrifying, there was something oddly charismatic about the man. Bit like a few of my exes back in the day.'

Rita shook her head in disbelief, walked over to the open-plan kitchen, ran water into the sink and popped the glasses in to soak.

Hilda waved her iPad in the air. 'And this, dear daughter-in-law, is my modern-day encyclopaedia. I hope Mr Jobby was proud of his invention.'

'It's Jobs.' Rita smiled.

'Well, it certainly wasn't Jory, was it?' Hilda flicked her cigarette into a clam-shaped ashtray. 'Messes with the kids' heads – all this on tap, incessant knowledge. Me and my Ralphy, all we needed to know was what the weather was doing. And when to bring the cows down from the top field. Much simpler then.'

Hilda butted her cigarette and took a swig of her drink. 'Let me explain something, Rita.' *Here we go*, Rita thought, ready for one of Hilda's rambling stories. She was sure that her cantankerous mother-in-law had always thought her lazy and assumed that she had all the time in the world to not only listen but be at her disposal. Whereas in reality, Rita had been the silent backbone of the farm. Fed the animals. Brought up two kids. Everything had been in such good order. Or so she had thought.

'Before I met your Archie's father and gave up my socialite lifestyle for a life of grain and bear it, I was a show girl in Monte Carlo and danced topless in a fountain with a Hungarian ambassador, I'll have you know. I've had my heart broken, my stomach pumped, and my jewellery stolen, but do you know what healed me?'

Rita shook her head in dreaded anticipation.

'Gin.' The old girl took a huge sip of hers. 'And distance.'

A laugh slipped from Rita's mouth before she could stop it.

'I'm serious.' Hilda's fading blue eyes managed a twinkle. 'People don't need meditation and green smoothies. They need distraction. Booze. Sex. A good old-fashioned stroll, a right good chinwag, or even better, some proper sleep and time away from their phones. None of this *let's-feel-our-feelings* rubbish.'

Rita took a deep breath as she poured herself a glass of water. 'I hear you, but that isn't going to pay the bills, so whether you approve or not, the Seahaven Bay Retreat is happening. I'm going to get the barn cleared, yurts erected on the High Meadow and people are going to pay good money to come here and feel their feelings.' Rita was buoyant. 'I've realised it's so much easier to create a simple website now compared to when I studied for my marketing diploma.'

'This is the same woman who can't even walk into her big lounge as it brings back too many memories, doing all this, is it?'

'That's cruel and it's very different.' Rita steadied herself.

Hilda sniffed. 'Well, as long as they don't do any nonsense near me, I don't care what they do.'

'You'll hardly notice, I promise.'

Hilda put another cigarette in her mouth.

Rita raised a finger. 'And what did Archie used to say to you about smoking in the annexe?'

The old lady flicked her lighter. 'He said I'll burn the place down but it's that or the grim reaper personally wrestling the cigarette from my lips, so I'll take my chances.' Rita rolled her eyes. Hilda then struck like a cobra. 'So, where's the money coming from for all this, then?'

Rita's subconscious did what it shouldn't have. 'If Archie hadn't racked up so much debt, it would be coming from our savings.'

'But you sold the contents of the cow shed including the cows and our one and only tractor to Hawthorn Acre.'

'Yes. I didn't want the bailiffs knocking. I never admitted to anyone but Archie that I'm allergic to them, and I have to live.'

'I still can't believe you allowed the bollocking Jenkens to benefit, though.'

'Hilda! I told you many times. I wasn't thinking straight. I was desperate.'

'No wonder your Thom was furious too... he was so close to Archie, that boy of yours.'

Rita thought back to how her firstborn, by three minutes, had mirrored Hilda's outrage, all because she'd acted without asking him first.

'And as for being too proud to ask your old mother-in-law for help.' A tutting Hilda Jory shook her head.

Rita looked at Hilda and decided enough was enough. 'Hilda, please tell me what happened between the Jorys and the Jenkens.'

Hilda's lips pursed. 'It's passed; it's gone now.' Rita could see pain etched across the old woman's face. 'I could have helped you. We'd have managed. But no, instead you lay dear old Stan off, and sell out to the Jenkens on a whim. I can't believe he's working for *them* now, and I doubt you'll find anyone half as good. He was practically family, Rita.' Rita knew that was the truth; the loyal handyperson had been Archie's sidekick and confidant for many years. But survival mode with a sprinkling of anger took over.

'I was hurt. Not thinking straight. How dare your son leave us so early and in such a bad financial way! We hadn't even written a will.' Rita's voice tightened. 'We have two children; we should have written a will.'

'Ah, there she blows. No wonder I've never seen you shed a tear with all that anger inside of you.'

'That's unfair. I loved him so much. You know that.'

Hilda's breath hitched. 'We all did, but it takes two to tango, dear. So, maybe that anger and blame needs to be directed at yourself.'

Rita harrumphed. She had kicked herself for not having had an open and honest discussion about this eventuality. But they were still young. Archie had been just fifty-five when it had happened. Death had seemed a lifetime away. All she did know, gleaned after one drink-fuelled evening together in the Winking Pilchard, was that Archie wanted to be buried in the Seahaven Bay churchyard, and that he was to be carried in to 'Life is a Rollercoaster' by Ronan Keating, which had certainly caused a few strange looks from the congregation.

Hilda Jory emptied her glass, replacing it on the side table with a loud clonk. 'And re this will that wasn't ever written. Maybe you need to look a little harder. Or you could always get a *proper* job to get you out of the mire.'

Rita swallowed down her anger.

Hilda picked up her paper to continue studying the obituary page. 'Ooh good, there's a funeral at St Margaret's next week. Maybe you could drop me into town for it.'

'You know the bus is easier for that side of town,' Rita replied through gritted teeth, still not understanding the old girl's fascination with death.

'Oh and... how about adding to the marketing nonsense that I'm sure you'll be spurting, *where the sea meets your soul?*'

And with that, Granny Jory pressed the button on her armrest and reclined like a queen refusing an audience.

Rita shut the door behind her and breathed in a huge glug of optimistic air. This was part of her new life: having to deal with Granny Jory alone. And despite all Hilda's bravado, and while the annexe might reek of mischief and gin, there was still pain. She wasn't a bad woman. She, too, was a grieving woman. Full of loss and longing of what could have been, for not only life with her husband but also her one and only son.

Also, to give her her due, the annexe had been Hilda's idea. Once it was ready, she had graciously transferred the deeds of the farmhouse out of her name and moved into the ground-floor rooms of the adjoining building, giving Rita and Archie, then newlyweds, their own space and privacy. And, ironically now, her inheritance.

Throughout their lives, Hilda Jory had been consistent in her outrageousness, and also weirdly dependable in her own way. Rita understood why Hilda had never remarried. Because once Seahaven Bay and the farm got under your skin, it stayed there. And that was why, she resolved, the Seahaven Bay Resort – 'where the sea meets your soul' – would happen. And whether she or the guests liked it or not, Granny Jory came as part of the package.

<h1 style="text-align:center">TEN</h1>

The next day Rita was awoken early by the soft light filtering softly through the gap in the heavy curtains. The house was still, except for the distant cry of seagulls and the faint rustle of leaves in the orchard. Even Nigel seemed quiet for once. But in her gut, after Hilda's strange comment about a will, a restlessness lay in her stomach like a badly kept secret.

Sighing, she pulled on her hooded light blue towelling dressing gown and made her way to the old oak desk in the study, the one place Archie had always kept important papers.

She knew she should have addressed this earlier, but grief had swallowed everything, making even the smallest of tasks feel impossible, and anything involving paperwork was a mountain she simply couldn't face. The whole administration side of death had nagged at the back of her mind for weeks. But every time she thought about picking up the phone to her solicitor, she would feel a pang of sadness, and she put it off again.

Her fingers trembled slightly as she moved aside letters, notebooks and an assortment of faded photographs. Nothing but memories. But it wasn't memories she was looking for. It was a will – a will that had never been discussed, if there even was one.

Next, she moved to the heavy metal safe nestled at the back of Sennen's old wardrobe. Kneeling, she wiped away a thin layer of dust and pulled open the door with a quiet creak. Inside were a few envelopes and the legal documents for the farm. Thinking something may have fallen down the sides, she searched again. Nothing. Well, at least this confirmed what she had thought was the case. He would have told her if he'd made a will; she was sure he would have told her. They had had no secrets, had they?

Determined, Rita went back to the study and searched every corner. The drawers, the filing cabinet, even the old shoebox Archie had once joked contained 'the secrets of the universe'. On opening it, she put her hand to her chest, moved at revisiting so many memories from their past. Inside were love letters and silly notes they'd passed over the years, a train ticket from a sex-filled weekend they'd spent in Edinburgh. A painting that Sennen had drawn of the farm and a clay miniature of Buddy, the labrador they had had before Henry, that Thom had made in his pottery class. Sweet, sentimental fragments of their life together. Despite the big man's stature and demeanour, Archie Jory had been an old romantic. And will or no will, she was certain that he had cared deeply, loved passionately, and would have fought a lion for her and those kids of theirs if needed.

With another weary sigh, she went downstairs, made herself some breakfast, fed the animals and, at nine o'clock on the dot, searched her phone for the family solicitor's number. Although Archie's share of the farm would automatically pass to her, the Land Registry still needed to be informed and today at last, fuelled by Hilda's will comment, she was ready to face it.

'Dickens, Bryant and Feathers, good morning,' the young female voice trilled.

'Oh, hi there. It's Rita Jory – is Malcolm there, please?'

The line went silent. A brief pause.

The deep familiar voice of Malcolm Feathers came on the line. 'Rita, how are you?'

'I'm OK.' She swallowed hard. 'I'm err... struggling to find Archie's will and thought you might have a copy?'

There was another brief silence on the other end. Then, the solicitor slowly replied, 'Yes... I did have a copy. But in fact... it's gone missing. I've been waiting for instruction from you on how to proceed, but when I heard the news of your husband's passing, I did go to pull the file out anticipating your call, but I'm afraid to say the file's disappeared from my office.'

'And you didn't think to ring and tell me this?'

Another silence. Rita felt the ground shift beneath her. There had been a will after all – but where was it?

'And what do you mean, missing? How does a will just... disappear? You're supposed to keep documents like this secure, aren't you?'

Malcolm stuttered. 'I'm as baffled as you. We're looking into it, but for now, there's nothing. I'm so sorry, Rita.'

'And you have no other records?'

'No,' Malcolm said softly. 'We keep one copy, and the client gets the other. In fact, I thought I would hear from you much earlier, because even if your husband has left everything to you in his will, you still need to apply for probate to access and transfer his sole-name assets.'

'But he didn't have any, did he?' Rita paused, then tightened. 'Malcolm, surely you can remember his wishes?'

'I'm sorry, Rita. It was a long time ago. But you will be the first to know when it shows up.'

Rita felt anger rising. 'Yes, I will be, Malcolm. This is diabolical, if you ask me.' She hung up and swivelled herself around on the office chair deep in thought. What on earth was going on here?

Outside, the morning sun climbed higher, casting long shadows across the courtyard. Rita showered off some of her anger, then made herself a milky coffee. As she sat at the kitchen table, she sighed deeply. It would be OK. She would do what she did best. She would work hard and make her own money. At least she knew there was a will now. But why had he not told her he'd written one and why was the key to Archie's final wishes nowhere to be found?

Wanting to keep her mind busy, Rita yanked at the barn door with both hands, her boots sinking into the muddy track as she did so, and with a resounding creak, the heavy timber gave way, sending a cloud of dust, hay and mouse droppings into the mid-morning light.

'Welcome to your sanctuary,' she muttered, coughing, before letting out a strangled laugh. She looked up and around. A high-beamed wooden ceiling soared overhead, and the panelled walls were softened by tendrils of ivy creeping through the cracks. At the far end, the showstopper: grand arched double doors opening out towards the fields that rolled down to the sea beyond. The old hayloft was still intact, its ladder worn smooth from years of climbing. An old iron oil lantern hung from one of the beams, long unlit, but still steady in its place. For a moment, a long-held fantasy flickered through her mind: the image of her and Archie tangled together in the soft, itchy, sweet-smelling grass. The thought passed quickly, but not before a fleeting smile touched her lips, remembering the night they had conceived Sennen Hayley and Thomas Barnaby. The origins of their middle names had remained a secret between Archie and Rita, one no one had ever guessed, not even hawk-eyed Hilda.

Rita's mind started to wander. With hard work, and vision, she had no doubt that the farm could easily become a seaside haven in which to rest, relax and recover.

The website, sprinkled with a few of Zenya's suggestions, was nearly finished, and Rita had been diving into yurt research, slowly coming to terms with just how outrageously expensive they were. Who knew a canvas tent could cost more than a small car?

She took in her surroundings, once central to the farm's success. The barn created a huge undercover space which would mean she could operate in all weathers. And this time, it could serve a whole new purpose, one that didn't involve her eyes streaming or her breathing like Darth Vader in the middle of a panic attack, thanks to her ridiculous allergy to Archie's beloved herd.

Rita pushed open the expansive double doors, tugged off her gloves, reached in her pocket for her mobile and took a photograph of inside the barn and the view from it. She immediately sent it to Sennen.

RITA

Welcome to the Seahaven Bay Retreat

A reply pinged almost instantly.

SENNEN

Are those pitchforks or murder weapons?

RITA

Ha! Well, I did say I was basing it loosely on The White Lotus.

SENNEN

You know you're meant to soothe people, right? Not terrify them. Soz. Got to go, the mother of a bridezilla is trying to reach me.

Rita smiled, slipped the phone away, and rolled up her sleeves. The smile didn't last long when she found a dead pigeon under an old tarpaulin.

By midday, she'd cleared out all the scattered junk, uncovering treasures as she went: a stack of forgotten apple crates (now earmarked for yoga mat storage), a couple of antique milk churns (potentially good for seating), and randomly a faded photograph of Sennen in her role of Ophelia during a brief stint of amateur dramatics. She gave it a fond smile, put it in her jacket pocket, then flinched on hearing a noise behind her.

'Don't mind me,' came the familiar rasp. She turned to see Granny Jory standing in the doorway, in a leopard-print dressing gown.

'What are you doing here?' Rita brushed dirt and straw from her hair.

'Thought I'd see what foolishness smells like.' Hilda stepped over a coiled hose with surprising agility for someone of her years. Rita looked to the old girl's bright pink Nike trainers and smiled. 'I was expecting crystals and chanting. Instead, I find rust and potential litigation.'

Rita laughed. 'Not quite at the chanting stage yet. I only started clearing today. Sennen, Alex, and Kelly are coming down at Easter to help, I hope.'

'And Thomas?'

Rita's face downturned. 'He's as elusive as his father could be at times, so who knows when we shall see that grandson of yours next.' Her words cut hard as she remembered that Thom hadn't answered her last two check-in messages. It really did feel like he was ignoring her. How long would it take, if ever, for him to forgive her for selling out?

Hilda surveyed the barn, looked out at the magnificent view that spread down to the clifftop, then fixed Rita with a shrewd gaze. 'You're actually serious about this, aren't you?'

'Yes. Very.' Rita nodded.

The old woman gave her a wry smile. 'Good. It's about time you did something silly.'

Rita blinked. 'That sounded almost supportive.'

'Don't tell anyone. I've got a reputation to uphold.' Hilda winked, pulling a fat brown envelope from her pocket and pressing it into her daughter-in-law's hand. Rita opened it and peered in, amazed. There had to be at least ten thousand pounds in fifties, maybe more.

Rita cocked her head. 'What's this?'

'Danger money.'

'Oh my. This is too much! I'll pay every penny back.' Rita's eyes brimmed with tears.

Hilda tutted. 'I feel insulted at even the offer.'

Tears started to flow down Rita's cheeks. Hilda was brusque.

'Get a grip, girl, and reserve all that nonsense for when you manage to open. And don't forget you will need some kind of insurance, I expect. And for God's sake, get your hair done or something; you'll be frightening the goats soon, let alone any potential punters.'

With the same elation she'd felt on having the idea of the retreat, Rita smiled. 'You're not going to be wandering around like that when the *potential* punters arrive, are you?'

Granny Hilda lit a cigarette and blew out a long plume of smoke. 'Only if they deserve it.'

A flicker of movement at the doorway made Rita turn. Zenya was standing there, hair scraped into a messy bun, boots spattered with mud, wearing an oversized army jacket that had definitely seen better days. She gave a tentative wave.

Hilda looked her up and down with a snort. 'Good Lord. I thought the scarecrow in the south field had got loose.'

Zenya raised her brows, entirely unfazed. 'Morning to you too. Love the dressing gown. Late night at the bingo?'

Rita clamped a hand over her mouth to stop a laugh escaping as Hilda narrowed her eyes like a cat preparing to pounce. 'Zenya, meet Hilda Jory, my indomitable mother-in-law.'

Zenya reached out her hand to a tut from the old woman. 'Well, Zenya, that's a name with bite. And I don't know why she says that, if not for you to assume I'm some kind of old battle-axe.'

Zenya didn't react, just looked to Rita. 'I was popping down to the bay and saw you were clearing out the barn.' She stepped over the tarpaulin. 'Thought I'd lend a hand.'

Rita flushed. 'Oh. I didn't... I mean, I didn't ask because I can't pay you yet.'

Zenya blinked. 'Who said anything about money? I'd like to help get you up and running.'

'She means she's cheap,' Hilda muttered, puffing on her cigarette. 'And anyway, you *can* pay her now.'

Hilda tapped the brown envelope tucked into Rita's jacket pocket. 'That's not for flapjacks and frippery, girl. It's seed money. So use it, and get decent bollocking staff on the payroll. Anyway,

I've got death notices to read.' With that Hilda Jory headed towards the door.

Zenya shouted after her. 'Just say the word, Hilda, and I'll happily balance your chakras.'

'You're all right, dear.' Hilda's eyes were twinkling. 'Last time someone touched my chakras I didn't walk straight for a week.'

ELEVEN

With a spring in her step from Hilda's generosity the day before, Rita headed out to feed the animals. April had been typically wet and blustery, full of its usual showers, but somehow wetter than most years. A positive for Rita as aside from conducting her necessary chores outside, it had allowed her to focus on finalising her business and marketing plan. Sennen had agreed that putting yurts up on the High Meadow was a brilliant idea. An opportunity to showcase the 'Seahaven on Earth' aspect of the sweeping views over the cliffs and horizon. It would offer guests a peaceful, scenic retreat, while also keeping them comfortably distanced from the bustle of Rita's everyday farm life.

Kelly had suggested her getting a business loan, but with owning half of Archie's debt Rita was doubtful she'd get any credit, not yet. Hilda's cash injection was a godsend, but yurts weren't cheap and she wanted to get opening and start the money coming in as soon as she possibly could.

For now, she would provide a couple of compost toilets in the yurt area so that guests wouldn't have to wander the good half mile down from the High Meadow in the dark. She would also give the outbuilding toilet and shower a good old scrub and daub of white paint.

Not ideal facilities, she realised, but she was selling the place as a rustic retreat – 'coming back to nature with no mod cons' – so hoped she wouldn't get too many complaints. And, once more financially secure, she planned to convert another of the outhouses into a fancier toilet and shower area and also construct a basic kitchen and dining unit.

With chickens fed and on her way to tend to the goats, Rita conducted her daily ritual of having a look in the barn to try and muster up further ideas. With all the rain they had had, it had seemed a gloomy outlook all around, but today, the sun was shining and despite not having waxed her shapely legs for at least two months she had even put on shorts with her wellies.

Looking around at the newly cleared barn, and with the help of Hilda's cash injection, everything somehow seemed less daunting now. There would be cushions. Lanterns. Maybe some fairy lights strung across the beams. She just needed to work out a timetable of what exactly the programme of classes would look like. Also, how she would cater for food and beverages. All of which would need to be high quality but not overly expensive.

As if her daughter was reading her mind, Rita's thoughts were abruptly interrupted by a message prompting her to check her email.

I love it. You're good at this, Mum! Sennen had typed. Just made a few minor tweaks to what you sent over. Here it is.

Rita began to read aloud.

'Escape to Seahaven Bay Retreat – where the sea meets the soul. Nestled in nature, our cosy, back-to-basics yurts offer a front-row seat to a view so breathtaking, it feels like heaven on earth. Step into our sea-view barn for rejuvenating sessions including gong cere-monies and yoga, or gaze at the stars and moon in quiet wonder. Embrace the wild with cold-water sea swims, then nourish your body with fresh, raw, healthy foods – or head to the picturesque harbour to find a charming local hostelry. It's time to lose your inhi-bitions and find your soul. Welcome to the Seahaven Bay Retreat – your rustic hideaway by the sea...'

'Lose your inhibitions, eh, Mrs Jory,' a deep voice enquired.

Rita nearly dropped her phone at the unexpected interruption. And on seeing who was in front of her she wished she'd tended to her hairy legs and sorted her hair, which was now almost two-tone.

Jago Jenken, proprietor of Hawthorn Acre, was the kind of man who turned heads without even trying. He had thick black hair and vivid green eyes, and one dimple that sat deeper than the other when he smiled, lending an uneven charm that made his grin all the more captivating. Even in worn work clothes and boots thick with mud, he looked better than most men in a dress suit. His voice was deep, the kind you felt in your chest, and his eyes held a mischievous twinkle that reminded her, achingly, of a younger version of her Archie. There was something about the way he carried himself, open and magnetic, that made it impossible not to watch him a moment longer than was proper.

'Everything OK?' Rita stuttered.

'I found one of your goats in my top field. Just brought her back and – hope you don't mind – just popped her in the pen. I hate to say it, I think she might have met my Cedric halfway. It is spring, mind.' Jago winked.

Was he flirting with her? He never had before. Then again, thanks to the long-standing Jenken–Jory feud, she'd barely exchanged two words with him before she sold him Archie's beloved cows and tractor. When Archie had been alive and their paths had crossed, she'd found her mind wandering, tinged with guilt, down deliciously forbidden roads, imagining all the things a married woman could only dream about. When it came to the tractor sale, she had been so consumed by grief that even if Matt Damon had appeared topless on a white charger, she wouldn't have noticed.

If he *was* flirting, he clearly believed beauty was only skin deep, because she looked like a pig in a wig today – and her legs were so hairy you could practically plait them.

'Shit. OK, thank you. I expect it was Camilla; she's trouble, that one. Has been known to ignore her constraints on occasion.'

'Naughty girl.' Jago smirked, his voice low and teasing. Rita's face reddened as the handsome one continued. 'You all right? Must be hard coping on your own.' Jago looked around the now-empty barn. 'You've done a good job getting this ship-shape, though.'

'Err, thanks.' Rita's words came without thought. 'And are you looking after those cows all right?'

'Looking after them like my own.' Jago hesitated for a second. 'Anyway, I thought you were allergic to...'

Rita was wide eyed. 'How did you kn—?'

Jago was swift in his reply. 'So... do you think you'll stay here? At the farm, I mean?'

Something tightened in Rita's chest. The question caught her off guard, touched a nerve she didn't even realise was quite so raw.

'I'm not selling to you, Jago Jenken.' Rita was sharper than she intended. 'Not now, not ever.'

Jago raised his hands in mock surrender, eyebrows lifting. 'Whoa. An angry Jory, I've seen a few of those in my time.' He softened his tone. 'That's not what I meant. I just thought...'

She cut in again, the words tumbling out before she could stop them. 'I wasn't born bloody yesterday.'

'All right, all right.' Jago sounded contrite now. 'I really didn't mean to strike a nerve.'

Rita blew out a breath, already regretting her tone. 'I'm setting up a wellness retreat, actually. So, if you want to come and release the stresses of farm life by screaming into a pillow, you'll be very welcome.'

Jago raised an eyebrow, the flirty spark returning. 'And you need a retreat for that?' He didn't look away, the one dimple flashing like a dare.

Her temper fizzled out like a match dropped in water, and she tried not to smile. 'Anyway, it's more than just pillow-screaming. There might be goat yoga too.'

'Ah,' he replied, mock serious, 'your Camilla's just had a bit of practice for that already.'

Rita rolled her eyes, but her heart gave a traitorous flutter. Damn him.

Jago smirked. 'Anyway. There was a gap she must've squeezed through. I roughly mended it. The whole goat pen really could do with a seeing to.'

'Couldn't we all,' Rita stuttered, followed by a rapid and embarrassed, 'I mean... but thank you, thank you for doing that.'

Another lopsided smile. 'Well, you know where I am.'

With that, all six foot one of deliciousness strode off towards Hawthorn Acre.

Rita let out a slow breath she hadn't realised she'd been holding. The flutter Jago Jenken had just stirred in her wasn't unwelcome. If anything, it reminded her she was still alive, but it unsettled her all the same. Archie's absence was still so raw, his presence lingering in every corner of the house. She wasn't ready to be feeling anything new, not yet. And yet there it was, a quiet spark, gently nudging at the edges of her grief.

TWELVE

The faded sign of the Winking Pilchard, a cartoonish silver fish with one eye cheekily closed, swayed gently in the breeze. On calm evenings, the pub's bench-lined terrace would fill with locals and visitors alike, pints in hand, waiting for the sun to drop below the horizon and another day to reach its final chapter. On stormy days, it was the place to hunker down, listen to the wind whip against the stone, and tell stories that grew taller with every round. As with a lot of the now few and far between old-fashioned hostelries, the Winking Pilchard was more than just a pub; it was a compass point in the lives of the Seahaven Bay folk. And nestled at the harbour's edge, it marked the perfect boundary between land, sea, and all the magic in between.

As the landlord gave Rita a huge, welcoming smile, the familiar scent of woodsmoke hit her like a wave, stirring a rush of nostalgia that caught her off guard and causing her breath to hitch. It was only the second time she'd set foot in the pub since Archie's wake, and the warmth of the place, once so comforting, now felt bitter-sweet. She hesitated, emotions teetering, until a sudden flurry of floral fabric and jangling bangles swept in behind her.

'Honestly, Reet,' puffed Kelly, brushing wind-blown hair from her face. 'That was not my kind of hill, in these heels.' She shivered. 'I can't believe it's April and so bleeding cold.'

'I did tell you to wear your trainers... and a coat.'

'You said we were going out, out.'

Rita laughed and smiled warmly at the landlord. 'You all right, Pete; you remember Kelly?'

Pete 'the Pilchard' Perkins slid two large glasses of cold French Sauvignon Blanc over the worn bar without a word. He knew their orders already. He knew *everything*.

'I never forget a face, you know me, and can I say, young Kelly, that you look as fit as a bargee's ferret this evening,' the strong Cornish accent conveyed. 'And these are on me.' He winked.

Kelly guffawed. 'I'll take it, whatever it is, I'll take it.'

'Never trust a man with mutton-chop sideburns,' Rita quipped.

The landlord's ample stomach wobbled. 'Oi! I'll have you know they've won competitions, these 'ave.'

'Cheers, Pete,' Rita said as she and Kelly laughed in unison.

They settled into what had been Rita and Archie's favourite corner booth, the one tucked just under the crooked window that looked out to the harbour, its glass slightly misted from years of salty sea air. A few regulars nearby raised their glasses in a friendly toast, their faces flushed from the warmth of good company.

Kelly squeezed Rita's hand. 'So, I don't want any of your many brave faces tonight. I want to know exactly how you are?'

Rita took a large glug of wine. 'I know it's been a while now, but it... everything still feels... off, you know. Like he's going to walk back in with muddy boots and a list of jobs I haven't done.'

'You were with him twenty-five years, darling.'

'I know, an age. And I still can't talk about the accident or anything about him with the kids, I just can't, and Sennen wants me to. Meanwhile, Thom hates me. I'm sure he thinks it was my fault. It's so hard.' Tears filled Rita's eyes.

'It was an accident. A freak fucking accident, and it wasn't your fault. And you must hold on to the fact that the investigating officer said he wouldn't have suffered. That it would have been quick.'

'But he was angry when he left, Kel,' Rita said quietly. 'He was bashing things around, in a right boot-stomping mood and what if he was angry because of something I'd done to annoy him, and I just didn't realise what.'

Kelly rested her hand on top of her friend's. 'We've been through this a million times, Reet. That coast road is fast; the drop is steep. Archie was at the wheel, not you. The type of relationship you had, you'd have known if it was you who'd upset him. And you can't live in the "what ifs", because that makes a slow death for yourself.'

'Sometimes I feel maybe I didn't know him at all.'

'Because of the debt, you mean?'

Rita took a huge noisy breath and nodded. 'I just don't get it. On the statements are cash withdrawals mainly, and you know what interest is like on these things. I'm living on credit cards – luckily ones that still have a bit of credit on them.'

Kelly nodded and took a drink. 'What exactly was he spending the money on; have you any idea?'

'Nope, not a scooby.' Rita sighed deeply. 'I realise now why he put that post box on the gate. So I never got wind of the new cards he'd applied for in both of our names!'

'Oh, Reet. Thank God you sold the cows and the tractor then.'

'Yes, I still feel such guilt for that, but I'm sure Jago Jenken paid over the odds, you know, so at least Archie's credit cards are paid off now.'

'Why would a Jenken do you a favour?'

Rita shrugged. 'I have no idea.' She chewed her lip. 'I flirted with him the other day. And, well... I enjoyed it. How bad is that!'

Kelly laughed softly. 'Reet, there's no harm in that. Grief doesn't come with a timetable. Doesn't check when it's OK to move on.'

Rita groaned, covering her face with her hands. 'Oh God... I'd never take it any further. Not a chance. Hilda would kill me for one.'

Kelly nudged her shoulder. 'Relax, you're allowed a little harmless flirt now and then. I have a world record for it.'

Rita smirked despite herself. 'I don't think Archie would've been impressed if he'd caught me daydreaming about Jago Jenken in nothing but his work boots.'

Kelly's grin was pure sauciness. 'Let's just sit with that thought for a moment, shall we?'

Their eyes drifted to the hearth, where a fiddle player was tuning up, the first notes of a catchy sea shanty cutting into their conversation.

'This music reminds me of the night we met Archie.' Rita shook her head.

'Oh yeah.' Kelly's eyes brightened. 'If I'd have agreed to Pete the Pilch's suggestion then my life story could have been a very different one.'

'I'm not sure some of it was even legal.' Rita snorted. Once she had stopped laughing, she put her hand on top of her friend's. 'That's better. I needed to forget my woes for a bit. Anyway, tell me. What's going on in fancy London, then?'

'What isn't going on is mine and Ron's sex life. He only brings out the meat and two veg for birthdays, anniversaries, maybe Christmas if I'm lucky, now. I told him I was going away for a few days, and he barely looked up from his Sudoku. I'm forty-five, and like you, not over the hill. In fact, my winking pilchard is constantly wet and ready for action.'

Rita nearly fell off her chair laughing. 'Oh my God, Kel, that is vile and hilarious in equal measure.' Her old London twang was suddenly overriding her muted Cornish one.

Kel wasn't finished. 'I didn't marry a man for warm cups of tea and reruns of *Antiques Roadshow*. I need a bit of... well, life!' She stood up. 'Another drink?'

Rita sat lost in thought, listening to the fiddler playing as Kelly ordered their drinks and then shimmied back with two large glasses of Sauvignon Blanc.

'There is something else.' Rita's face was serious.

Kelly leaned into her friend. 'Go on.'

'The other day Hilda insinuated that maybe Archie had written a will. I'd never thought to look because as far as I knew he hadn't made one. So, I searched everywhere I thought it might be, but nothing. Then I called our family solicitor, who said there was one and it had gone missing.'

Kelly was wide eyed. 'What the fuck?'

Rita grimaced. 'I know. It's hurting my soul.'

'I'd be hurting the solicitor if he doesn't get to the bottom of it.'

'I know, I know but my trust for Archie was our golden bind.'

Kelly raised an eyebrow. 'Wasn't it the great Bard who said, "All that glisters is not gold"?'

'Blimey, Kel. I thought you hated English Lit.'

Kelly shrugged. 'I did, until that hot young English teacher started when we were in Year Eleven. Remember. Mr Hayes, wasn't it? I'd have been his Juliet anytime.' She took a large swig of wine. 'Oh God, thinking of him, I so need a shag.'

They both laughed again, and Rita felt her tension loosening.

'Look' – Kel's voice was full of care – 'there will be an explanation. Archie was a good man. He loved you, Rita. If I mysteriously disappeared tomorrow, Ron wouldn't even notice. Maybe I'll come and live down here with you. Help with the retreat. Read crystals and pretend to know what "retrograde" means.'

'You'd terrify the guests,' Rita said, smiling. 'But I'd love that.'

Kelly raised her glass in an impromptu toast. Rita followed as her friend announced, 'To Ron's vanishing libido, Archie's vanishing will, and most importantly, to the Seahaven Bay Retreat.'

Rita grinned and they both said in unison, 'The Seahaven Bay Retreat.'

THIRTEEN

In the dead of night, a furious knocking rattled the farmhouse door, jolting Rita awake. Heart hammering and feeling decidedly groggy after drinking at least a bottle of wine earlier, she reached instinctively for the shotgun that Archie had insisted should always rest beside their bed. For a moment, she froze, breath held, terrified of what she was going to be confronted with. She could hear Kelly oblivious to it all, snoring like a warthog in Thom's old room across the corridor.

Then came a voice, muffled but unmistakable. 'Mum! It's me, it's Sennen!'

Rita threw back the covers and charged down the stairs, gasping as her feet hit the cold kitchen flagstones. She unlocked and whipped open the door. There stood her beautiful daughter, tear-streaked and shaking.

'Alex has dumped me,' she choked, eyes red and swollen. 'And I don't know what to do.'

❦

The next morning Kelly sat hunched at the kitchen table, nursing a mug of sweet black coffee, while Rita leaned against the

Aga, eyes half shut, her smudged eyeliner giving her the look of a panda. Sennen moved quietly around them, setting the table, her usual spark dimmed, her movements slow and mechanical. Yet, even with her long auburn hair scraped into a messy bun, her flared jeans and a baby pink WEDDINGS BY SENNEN T-shirt showing off her petite frame, she still looked like she'd stepped straight out of a magazine shoot.

'Jesus. I come home hoping for a bit of nurturing and end up playing mum to two fully grown adults,' she sighed. 'And you're getting just bacon sandwiches; I don't have it in me to coordinate a full fry-up.' She grabbed the ketchup from the fridge and plonked it down on the table, followed by the two plates of delicious-smelling food.

Kelly tucked in hungrily, while Rita, aware she was a delicate shade of green, didn't move to touch hers. Sennen busied herself by washing up at the sink.

Between mouthfuls, Kelly looked up. 'Great to see you, Sen, although of course I wish it were under better circumstances.' She took a sip of coffee. 'You know he's a dick, right? Alex. Always has been. It's just now you see it.'

Rita jumped in defensively. 'Kel! Not now.' She put her hand on her daughter's shoulder. 'Tell me again, love, what happened. I was sleepy last night. I'm sorry.'

'You were still drunk, Mum,' Sennen tutted. 'He told me on Thursday night he couldn't cope with me moping about Dad. So, I stormed off. Luckily, I was at a wedding I'd planned yesterday and had budgeted for a hotel. But I got to the room and couldn't bear to be on my own, so I drove straight to you.'

'Oh, baby girl.' Rita felt her pain as her daughter went on.

'He also said that maybe I'd moved in with him too soon. I mean, we're twenty-three, not eighteen!'

'That's still *quite* young,' Kelly offered.

Rita glared at her friend, who, under her breath, said, 'Oops. Not now, OK.' Kelly pretended to zip her mouth shut.

'I mean, let's give grief an expiry date, shall we?' Sennen

bashed her hand down on the draining board, then burst into ugly snotty tears. 'It's not fair. I miss Dad so much.'

'Oh, darling. It's so awful, I know, but I'm here and you can stay as long as you want to. Come on, wipe your hands and let's sit down. I'll sort that later.'

Sennen did as she was told. 'Alex wasn't always this horrible. He just... didn't know how to deal with my emotions. With all this.' She gestured down at herself, as if her grief were something she carried like a second skin.

'Well, maybe he should've tried a little harder,' Rita said, voice croaky from too much wine and too little sleep. 'That's what you do when you love someone. You don't walk away just because it gets a bit dark and difficult.'

Kelly felt she could speak up now. 'Didn't Marilyn Monroe say something like, "If you can't handle me at my worst, you don't deserve me at my best"?'

'Still not helping,' Rita murmured.

Sennen blew her nose loudly with the kitchen roll handed to her by her mother. 'I have been a nightmare. I know it was like the old Sennen disappeared, but he didn't want to make the effort to look for me.' She started to cry again.

Rita reached out and squeezed her hand. 'You're still in there, darling, and we see and hear you loud and clear.' She then stood slowly. 'Right. We need air. I've got a spare pair of wellies. Let's walk off these hangovers and heartbreak, shall we? Kel, you coming?'

'The only place I'm walking is back up those stairs to bed, and I'm staying there until lunchtime.' Kelly took a bite from Rita's sandwich.

'Cock-a-doodle-doo!' came Nigel's raucous tones from the orchard.

'And put a gag on that sodding bird while you're at it,' Kel groaned. 'He woke me at six o'-bleeding-clock this morning.'

Rita and Sennen exchanged a knowing smile as they pulled on their wellies.

As Rita and Sennen reached the High Meadow, the sun came out. They approached the edge of the cliff and, at the sight of the expansive ocean below, Sennen started to run, arms outstretched towards the majestic old sycamore tree.

'Come on, Mum, let's sit under the Singing Tree like we used to when me and Thom were little.'

Rita threw down her mac, and two generations of Jory women sat side by side at its base, where the roots bulged and twisted like legs poking through the ground. The soil beneath the tree was soft and cool. Above them, the sycamore's fresh spring leaves shimmered in the light, each one the size of Rita's palm.

'Your dad used to leave me little love notes in this tree, you know. When we first got together and even when you two were babies. Following that on every wedding anniversary.' Sennen was wide eyed. 'It felt such a treat for me to come up here and see what he'd hidden.' Rita made a funny whining noise. 'He knew it was my "healing space".'

'Oh my God, Mum, that's adorable.'

'I would quite often come up here when the weather was good to feed you both, to escape the monotony of the farmhouse. It was hard, having two of you to look after. I don't think I've ever known tiredness like it. And this view gave me some head space.'

They both took a minute in silence to look out over the wild, endless, and achingly breathtaking view. To take in the soothing cries of gulls and distant screeches of kids playing on the beach as they enjoyed the freedom of the Easter holidays. The horizon stretched wide and calm, with the pale sky gently kissing the now-shimmering sea.

Rita sighed. 'Your dad would be so busy, but he would always have time to show that he was here for me.' She let out a little groan. 'So many memories. You first crawled by this tree, then ran, then played...'

'Who crawled first?' Sennen asked quietly.

'Thom.' Rita shrugged.

'Of course he bloody did!' Sennen laughed.

'But only a week before you.' Rita's voice lowered. 'And then in what felt like the blink of an eye, it was time for you to run away from Seahaven Bay.'

'I never ran far.' Sennen grabbed her mum's hand. 'I love you, Mum.'

Rita welled up. 'I love you too, darling.'

Sennen jumped up. 'Show me where Dad hid the notes. I wanna see.'

Rita smiled. 'Down here.' She leaned back against the trunk, fingertips grazing the bark. Just above root level was a small hollow, a natural little letterbox, hidden beneath a strip of peeling bark. He'd once covered her eyes with his hands and led her to it, one golden summer evening, the same summer they'd shared their first kiss. Inside had been a tiny note, folded small and sealed with a heart sticker. She still had it, tucked safely away in her memory box, along with all the others.

In his crooked scrawl, it simply read: *To the woman whose kiss ruined all the others.*

Short. Honest. Utterly him.

Sennen jumped down and crouched beside the base of the tree. 'Just imagine if we actually found a note in here,' she said, grinning as she reached casually into the deep hollow. Nothing. Undeterred, she reached in deeper, more carefully this time, and let out a loud shriek as her fingers touched something. 'Oh my God!'

She pulled out a filthy, thin strip of paper, folded tight. Both women stared, mouths open like startled goldfish. Rita grabbed it from her, her hands shaking.

'What does it say?' Sennen whispered.

Rita unfolded the paper slowly, her voice catching in her throat as she read aloud the words printed there: '*Ask Stan. He knows everything.*'

Sennen stared at her, eyes wide. Then she smiled. 'Grandad

Brown always said the stories of our lives have already been written, didn't he?'

Rita couldn't reply. She just nodded, holding the note like it might dissolve if she breathed too hard. 'Not literally, though.' Rita's hands were shaking. 'And your dad never used a printer.'

'Well, whoever put it there, Mum, I mean, they knew it was somewhere you may look and find it.'

Rita looked around, half expecting someone to appear from behind the gnarled trunk. Who would leave a message here, in this quiet, hidden spot? Was it a random kindness, or something more? A secret admirer? A warning? Her mind spun with questions, none with answers yet. Who even knew that Archie used to leave her notes?

'Grandad was *always* right, though, wasn't he?' Sennen was oblivious to Rita's inner turmoil.

Rita's thoughts drifted to her dear old dad, who had passed away just five years earlier from cancer. Her parents had had her late in life, after years of trying; her mum, a twin herself, had fallen pregnant at forty-four and along came Rita Joan Brown. She never remembered a single cross word between them, not with each other, and certainly not with her.

Her mum had died six months to the day after her father, on the very same day as her auntie Jane, her mum's twin sister. Rita was still convinced it hadn't been coincidence, but broken hearts that had carried them both away.

'Mum, are you listening to me?' Sennen said moodily.

'Yes, yes, darling, of course. Grandad was quite often right, yes.'

Sennen was looking around her at the view. 'Thinking on it, it's perfect up here for your retreat idea. Guests can come and sit and meditate in the shade. Listen,' Sennen whispered as a blackbird's song rang out, clear and mellow, a rich, flute-like melody that drifted through the morning air. A thread of breeze caused the branches to sway and creak.

'The tree really does sing, doesn't it?' Rita smiled broadly.

'It does.' Sennen smiled back. 'So how about this for your

marketing stuff? We could maybe put a little sign up here too.' Still standing, Sennen dramatically announced, 'The Singing Tree – a place to sit and listen. A quiet sanctuary for you to meditate, to read, to write, or just to be at one with nature.'

'Imagine how lovely wind chimes would sound under here too,' Rita added breezily, despite still reeling from the note.

'I'm proud of you, Mum; the whole idea is such an inspiring one.'

Rita felt a rush of pride surge through her dark thoughts. 'And one I'd better get a move on with. It'll be May soon.'

'Could you be ready for guests to arrive in July, do you think? At least the weather should be milder by then.' Sennen moved out to the edge of the tree and put her face to the sun.

Rita nodded. 'I think so, yes. I'm ready to go with the marketing stuff. I've set up an Instagram account and created a basic website. People can pay me via PayPal to keep it safe and simple. I just need to add a few classes, but we can do that as a top line without any detail for now. We need to discuss prices and of course offer an introductory discount, even though I will ensure the money is right for what I need. I've even sketched out a retreat map so people don't get lost but I keep adding areas so it's not final yet.'

'Go, Mum!' Sennen beamed, genuinely impressed. 'You've done loads already. And what about putting up the yurts? Have you thought about when that'll happen?'

'I'll work it out.' Rita felt in control. 'They haven't even arrived yet. They're being delivered, along with the mattresses at the weekend.'

Rita had used the majority of Hilda's money and had taken the risk of maxing out another credit card to keep her dream alive.

'We need some kind of shelter around the compost toilets, plus I've yet to give the outbuilding loo and shower a proper clean-up. Once I've titivated the barn, we're nearly there. Thankfully, I've got Zenya on board, whom you must meet, but I really could do with one other person, as she's not qualified to teach yoga.'

'It's peak wedding season for me,' Sennen said, biting her lip.

'But maybe I could somehow come and help in the summer. Base myself down here for a bit. I mean, it's probably unrealistic with all the bookings I've got, but... I could shuffle things around, work remotely on the admin stuff, and lend a hand where I can. I'd love to be part of it, Mum.'

Rita could see the cogs whirring in her daughter's mind. 'You've got your own life, darling. And as much as I adore you and would want you around all the time, I have to do this for me. Actually, we haven't even talked about you and Alex. What kind of mother am I?'

'A brilliant one. That's what you are. You bringing me up here this morning, it kind of puts everything into perspective, doesn't it? This view, the horizon. Who knows what's beyond it. I need to go home and have a chat with him. He can't just throw me out on the street. My life is in Reading; I like it there. But I guess I can work from anywhere. I just need some time to fathom stuff. I may just rent a studio flat somewhere and get back on track.'

'You're being very grown up about it.' Rita went to her daughter and squeezed her shoulder. 'And our door is always open.' She stuttered on the word 'our'. 'You know that.'

Sennen pulled her shoulders back. 'Mum, nothing can be as bad as Dad dying. He wisely taught me that there is always a solution to everything; the ironic bit is he used to add "except for death".'

Sennen's sentimental statement was lost in the wind.

As the pair started to walk back down towards the farmhouse, a single gunshot shattered the peaceful morning, causing all kinds of birds to scatter and shriek in fear. The chickens had all run into their coop and the goats were cowering at the back of their winter hay shelter.

Sennen was wide eyed. 'Where the hell did that come from?'

'Stan probably just saw a pheasant; your dad used to be the same.'

They then heard a low monotonous wailing. Rita, now worried herself, started to run towards the chicken coop, Sennen in tow, to find Kelly, in her oversized sunglasses and Rita's hooded dressing gown, shotgun in hand, shaking all over. Nigel the cockerel lay motionless at her feet.

'I didn't mean to do it,' Kelly whined, throwing the gun to the ground in fear.

'What exactly did you mean to do then?' Rita's voice rose in anger.

'I just... I thought if I fired out of the window into the sky, he'd shut up. You know, scare him a bit.'

Sennen crouched down to inspect Nigel. 'Well, it looks like you've definitely scared him... permanently.' She held back a snort. 'He's clearly died of shock.'

'Oh, no, oh no. My hangover was raging, I'd just got back off to sleep, and there he is crowing like he's auditioning for *The Voice: Poultry Edition.*'

'He was a cockerel. It's literally his job,' Sennen replied matter-of-factly.

'Well, he's certainly retired now,' Rita said curtly. 'But if it helps you to sleep at night, he was nearing the end of his life anyway.'

'I'm a monster.' Snot was now everywhere on Kelly's face.

'Yes, you are,' Sennen replied bluntly.

They all stared down at the lifeless feathery body.

'You're not going to report me to the RSPCA, are you? You can if you want. I will deserve everything I get.' Kelly wiped her face on the arm of Rita's dressing gown.

As the hens clucked uncertainly nearby, a lone tear fell down Rita's cheek as she gently picked up and cradled Nigel's lifeless, slightly wonky body. 'We shall bury him in the orchard graveyard next to our dear Buddy.'

'I'm so sorry,' Kelly wailed again.

'And we must never mention this to anyone,' Rita added. 'If anyone asks, our feathery alarm *cock* died of natural causes.' Tears began to run down Rita's face.

'Not by some madwoman with a hangover,' Sennen added. 'And Mum, I think it's time you got rid of that gun.'

Rita nodded, a little laugh slipping out at the insanity of the situation. 'What, before she takes out the goat herd too, you mean?'

FOURTEEN

Three weeks later, Rita stood in the middle of the barn, a mug of tea going cold in her hand, and breathed a deep 'breath of peace' from her stomach, the kind that Zenya had taught her to execute when feeling anxious.

The impressive old structure had been scrubbed to within an inch of its life, walls cleaned of cobwebs, floor swept and mopped three times over, and the smell of mildew and cow poop replaced (mostly) by lemon oil and dried lavender. String lights twinkled along the main beam and a huge rug she'd rescued from the attic and beaten senseless in the garden made for a centrepiece. She'd also found an assortment of scatter cushions in the harbour charity shop. Upturned milk churns, for which she had fashioned a soft seat, provided further seating if required and the old apple crates she had found were now the home for yoga mats, meditation cushions and blankets.

The hayloft had been sectioned off with a floral curtain that Zenya said looked very boho, although Rita privately thought it looked like a shower curtain from a 1990s caravan, but she wasn't going to argue aesthetics. Not when she was so close to opening and with the newly cleaned-up and clothes-washed Zenya being the epitome of woo-woo and so perfect for the retreat. She checked her watch. The ever-talented health guru was also cooking her an early dinner and she mustn't be late.

Her thoughts were disturbed by the sound of tyres crunching on the gravel. Realising it was the familiar cough of Stan Bodkin's battered old Land Rover, she tentatively walked outside and, shielding her eyes from the sun, saw him step down from the driver's seat, his tweed cap pulled low. He walked slowly towards her.

'Morning, Mrs Jory,' he called out with his strong Cornish accent. 'You got a minute?'

She tentatively met him halfway. 'What's all this? I'm surprised you're even talking to me.'

Stan looked her right in the eye and just the familiarity of having him back on the farm caused a surge of emotion to run through her. Her ex-farmhand was older than Archie, early sixties now, if Rita remembered correctly, with a kind and open face, weathered by a lifetime of hard graft under open skies, eyes lined through squinting beneath the shadow of a battered cap, and his hands, large and calloused. A slight limp from a motorbike accident when he had been a teenager but with the reliability of an ocean tide. Rita had always loved the quiet gentleness of the man in the way he talked to animals and the overwhelming loyalty to Archie and herself that had run deep for over twenty years.

On hearing his voice, Henry ambled over from his sunbathing slot behind the barn, and they made a fuss of each other.

Stan gestured to his Land Rover. 'Come on, the pair of you, get in. I've got something for you...'

Rita frowned, intrigued, and climbed into the car. They sat in silence as they made their bumpy way up to the High Meadow, where he stopped right next to the Singing Tree, Henry sitting upright on the seat as if he were back in one of his rightful places. After opening the door for Rita, Stan went to the back of the vehicle and tugged at the tailgate. With a loud grunt, he slid out a handmade wooden bench, smooth and sturdy, the grain of the oak glowing honey-gold in the morning light. Rita's heart lurched as she stepped closer. Along the top rail, carefully carved in neat, shallow letters, were the words:

IN LOVING MEMORY OF ARCHIE JORY – MAY YOU ALWAYS HEAR THE SEA

Rita brought her hand to her mouth, blinking quickly. She couldn't stop shaking her head in disbelief.

'That noddle of yours'll fall off in a minute, if you don't stop doing that,' Stan said matter-of-factly. 'I had some offcuts in the barn up there.' Stan gestured towards Hawthorn Acre. 'Figured the old sod might like to rest up here. He quite often used to sit here with a flask of tea and a scowl, in times of trouble.'

'I didn't know that.' Rita felt tears pricking her eyes.

'Sometimes there's things in life we don't ever need to know.' Stan paused for a second. 'Your Archie, he said the wind in the branches helped him think.' The wise man looked up into the tree's vast canopy, where the leaves shimmered and whispered their own secrets. 'So, it's the right place.'

They carried the bench together, placing it to look out where the view opened wide to the sea, sky, and the endless pull of the horizon. Henry plonked himself down under it and whimpered.

Rita ran her fingers over Archie's name, then sat down slowly, letting the silence settle. She could almost feel him beside her, grinning that lopsided grin.

'I'll add it to the retreat map,' she whispered. 'A place for remembering. For listening. For love.'

Stan tipped his cap. 'Not sure what he'd have said to them kind of words.' He smiled. 'But you'll have to tell me all about this new business of yours.'

Rita's voice cracked. 'Stan, I'm so sorry that I had to let you go.'

'Apologise when you're wrong, not when you're real, love – and well, Jago, he says he can spare me for a couple of days a week, to help you with this retreat malarkey and any other bits you may need.'

'Really?' Rita felt a warmth go through her.

'Yep! I can spread my time across every weekday, if you like, if that helps an' all.'

'Oh, wow, that would be amazing, but I'm not sure I can pay you right away, Stan.'

Stan put one of his big hands on top of her small one. 'It's covered.'

'No, that's not fair.'

'Nor is the weather that often up here, but we just get on with it, don't we?'

Rita smiled warmly. 'I have to ask you something.'

'More, she wants more.' Stan laughed.

'Did you leave me a note in here?' She pointed to the hole in the tree.

'A note? What kind of note?' He screwed up his face. 'I barely have time in the day to brush my hair.' He winked as he took off his cap and rubbed his bald head. 'Your Archie loved you like the tide loves the moon, you know. And maybe that's all you need to know.'

Rita started nodding furiously again, her eyes filling with tears.

'Now come on.' Stan opened the passenger door. 'I've got a goat pen to fix properly before that Camilla becomes even more of a four-legged scandal.'

FIFTEEN

Rita opened the annexe door to a smell of garlic, rosemary... and something burning.

'Don't panic.' Zenya fanned the smoke alarm frantically with a tea towel. 'It's only the edges.'

'I don't know.' Hilda held court from her velvet recliner. 'I let you use my facilities, and you burn the pigging place down.'

'I thought you'd appreciate the company, and it beats you cooking for yourself, I guess.' Rita smirked. 'How was the funeral today, anyway?'

'It was marvellous. Eulogy too long and very dull but they'd got caterers in for the wake. A proper job it was. Sausage rolls that even Mrs Munroe couldn't find fault with. And I think Betty Bloom must have provided the scones, because they were to die for.'

'I'm so sorry for your loss,' Zenya piped up, pushing the sleeves of her flowing green smock up with her chin as she began to prepare a green salad.

'Oh, I didn't know him, dear. He was a husband of a woman I used to go to primary school with.'

'Don't ask,' Rita mouthed at Zenya's perplexed face.

Rita peered into the oven behind her. 'So, what exactly are we having, then?'

'Rustic vegetable tart,' Zenya announced proudly.

'Heavy on the rustic, by the smell of it,' Hilda piped up, moving herself to the pine table in the kitchen, where she sat down, glasses perched low on her nose, this week's obituary page open. She didn't look up to speak. 'If the bottom's not soggy and it's got no unidentifiable herbs in. I'll try it. I read recently about a woman taking nearly her whole family out with wild mushrooms.'

Zenya laughed. 'I promise not to kill you, Hilda; I'm too looking forward to working with your daughter-in-law.'

The tart hit the table with a dramatic clatter, accompanied by a mismatched salad, a bottle of cheap white wine that Rita had brought with her, and three tumblers that had once belonged to Hilda's mother and had survived the Blitz and two marriages.

Rita poured, then raised her glass. 'To surviving the week and officially welcoming Zenya to our dysfunctional farmhouse family.'

'To being fed and having a bit of company,' Hilda added.

'To chaos, women, and wellness spa dreams.' Zenya laughed.

'Presently powered by cheap wine and sheer delusion,' Hilda cut in.

They clinked.

For a while, there was only the sound of cutlery scraping plates and soft hums of approval. The tart, against all odds, was rather good.

'Ooh.' Hilda grimaced. 'I can taste some kind of herb I don't recognise.'

'It's probably tahini paste that I stole from the restaurant I was washing up at last summer.'

'Oh, you do work sometimes then?' The old woman stuffed another forkful in.

Rita shook her head. 'Hilda! Do you have to be so rude, all the time?'

'Rude, dear? I prefer "honest with flavour".'

Zenya grinned. 'I've done a lot of kitchen work. It suits my transient lifestyle. But I've also picked up a few cooking skills along the way, which have proved useful when surviving on not a lot.'

'I admire your grit.' Hilda took a large swig of wine and wrinkled her nose.

'Thank you,' Zenya acknowledged. 'And Granny Jory, for the record, I officially love you. I can feel that you've alchemised your pain into something the rest of us get to smile at.'

It was the first time Rita had known Hilda lost for words.

Later, as Rita loaded the dishwasher, she found herself watching Zenya chatting away to her mother-in-law. The young woman tilted her head when she listened like she really did care. There was something magnetic about her, something wild and deeply kind.

With Hilda moving to her bedroom, Zenya got up from the table and stretched. 'I'd better hit the hay. I'm going to make a proper start on the vegetable garden tomorrow.'

After finishing tidying, Rita made drinks and took them outside. The moon hung low, silvering the tops of the waves way in the distance and catching the tips of the long grass that covered the orchard. She had suggested that Zenya move into the spare room in the upstairs of the annexe above Hilda's flat, and was happy to pay her bed and board and give her a fee for each session she was going to be running. But the free-spirited thirty-year-old wasn't having any of it. She would accept being fed and getting the going rate for her services. Plus, the use of the amenities in the annexe would be a bonus, but it was under the stars where she was quite happy sleeping. She was also delighted to be introduced to the vegetable patch and with May being a prime time for planting, she had said she would gladly help getting it back to its full growing and eating potential.

Her tent, now tucked at the back of the orchard, still with a view of the ocean, was positioned next to the low stone wall for a bit of shelter. She had made it cosy with bunting, solar lights, and two old wicker chairs from the barn. Zenya now sat on one of them wrapped in a blanket. She looked entirely at home when Rita appeared wearing a night torch on her head.

'It's still a bit nippy for May.' Rita held out a mug. 'Thought you might like something to warm you up.'

Zenya took the mug with both hands. 'You read my mind.'

'Isn't that your job?' Rita's lips turned upwards in a half smile.

The wild woman smiled. 'Hot chocolate, too, what a treat.'

They sat side by side for a while in companionable silence, listening to the soft bleating of sheep drifting over the fields, mingling with the distant call of gulls and the gentle, steady rhythm of waves lapping against the cliffs down below. The occasional cluck of a nearby hen completed the quiet symphony of farm and sea. The goats were clearly sleeping.

Rita broke the silence. 'You really like it out here, don't you?'

Zenya nodded. 'I do. It's quiet. Simple.' She looked up to the sky. 'And the stars don't ask anything of me.'

Rita gave a small laugh. 'A caravan is about my limit.'

'I tried that.' Zenya breathed a big breath. 'But even then I felt like the walls were closing in on me.'

'Have you lived like this for a long time?' Rita enquired gently.

Zenya took a sip of her drink. 'I was in foster care, mostly, as a kid. Never stayed anywhere long. Five homes by the time I was ten. When I was old enough to leave, I didn't want anything permanent. I'd had enough of people telling me where I should be, how I should behave, what I should want.' Her voice tailed off.

Rita quietly absorbed the woman's pain.

'Society with all its boxes. Wife. Career. Mortgage. Kids. It doesn't know what to do with someone who colours outside the lines.'

'So why Cornwall?'

Zenya shrugged. 'I love the landscape and being by the sea just fills my soul with joy. Plus, people tend to stare less down here when you say you live in a tent and believe in the healing power of plants.'

Rita smiled. 'We stare a bit.'

Zenya laughed. 'Yes but give me curiosity over judgement any day.'

Rita took a drink. 'You're braver than me. I'm staying exactly where I am to try and rebuild my life.'

'And I ran from everything and ended up in your field. Maybe we're just two sides of the same storm.'

Rita looked up. The stars were bright tonight, clear and sharp. Somehow, beside Zenya and under the open sky, things didn't feel quite so tangled anymore.

'Maybe we are.' Rita sighed, and took a sip of her hot chocolate.

SIXTEEN

Rita cast Stan a huge smile as she saw his Land Rover rattling towards her at the top of High Meadow. It was early and the sun was already up, causing sprinkles of golden light to seep through the dense branches of the Singing Tree, where they shimmered and danced on the earth below. With a cheery nod, Stan doffed his cap, then heaved the two large canvas yurts, their wooden frames bundled up like giant puzzles waiting to be solved, off the roof.

Rita grimaced. 'Shit, they look bigger than I remembered. Yurt assembly is a two-man job, apparently. But I'll do my best.'

'I gotta get the bases up 'ere first, Mrs Jory. Made 'em myself for you, I did. I read that having the platform elevated eighteen to twenty-four inches above the ground will create a handy crawl space to access plumbing, wiring or storage for you later on, if you go that way.'

Rita bit her lip. It had cost more to get the ones with bases included. 'I don't know what to say.'

'Don't say anything; Jago provided the materials, and we haven't put the buggers together yet.' Stan grinned. 'I think it'll take us at least a couple of days to get you right with the five.'

Rita was just perusing a YouTube video she'd found the night before on yurt erecting and positioning, when she heard the distant chug of a tractor drifting over the meadow, growing louder until Jago Jenken came into view, perched proudly at the wheel of Archie's smart Massey Ferguson, a sheepdog by his side. Behind him, a battered trailer rattled along, piled high with the heavy wooden bases for the yurts. He gave a theatrical wave as he approached, his grin as wide as the ocean below.

'Good morning, Rita. You didn't think me and Meg would miss out on this great erection, did you?' Jago called out, jumping down from his perch, while Meg barked and ran towards Henry, who was now off towards the gorse hedge at the edge of the field.

Stan gave a grateful nod. 'Perfect timing.'

Rita felt herself blushing. 'Err. Thanks for bringing these up, Jago, but me and Stan can manage, thank you.'

'If I'm paying for Stan to help, then getting the job done quicker is a benefit to us both, don't you agree?' Jago clapped his hands together. 'Let's raise some yurts, shall we?'

Archie had always told her never to assume. She also realised that pride or no pride she needed this help. Maybe the Jenken family weren't all bad. Maybe Hilda's opinion was a skewed one. Like she did with bookshop Jude, she would take Jago Jenken at face value. Innocent until proven guilty and all that.

As the two men began unloading the bases, Rita gestured to where she wanted them positioned. The whole ethos of the retreat was about connecting with nature, so it made sense to have all the yurts facing the breathtaking ocean view. Not too close, for privacy, but near enough to suggest a gentle sense of community. It was a sweltering May day, and as Jago peeled off his T-shirt to reveal a tanned, toned torso, he threw Rita a lopsided grin.

Rita was unable to stop her words, or a smirk from escaping. 'Who do you think you are, Ross bloody Poldark?'

Jago stopped what he was doing, shook his dark curls out of his eyes, and wiped his now-sweaty brow. His green eyes were twinkling. 'I'll be whoever you want me to be if it earns me a cup of tea and a scone later.'

'That easy, eh.' Rita laughed, shaking her head. 'You'd better get on with it then, Jago Jenken. These yurts won't build themselves.'

'Right you are, Demelza.' He tossed her a wink before hefting one of the circular base panels effortlessly. 'But I'll expect extra jam on mine.'

Rita took a breath. Unchaste thoughts of a topless Jago Jenken smearing jam all over her began to circle her mind. 'If you're lucky,' she stuttered as she hotfooted it to the Jimny, her face as red as a strawberry.

Rita had headed back down to the farmhouse and was in the kitchen making a large flask of tea and putting ice in water bottles when she heard footsteps on the gravel outside. Expecting to see Zenya or Hilda, she was surprised to spot a young man, with a huge travel backpack, looking into the sky as if trying to decipher where exactly he was.

At just over five foot seven, the dark-eyed, dark-haired, and undeniably handsome twentysomething carried himself with the easy confidence of someone twice his size. He had the kind of sun-kissed skin and sculpted cheekbones that you could only wish to be born with. He wore a pair of beige tailored shorts, effortlessly chic in that way only European men seem to manage, and a black fitted vest that clung to his impeccably toned physique. What did look slightly out of place, though, was one of those geeky transparent plastic map cases designed to be worn over the head, hanging flat against his chest on an adjustable strap.

With a raised eyelid from Henry, who was asleep on his bed in the kitchen, Rita opened the front door before the young man got to it.

'Hey, you OK?'

The man jumped. '*Hola*,' he called out, slightly out of breath but beaming. '*Perdona*, I mean, sorry, can you help me, please? I think I am... how you say, completely lost.'

Rita raised an eyebrow, slightly amused. 'Where are you looking for?'

'I am on tour of Europe. I was hiking.' He gestured vaguely behind him. 'So beautiful, here.' He looked to his map again. 'So, this is Seahaven Farm, yes?'

'That's right.'

'OK, *bueno*. But now I look for the harbour and for some fish and chips. And it has disappeared, I think.'

Rita laughed and pointed to the left. 'It's about a mile down the hill that way. So, you're not far. Is it your first time here?'

He nodded eagerly. '*Sí*. First time here, and I love it already. The sea, the air, the English boys.' He cocked his head to gauge Rita's reaction. It came in the form of a smile. 'I want to stay. Maybe find work if I am lucky.'

Rita's ears then pricked. 'What kind of work are you looking for?'

'I am fitness trainer now.' He puffed out his chest. 'Before, I was jockey. Horses, racing... since I was sixteen. But I fell and my shoulder is how you say, fucked. But now I train people instead. No saddles,' he added with a wink and held out his hand. 'Mateo Serrano, but everyone can call me Teo.'

Thinking that her upcoming guests, female and possibly even a few of the men, would absolutely adore him, Rita shook his hand.

'Rita. Rita Jory.'

'Ree-tah,' he repeated slowly, letting the syllables roll off his tongue. 'Now that's a pretty name. And also, the name of my *abuela*.'

'Your granny?'

'*Sí, sí*. You speak *español*, ah Rita.'

Rita laughed. 'Hardly. GCSE was my limit.'

'You are not just the pretty name or the pretty face.' Teo grinned.

Rita felt herself blushing, again! What was happening to her today? He'd already insinuated he was gay and was a similar age to her son, and she was acting like Camilla.

'Could you teach yoga or Pilates do you think?'

Teo cocked his head. 'Why you ask?'

'I've got a retreat opening soon. Meditation, yoga, all that healthy stuff. Here at the farm. Could be right up your street.'

His molten brown eyes lit up. 'This is... how you say, fate?' He brought his hands together in a prayer pose and added with a grin, 'I teach yoga. Vinyasa and Hatha.'

Rita, having no clue what either style involved, nonetheless grinned broadly. 'Amazing!' she replied, with the kind of enthusiasm normally reserved for fireworks or winning raffle tickets. Just then, Hilda, dressed in black from head to toe, arrived, her sharp eyes giving Teo the complete once-over. Rita cringed at what might come out of her mother-in-law's mouth. 'Morning, Hilda. This is Teo Serrano, hopefully soon to be our new yoga instructor.'

Hilda, a shade under five foot, peered up at him with mischievous eyes. 'Serrano, eh? Tasty, just like the ham.'

Rita looked horrified. Teo laughed. '*Gracias, señora.*'

Hilda's face remained straight. 'Don't *señora* me; I'm off to a funeral, not a flamenco class.'

It was Teo's turn to look horrified.

Rita was curt. 'Another one?'

'Yes. George Lewis. Lovely man. Lived in the last house on Cliff Street. The bus is about to go down to the bay, so I'd better toddle off.'

Rita shook her head. 'She's got more front than half the seagulls in this town, that one.'

Teo waved his hands in the air. '*No comprendo, pero* I like her. She speak the truth and the truth is...' He hesitated. 'The truth is what connects us, whatever the language.'

'I think you're going to fit in here, just fine.' Rita smiled, handing him a newly printed retreat flyer. 'Now why don't you get your fish and chips. If you run, you will catch the same bus as Hilda and how about you come back here for dinner, and we can discuss everything. Say seven p.m.?'

'Do you do B&B here, too, Señora Jory?' Teo tilted his head cheekily.

Rita gave a wry smile. 'Not officially. But if you don't mind creased sheets and a snoring labrador, I might be able to rustle something up.'

Teo held out his hand. '*Perfecto*, I see you later. Now give me some more of those flyers, for surely we must sell, sell, sell?'

SEVENTEEN

Exceedingly early the next morning, up at High Meadow, the sky blushed with the first streaks of dawn. A light mist still clung to the lower fields, and the dew on the grass soaked through Rita's trainers as she twisted her hair into a knot and secured it with an old elastic band she'd found in her jeans pocket. She really must get to the hairdresser's but there was just too much to do at the moment and despite Hilda's 'danger money', she still classed having her hair done as a luxury item.

Birdsong drifted lazily from the Singing Tree, and somewhere in the distance, a horse whinnied. The girls and the chickens had been delighted at their early feed. After a quick walk, Henry had gone back to his bed in front of the Aga, where Rita had left him snoring.

Stan ambled into view, a roll of guy ropes slung over one shoulder like a reluctant Scout leader. His face was already pink from the short walk from his Land Rover.

'Jago can't make it today,' he puffed.

Rita stifled a yawn and tried not to let the disappointment show, but it landed anyway. 'Oh,' she muttered, keeping her eyes on the mallet she'd just picked up. 'Well, we'll just have to manage, the pair of us, Stan, won't we?'

She looked ahead to the work they had achieved the day before, willing herself to focus. She had always hated the manual side of the farm work, in fact, rarely did it. But the resort was her baby, and she wanted it to succeed, not just for financial purposes but for own sense of purpose too.

Just then, the thud of footsteps on damp earth caught her ear, and she glanced up to see Teo jogging over the crest of the hill, grinning, a half-eaten banana in one hand. He wore a sleeveless T-shirt and his well-fitted European shorts again. His tanned skin glistened with the fresh sheen of effort.

'Today, we conquer the roof circles, no?' he declared, arms raised in mock triumph as he approached.

Rita blinked in surprise. 'Teo? I didn't expect you here this morning.'

He grinned, taking another bite of banana. 'Well, nobody brought me breakfast. And I said I would work for that.' He actioned a theatrical shrug. 'And the secret to happiness, *amiga*, is low expectations, so we are all happy, *si?*'

He laughed at his own joke with such good-natured charm that even Stan, who rarely smiled before 9 a.m., let out a quiet chuckle.

Rita shook her head, but a reluctant smile tugged at her lips, too. Teo was already worth his weight in gold. Perhaps with him and Zenya now on the payroll she really could manage after all.

By lunchtime, Rita was in the Jimny ready to take lunch supplies to the High Meadow when Zenya, barefoot and muddy-kneed, waved and beckoned her over to the vegetable patch where she'd spent the morning digging and planting.

Rita stood at the edge, hands on hips, her face agog as she squinted slightly in the midday sun. The air was rich with the scent of freshly turned soil and mint. 'Wow! I can't believe what you've achieved in such a short time.'

Zenya's face lit up with pride. She brushed a loose curl from her forehead, leaving a smudge of earth on her cheek. 'I've enjoyed every second. We've got courgettes, cucumbers, and tomatoes in the greenhouse, and beetroot, lettuce, and radishes in the ground. I thought a herb garden would be sweet, too, nothing fancy, just the basics. Plus, I love green beans. And runner beans. I just need to find some sticks for these.'

'Look in Archie's workroom, blue door.' Rita pointed towards the courtyard. 'You'll probably find everything you need in there. That's where the tools were, right?'

'Yep. Brilliant, thanks! We need to find a piece of glass from somewhere and I'll fix the pane in the greenhouse too.' Zenya wiped her hands on her jeans and glanced towards the far end of the meadow. 'And are you sure you don't need any help up there with the yurts?'

'No, honestly, you doing this is more than enough.' Rita smiled and leaned against the fence. 'I'll introduce you properly to Teo later too. He seems like such a good lad.'

Zenya raised an eyebrow. 'Don't you go trying to set me up, Rita Jory. I'm not exactly in the habit of letting anyone in these days, in fact, ever. I'm happy on my own. And aside me not *ever* having had sexual relations with a man shorter than me, he looks about twelve.'

Rita laughed. 'Calm down, he's twenty-five and likes Manuels not Marias, so you're safe there.'

'Oh.' Zenya grinned.

'Right, onwards and upwards.' Rita walked towards the Jimny, then turned back. 'I'm so happy we met, Zenya. I really mean that. And I'm so grateful for what you've done here, already; it's a miracle.'

If it weren't for the beating sunlight, she was sure that she could see tears in Zenya's eyes.

EIGHTEEN

Two weeks later, the yurts were up, the compost loos ready for bottoms, and the outbuildings and barn scrubbed and fit for purpose. The promotional leaflets had been passed around locally, and the Seahaven Bay Retreat was already getting attention online.

Before Archie had passed away, Rita had never been an avid user of social media, but with more time on her hands, she had become what Sennen called a 'reluctant scroller'. She'd had to get extremely au fait with Facebook and Instagram as marketing tools, and although she wasn't quite brave enough to post a live Reel, Rita had to admit the retreat's Instagram page scrubbed up nicely, thanks mostly to Zenya's filter-fancy thumbs and Teo's insistence on '*luz natural* only'.

Today's marketing blurb had gone out with the headline announcing: *Book today for an extraordinary one-off introductory rate of 25 per cent off for our month-long SEA, BREATH AND SOUL ESCAPE starting on 1 July. Just five places left!*

Rita figured no one need know there were just five places in total and if the miraculous happened this month and they were oversubscribed, they could offer those interested parties other dates.

Now, it was just a waiting game.

The yurts looked like something out of a bohemian fairy tale. Each one was kitted out with thick, patterned rugs and gloriously squashy mattresses – Rita's decision, which she stood firmly by, even if it meant blowing half the budget on memory foam. She'd reasoned that if people were going to be predominantly using a compost toilet and having to share a shower, they at least deserved a good night's kip. She'd originally planned to use real candles, but after reading about the fire risk in a yurt, she wisely switched to some surprisingly effective fake ones. And no one need know the rugs were half from the charity shop; the other half she'd found rolled up in the hayloft.

Figuring hungry guests wouldn't be happy guests, she didn't want to starve anyone either. It wasn't a fitness or weight loss retreat after all, more of a massage for the mind. Betty had agreed to supply daily breakfast hampers, Betty's Tearoom style! They were to consist of Seahaven Bay Retreat branded cool bags, filled with two flasks, one with coffee and one with hot water, English breakfast tea bags, plus a selection of herbal ones, plus a mini milk bottle. A cinnamon bun and a scone with jam and cream provided the tasty treat. Just in case guests moaned at the thought of putting white flour and sugar down their crops, there would be a large bottle of mineral water. Plus Rita had done a deal with Hawthorn Farm down the road to include fresh strawberries from their 'pick your own' field – a fruit which would take them up until August at least and then she could revert to apples and pears from the orchard as the healthy option. To finish off the feast, a natural yoghurt. She had put a couple of picnic tables outside the yurts so if guests wanted to eat together then they could or if they wanted solitude, their sea-facing yurts had a chair and small table outside also.

To benefit another local business, she had also thought that leaving a book in every yurt would be a nice touch and an added takeaway. Jude had obviously been delighted, and Rita had entrusted him with choosing exactly the right words required to fit the setting.

To keep costs down, and perhaps to avoid any unexpected barbecue disasters in the High Meadow, Rita had opted to go fully vegetarian. Zenya had agreed to be resident chef and would offer salads and rolls for lunch and a freshly cooked evening meal. This would be prepared in the farm kitchen. They had yet to decide where to serve it. And if anyone couldn't go without meat, fish, or alcohol then Rita figured they could get the bus down to the harbour and the Winking Pilchard, for which Pete the landlord had gladly given her a load of 'buy one meal get a drink free' vouchers. She really must get around to seeing Jilly again to see if she may do some sort of discount on the Pilates sessions too.

As it was Sunday and her semi day of rest, with chickens and goats fed, social media duties signed off and a cup of tea drunk, Rita wanted to enjoy the balmy June weather. Pulling on a summer dress and trainers, she headed towards the High Meadow with Henry the labrador at her heels.

She was surprised to see Teo busy draping fairy lights from one yurt to another with the precision of a Formula One driver taking a bend. Zenya, in a haze of lavender oil and eucalyptus, was arranging jars of dried wildflowers and placing little handwritten notes onto pillowcases that read, BREATHE IN. BEGIN AGAIN.

Stan had crafted two rustic wooden signs, one that he'd fixed to the main gate and another that was now stuck in the ground in front of Yurt Avenue, Rita's new name for the row of fancy tents, which, thanks to Hilda's input, read, SEAHAVEN BAY RETREAT – WHERE THE SEA MEETS YOUR SOUL.

Zenya and Teo stopped what they were doing and joined Rita on Archie's bench.

The breeze had picked up, carrying the scent of salt and lavender. Henry sat at their feet and gave a sleepy sigh. The cliffs rolled away in rugged folds, sun-bleached and dappled with golden gorse. Tiny white sails bobbed in the bay, and gulls wheeled lazily overhead. It was one of those quiet, golden June afternoons when time seemed to pause, just long enough to remind you how beautiful the world could be. Rita could even smell that summer was well and truly here.

She broke their unified silence. 'I don't expect you to work on a Sunday when a retreat is not on, you know.'

Zenya replied first. 'I want to. You have given me peace and security, Rita. Something I have been searching for, for a long time.'

Teo smiled. 'And me, well, you have opened me up to a new life in a different country. I love this. And I love this place.'

'You might not be saying that when the guests start arriving. It could be interesting,' Rita quipped.

'I will soon woo-woo them back to ground level,' Zenya replied, smiling.

Teo's voice softened. 'And you sure it still OK for me to stay in the upstairs annexe?'

'Of course.' Rita nodded. 'I must get Stan to put a lock on the door for you.'

'*Sí, sí*, as I am a little worried about Hilda getting risky with me.'

Zenya laughed aloud. 'I think you mean frisky.'

Teo stood up and stretched his perfectly taut arms to the sky and with a noise of complete contentment, quoted, '*La vida es más divertida si te arriesgas un poco.*'

'Life is more fun if you take a few risks,' Zenya immediately translated. Teo and Rita's mouths dropped open.

'Or frisks,' Teo stated, causing them all to crack up.

NINETEEN

Rita had just got in from feeding the animals and was tucking into tea and toast at the kitchen table when it happened.

Ping!

She paused. Email alerts usually heralded spam, a newsletter she never signed up for, or a flash sale on beauty products she didn't need. But something about this ping felt... different. With a deep breath, she reached across the table for her laptop. She tapped the trackpad and squinted at the inbox.

Subject: Booking Confirmation – The Seahaven Bay Retreat

She stared at it. Then blinked. Then stared again.

Booking... confirmation. She whispered aloud then gasped. For there it was. A real person by the name of Emily Budd had booked the month-long Sea, Breath, and Soul Escape. She'd even paid in full. There was a message, too:

Hi! I found your retreat on Instagram and fell in love with it instantly. I'm so excited to spend a whole month by the sea. Hope there's decent coffee! Emily x

Rita let out a stunned laugh. Her hand flew to her mouth. 'Oh my God.'

She whirled around the kitchen, emitting little screams, pulse racing. This wasn't just someone saying 'interested' or asking how far it was from the station. This was a real booking. A real guest. Someone who'd looked at the photos, read her blurb, and decided *yes*.

She had imagined this moment so many times during late-night doubts and early-morning 'what am I doing?' spirals. But now it was real, it felt entirely surreal.

She did a little jump on the spot, a ridiculous half dance that caused Henry, who was sleeping in his bed, to open one eye then close it again with a harrumph.

She grabbed her phone, and clutching a tea towel like a victory flag, opened WhatsApp. She tapped out a message.

RITA

Guess who just got her first ACTUAL guest booking!!!!

A reply came almost instantly.

KELLY

AAAAAAAAAAAAAAHHHHHHHHHHHH!!!!!! I'M SCREAMING. I'M CRYING. I'M SO PROUD OF YOU MY FRIEND XXX

Rita grinned. She typed back one-handed while pouring herself a celebratory glass of non-alcoholic elderflower fizz, the one she'd been testing for guests.

She sat back down at the table. She had done this. Against all logic and fear and through all-consuming grief, she had created something. Rita Jory, once the woman who could barely get out of bed, who didn't know where she ended and her sadness began, had set up her own business.

The Seahaven Bay Retreat was officially (well, nearly –

because she could really do with four more guests) open for business.

Her hand rested on the edge of the table, her thumb tracing the grain in the wood. There was a hum in her chest, like something deep and joyful trying to make its way to the surface. But it wasn't joy alone. It was everything.

She didn't realise she was crying until a tear dropped silently onto the table. Then another and another, until she found herself full-on sobbing.

Then behind her through the open front door, she heard a voice. 'Rita. Oh, Rita. No. No.'

She quickly wiped at her cheeks with the sleeve of her cardigan before turning, but it was too late. Teo stood in the doorway, barefoot and gentle as ever, wearing loose cotton trousers and a faded T-shirt with the word NAMASTE peeling across the chest.

'I'm OK,' she managed, her voice cracking.

The handsome Spaniard didn't speak at first. Just walked over, placed a hand softly on her shoulder, and crouched beside her.

'Rita,' he soothed. 'You do not cry like this because something is wrong, am I right, please say I am right.'

She let out a shaky laugh through the tears. 'I think I'm happy. Honestly, I think I'm *so* happy. It's just... it's all a bit much. You know.'

'You are happy and sad at the same time,' he said with a wise little nod. 'That is how healing feels.'

She looked down at him, her heart full and aching. 'Do you think he'd be proud? My Archie, my husband, that is.'

Teo nodded thoughtfully. 'I expect he'd be proud of you whatever you did.'

Her chest tightened, but this time it didn't break her; it lifted her. She let out a long breath, nodded, and sniffed loudly.

'Come,' Teo said gently, rising to his feet and handing her a piece of kitchen roll from the side. 'The sun is up, the sky is blue and my beautiful Rita, she need to feel grounded. You are coming with me to the orchard.'

Rita dutifully followed the young Spaniard out through the back door, into the cool hush of early morning. The orchard was bathed in soft, pearly light, dew clinging to the grass like scattered jewels. Teo led her to the clearing between the trees, where the grass had been flattened from his own previous yoga session.

'Lie down,' he crooned. Rita, feeling hypnotised by this charming man, did as instructed, not even caring that she was lying in the damp. Teo knelt beside her, guiding her limbs until she lay completely still, with her palms facing upwards and her feet falling naturally outward. 'Now close your eyes and breathe normally. Focus on releasing tension from your foots up to the top of your head.

'*Savasana*,' Teo whispered, in his special tone, the one as if nothing in the world could ever truly be urgent. '*Savasana*.'

At first Rita resisted, thoughts spinning around her head at one hundred miles an hour.

'Flow with the breeze, just flow, just relax,' Teo soothed.

Rita felt her body grow heavy, her eyes closed, the breeze brushing her face like perfect kisses. And for a few glorious minutes, she let herself just *be*. No worries, no lists, no more grief dragging behind her like a shadow.

Teo continued his soothing mantra. 'Just breathe. Just peace. Just now.'

Then, all of a sudden: chug-chug-chug-chug. The unmistakable sound of Archie's old tractor cut through the stillness like an unexpected thunderclap.

With a deep sigh, Rita opened her eyes. Teo took her hand to help her up. 'I think your cowboy is here.'

Rita groaned softly as she sat up. 'He's *not* my cowboy.'

Teo nodded wisely. 'So, I overhear your good guest news. I shall go and tell Zenya, *si*.'

'Thank you, Teo, you really are a star.'

Rita sloped across the courtyard, her hair everywhere, tear

streaks still evident. But she felt younger somehow, as if the burden of the last few months had been gently lifted. Like a natural beauty was shining from within.

She couldn't help but smile back at Jago's lopsided grin as he climbed down from the tractor, pushing his wild dark curls back to show off his piercing green eyes. 'Hope I didn't interrupt some kind of sacred ritual.'

'You'll be the first on my list if there's a public flogging.' She quickly wiped at her face and scraped at her hair to try and get it into some kind of order.

Jago laughed. 'Here I am going out of my way to help you again and all I get is full-on abuse.'

Rita pointed to the trailer attached to the tractor. 'What you got on there, anyway? I've got enough yurts, thanks.'

'Hold your horses, madam.' Jago peeled back the tarpaulin covering the long, unidentified item with a flourish. 'Stan told me you needed somewhere for the guests to eat. It's a marquee and a couple of long bench seats. My old man used to use it for family parties, but being on my own now, I don't seem to have had time to follow that tradition.'

Rita blinked, her throat tightening. 'Why are you being so good to me? I know that you and Archie were never the best of friends but I kind of never asked why?'

Rita was sure that she could see a tear in big Jago Jenken's eye. He looked away and coughed loudly.

Avoiding her gaze, he began unstrapping the frame. 'I just thought it might help.' His voice tightened. 'No big deal if you don't want it.'

'You've already helped with the yurts, fixed some fences and are paying for Stan to help me... and now this?'

And just like that, her composure cracked for the second time that day. Maybe it was the *savasana*; maybe it had loosened some-thing deep inside her, unknotted a part of her she'd been holding tight for too long. Whatever it was, the tears came again before she could stop them. Quiet at first, slipping down her cheeks in silence, then with that awful hitching breath that a big sob courted.

'Oh God.' She wiped her face with her sleeve. 'Ignore me. I don't know what's up with me today. I was on cloud nine earlier.'

'Hey.' His voice had lost its usual swagger. He took a cautious step forward.

Rita turned her face away, wiping at her cheeks with the back of her hand like it might undo the moment, but it was too late. The crack had widened. She felt exposed, embarrassed by the rawness of it all.

Jago didn't try to joke, didn't offer some clumsy one-liner. He just stood there for a second, uncertain, then closed the distance between them.

'Rita, tell me. What's going on?'

She shook her head and sniffed. He reached out, slow, and deliberate, placing a hand gently on her arm.

'You don't have to tell me anything if you don't want to,' he said, his voice soft, encouraging.

And that's when she looked up at him, like really looked. His face wasn't mocking or smug or amused. It was open. Concerned. And maybe something else too. The silence between them stretched, and in it, something shifted. Jago brushed a thumb beneath her eye, catching a tear. The contact was feather-light. She didn't move. Maybe she couldn't.

Then his hand moved to her chin, cupping it gently, like he was giving her every opportunity to pull away. But she didn't. And before she even had a chance to think if she wanted to, it was happening. Jago Jenken was leaning in to kiss her.

It was soft, tentative. There was no swagger in it. Just warmth. Sincerity. And something that felt a little like longing. For a moment, Rita kissed him back.

But then panic flared in her chest like a struck match. She stepped back sharply, breath catching, eyes wide.

'I – I can't, Jago, it's too soon. I'm so sorry. It's just... What are you doing?'

He froze, hurt flickering across his face so quickly that Rita missed it. Then he nodded once, jaw tightening.

'Yeah. No. Of course not. What was I thinking?' He took a step back, clearing his throat. 'I should go.'

He turned and headed back to the tractor, boots crunching against the gravel. She watched him climb in and drive away, the marquee and benches rattling on the trailer, the released tarpaulin flapping in the breeze.

Rita stood frozen, heart thudding, lips tingling from a kiss that had not only taken her completely by surprise but had left her unsure what to feel.

TWENTY

It was a blistering hot day. Rita sat beneath the Singing Tree, knees hugged to her chest, her back against the inscription on Archie's bench. The wind moved through the leaves above, setting them whispering in a way that always felt like they were trying to tell her something she wasn't quite ready to hear.

She stared out across the ocean. Gulls were screeching into the wind; the horizon looked back at her, its perfect line a leveller for any human being. She let her mind drift, inevitably, to the kiss. She hadn't seen him since. She touched her lips absently, remembering how unexpectedly tender it had been. How Jago had looked at her, not like someone to fix, but like someone already whole. And how, despite everything in her that had wanted to lean into it, her feet had carried her the other way. The truth was, she didn't really know much about the man at all, only that he lived across the meadow and that he belonged to the Jenken family. And while the historical feud between the Jorys and the Jenkens wasn't spoken of often, it ran deep enough to still cast a shadow.

It was when Archie was still alive that she'd first read – through the ever-entertaining Queen of the Seahaven Bay Facebook Gossip Group – that Jago Jenken had once been married. The post had been tucked between a photo of someone's lost cat and a heated debate about seagull-proof bins. At the time, Rita had skimmed past it, but now, with that unexpected kiss lingering on her lips and Jago's quiet acts of kindness stacking like Russian dolls, she found herself wondering about the woman who'd come before. What had happened between them? And in a town as full of gossip as Seahaven Bay why she had not heard more.

What would Archie want for her future, she wondered. He had never been a jealous man; a selfish one sometimes, but he always had her best interests at heart. He had always encouraged her to do more if she wanted to. But she had been happy with her life, the majority of the time, and had taken to motherhood well. She had enjoyed being the organiser. And even though now she really was the organiser of her own destiny, a new relationship had been the last thing on her mind.

For she'd built something. Something *real*. And tomorrow five paying guests would arrive with bags and expectations and a need for peace, and she was ready (she hoped!) to meet them with everything they needed for a truly relaxing escape.

The melodic song of a blackbird above drew her gently out of her thoughts. As her eyes drifted down, they landed on the cubby hole. On impulse, she crouched and reached in, not expecting to find anything. Then after a good root around, her fingers brushed against something, causing her to act as if she'd been burned.

'No bloody way.' She laughed. Slowly, carefully, she drew out a small white piece of folded paper, her curiosity rising like a tide.

If you don't know what to do, do nothing and let the answer come to you.

No name. Typed again. Just that single, steady sentence.

Rita stared at it, her heart twisting. For a fleeting moment, she wondered, could it have been her husband? Maybe, somehow, he'd left it behind. Maybe she'd missed it when she was here with Sennen before. A message from the past, waiting to catch her just as she was about to fall. She smiled, because wasn't that exactly how the retreat idea had come to her? Out of nowhere, just when she needed it most.

Tucking the note into the pocket of her jeans, she headed to the yurts. She opened up all of the flaps to let the morning air drift in then headed back down the meadow path toward the barn. As she came around the corner, she stopped dead.

The space behind the barn, just yesterday a bare patch of concrete, now stood adorned with a smart white marquee. The front was rolled open, and she could see picnic benches had been arranged snugly inside. Fairy lights were strung inside and out. Her hand flew to her heart. Her bottom lip wobbled. There was clearly more to Jago Jenken than met the eye and on this occasion, his actions spoke louder than any words ever could. She stood for a moment, overwhelmed, then turned at the sound of gravel crunching.

A taxi pulled up on the courtyard and out tumbled Kelly with a bright pink wheelie case, owl-like sunglasses pushing back her thick blonde locks and red lipstick perfectly in place.

'Reeeeeeeet!' she squealed, flinging her arms in the air like a game show host. 'The glam squad has landed!'

Rita blinked, then burst out laughing.

Kelly marched toward her, lifting a giant red tote bag. 'Voila! One beauty kit. Hair dye, face creams, mini mani station, and my best chat. Hope you've got the *vino blanco* on ice.'

Rita opened her arms and let herself be hugged, hard and fast, nearly choking on the familiar sickly perfume that her best mate had been drenching herself with daily for years.

'Wine, yes. Sanity, debatable.'

Kelly pulled back and beamed. 'Doesn't matter. You've got me now.'

TWENTY-ONE

Rita sat stiffly on an upcycled kitchen stool, a towel draped around her shoulders, while Kelly prowled around her with the focus of a seasoned stylist prepping a celebrity for the red carpet. A bottle of wine on the go.

'I don't know why I let you talk me into this.' Rita laughed, eyeing the array of products on table. 'I'm more wheelbarrow chic than runway sleek now.'

'You never used to be like that and honestly, Reet, your hair. Even Vidal Sassoon would have struggled, the state it's in.'

'I know. I know. And before you say it, who'd have thought crows even had feet this big.'

'Rubbish.' Kelly double checked the hair dye instructions and took a slurp of wine. 'You've got cheekbones that hardly even need a contour. And a wodge of moisturiser will sort out those fine lines. Now sit still and trust the process. You're going to look like the mermaid of Seahaven Bay by the time I'm done. Actually, shit, I have a little gift for you.' Kelly rooted around in her tote then pulled out a bright yellow rubber chicken.

'Meet Nigel the second. You can take out all your rage on something that isn't me.'

Rita gave it an experimental squish, causing its eyes to pop out dramatically.

'Dear God.' Rita's shoulders started to shake. 'Actually, this is disturbingly satisfying.'

'And a lot quieter,' Kelly added, gauging Rita's reaction. 'I also got you a back-up in white, in case Nigel Mark II explodes under pressure.'

Rita half smiled. 'You're still not forgiven. Bless that poor bird.'

They both laughed, the sound echoing through the kitchen and out into the early evening. Rita let her shoulders drop and closed her eyes as Kelly began to work her magic.

After a prolonged period of silence, her knowing best friend asked, 'Are you all right, Reet? I mean, really all right.'

'Yeah, just tired. Lots to think about and do, you know.' Rita refilled their glasses.

'I guess grieving could become quite draining, but you know you can tell me anything, right? Is it the will?'

Rita's throat tightened. She knew she could trust Kelly with even the messiest parts of her life.

'No. I haven't even thought about that for a while, to be honest. Haven't got time to. I need money now and it's quite obvious all he's left me is debt anyway.'

'Shit, I didn't mean to make you think about it again, Reet.'

'It's fine.' Rita took a deliberate slurp of wine. It had nothing to do with the will. It had everything to do with Jago Jenken. His kiss had knocked something loose in her, stirred up feelings she'd thought were long buried beneath grief and practicality. Everything felt tangled up with guilt and confusion. And she wasn't quite ready for the questions. Or the answers. Or the weight of what it might all mean if something were to happen between them.

'Fine or fine? Whatever it is, I've got your back, mate.' Kelly squeezed Rita's shoulder.

'I know.' Rita sighed as Kelly repeated the mantra they had used throughout their many years of friendship.

'I'm always here with an ear.'

A couple of hours later, Kelly's magic had been worked. She held up a mirror with a flourish. 'Now. Prepare to fall back in love... with yourself.'

Rita gasped. Her hair, now a shiny and soft chestnut brown all over, sat in waves around her face, her skin glowed and her eyes looked brighter. More awake somehow.

'I look like... well, I look like me. The pre-Archie-going me.'

'You look like you're about to host the most fabulous retreat this county has ever seen.' Kelly beamed.

With Kelly now relaxing in a hot bath, Rita rang the annexe doorbell with her nose, whilst balancing a plate with two slices of pizza. The scent of pepperoni and roasted vegetables wafted up as she waited.

Hilda opened it in her leopard print dressing gown, eyebrows already raised. 'I don't recall asking for meals on wheels. And definitely not at this unearthly hour.'

'Don't get excited, it's just shop-bought pizza. Kelly is staying, we had some left over and I know how much you love it.'

Rita could hear the faint sound of grime music coming from Teo's room above. Hilda took the plate, eyeing Rita over the rim of her glasses. 'You've done something to your hair.'

Rita hesitated. 'Yes. I've had the full Kelly effect.'

'Oh.' Hilda's gaze didn't soften. 'It looks nice. Bit of rouge always did make a difference to you. One wonders who you might be doing this for?'

Rita tutted. 'The retreat is open tomorrow, so Kel, well, and I, thought I should look the part.'

But Hilda had already turned toward the little kitchenette, setting the plate down with a clink. 'Don't think I don't see what *he's* doing. All that helping out, turning up conveniently with things you didn't ask for. Wrapping you round his little finger, one favour at a time.'

Rita crossed her arms. 'You're being ridiculous; he's... he's just being kind.' Praying that her hawk-eyed mother-in-law hadn't seen *the kiss*, a stab of fear stung her.

'You know who I'm talking about, then?' Hilda turned slowly. 'And am I being ridiculous? First it's the yurts, then a marquee, then... who knows? He'll have you signing something before you know it. You wait. Next thing, you'll be handing over the farm and all that my Ralphy and your Archie worked for will be for nothing.'

Rita's jaw dropped. 'No!' She could feel her anger rising. 'I would never...'

Hilda's expression didn't change; however, her voice softened. 'Just keep your wits about you, that's all I'm saying. You've been through a lot. And sometimes we mistake kindness for something else. I just don't want this to be a lesson to you for the bad.'

Rita stared at her, the words still stinging. 'You think I'm that stupid?'

Hilda gave a small shrug and picked up her plate. 'I think you're still grieving. And that *he's* far from stupid.'

Rita felt deflated. 'Maybe if you explained to me exactly what happened between both families then I would be able to understand your fury.'

Hilda pursed her lips. 'Not now, Rita. There's a bottle of something fizzy on the top shelf of the fridge. Take it to celebrate tomorrow; you deserve it. Though technically, I paid for it... so raise a glass to me while you're at it.'

Realising that was all she was going to get, Rita replied tightly, 'Thank you, Hilda.'

'And I shall look forward to meeting your guests.' The old woman's lips twitched. 'I promise not to embarrass you. Much.'

Rita couldn't help but smile. Hilda put her free hand on her daughter-in-law's shoulder. 'Just be careful, Rita. That's all. Some people wear the face of an angel but have the mind of a devil.'

With that, she reclined on her chair, turned up the news and shoved a piece of pizza in her mouth.

As Rita walked back to the farmhouse, Hilda's 'face of an angel... mind of a devil' comment echoed loudly around her mind. She didn't want to believe it, and shook her head as if to physically dislodge the doubt. Didn't want to think Jago's warmth, his help, *the kiss*, could be anything other than real. Maybe grief had left her soft in places she used to be sharp. That scared her. She was a bright woman; surely she wouldn't be fooled, wouldn't fall for charm or convenience. And yet... she had never felt the need to ask why there had been such a rift between the families.

She glanced up at the silhouette of the barn, the marquee now casting long, soft shadows in the field behind it. She took a huge breath. *Please let me not be a fool*, she thought, as she reached the farmhouse door. *Please let me be right about him.*

TWENTY-TWO

The sun shone down over Seahaven Farm as if knowing that today had to be exactly right for the grand opening. Even the goats and chickens had surprisingly behaved themselves at feeding time, which she had managed at record speed.

Rita had checked on all the yurts, which were now looking so homely and comfortable, and had just met with Zenya and Teo in the food marquee, which had been signposted by Stan as the Snack Shack, to go over final arrangements.

Once she felt everything was in order, she showered (keeping her hair dry as it still looked so beautifully styled from the night before). She donned a long flowery midi dress that she'd found at the back of her wardrobe and old white leather pumps, which she'd cleaned up with hot water and a cloth. Putting on a smudge of pale pink lipstick and a swipe of mascara, she took a look at herself in her bedroom mirror and smiled. For the first time in ages, she felt that she looked good, which meant she felt good too.

She was just about to knock on Kelly's door to check she was getting ready when Sennen phoned, voice panicked but trying to stay calm.

'Mum, you're not going to believe this. The groom's mum has accidentally sent the cake to the wrong address. Apparently, it's sitting in someone's fridge in Brighton. The wedding is in Brampton! The bride just found out. She's losing it. I'm trying not to. A courier is going to cost a fortune, and as it's a replica of the Eiffel flipping Tower, they are saying that they can't guarantee it won't get damaged. So, I said I'd drive there and get it.'

Rita couldn't help but laugh. 'Well, at least it's not the wedding dress, I guess.'

'Bless you being so jovial.' Sennen sighed. 'But it means I really need to sort this and by the time I've driven to you it will be late and...'

'Sennen. My beautiful girl. Take a breath. I'm glad you're not coming; how about that.'

'What?' Sennen sounded slightly perturbed.

'I know you're super busy and wanted to make an effort for me, but it's too much driving all this way when you've got so much on. Wait until you get a proper break and see me then. Teo and Zenya are doing me proud, and I've got Kelly here for a few days. I'm totally covered.'

'Oh, Mum. I love you for always making things easy.'

'That's kind of my job.' Rita felt herself welling up at the appreciation. 'How's your new flat, quickly before you go?'

'I love it. It's small but I'm still Reading central, can walk to the station now, so it's worked out brilliantly.'

'I'm so pleased. Now go and get the Eiffel Tower. Oh, and any word from Thom?'

Sennen hesitated. 'He called me. Erm...'

'And...' Rita felt uneasy.

'He's fine.'

'Sennen?'

'He's fine, Mum.'

'Did he say anything about opening day?' Rita pushed.

'Mum, just have the best day ever and I will call you as soon as I can to find out how it went. Love you!'

All of a sudden, Kelly charged past her towards the bathroom, all white towel and wobbling bosom, with a loud, 'I won't be long, Reet, pinkie promise.'

Rita was just walking downstairs wondering why Sennen was keeping such a close allegiance with her brother when the doorbell rang. She went to open it but there was nobody there; just as she was about to close it again, something fell against her feet. On seeing it was a beautiful bouquet of long-stemmed pink roses, and sweet-scented white freesias, her heart did a little leap. She ripped at the mini envelope poked inside and then put her hand to her chest at the handwritten note.

Some things are better felt than said. Good luck today. Jago x

With a sudden feeling of being watched, Rita looked in the direction of the annexe to see a stern-looking Hilda slowly shaking her head.

Rita was adjusting her hair for the fifth time, as cars – including the only three taxis that serviced the bay – crunched one after the other up the gravel drive. She had asked them all to arrive at three thirty and remarkably all five of them had turned up bang on time.

Her heart hammered against her ribs. This was really happening. Actual paying guests. For one terrible moment, she wondered if she'd completely lost her mind, but then she saw people stepping out, stretching their legs, pointing at the sea view with delighted faces. The nerves loosened, just a touch, and excitement rushed in to take their place.

Stepping out of the Snack Shack marquee, she fixed a beaming smile, quietly repeating under her breath, 'You've got this, girl.'

She mouthed, 'Take a seat' to each of them as they filed in

whilst Teo arranged their luggage at the back of the marquee ready to take up to the yurts in Archie's Land Rover.

Kelly appeared from the side door, precariously balancing a tray dotted with champagne flutes filled with pale, fragrant elderflower fizz. She nodded to Rita, who signalled back to her to start handing them around.

Rita took in a huge, visible breath. 'Welcome, everybody, to the Seahaven Bay Retreat. I'm Rita Jory and this place is my new baby, so to speak.' Another deep breath. 'The plan is to run it like clockwork, of course, but you need to bear in mind we are on a farm, where the animals don't respond to "No noise please."' She paused to add, *Especially Nigel the cockerel*, then sadly remembered his demise.

A ripple of polite laughter moved through the group. 'And, secondly, we are in Cornwall where our microclimate doesn't respond to' – Rita assumed a thick Cornish accent – '"no rain or mizzle please", either.'

More polite laughter.

'As well as chickens, we've got goats. Camilla, the pure white one, has a knack for escaping. In fact, I wouldn't be surprised if she told me she was pregnant by the end of the week. So, if you do see her on the run, please let one of the team know.'

Stronger laughter.

Rita lifted her glass. 'A little something to celebrate new beginnings for us all – non-alcoholic, may I add. To get you going before the real work begins.'

'Work?' a big-busted woman in a flowery kaftan repeated. 'I'm only here to have a good time and maybe find myself a handsome distraction, if I'm lucky.'

Rita chuckled to herself, but when one of the two men in the group took a swig of the fizz and then casually slipped a tiny bottle of vodka from his pocket to top it up, she couldn't help but wonder exactly what she'd let herself in for.

Zenya and Teo had now joined her up the front.

'I'd like to introduce you to Zenya and Teo.' The beautiful pair smiled broadly. 'You will be seeing a lot of them around the place. Teo is our yoga guru, and as well as some stretching and soul work, he will be taking those of you who like a wildlife hike on some amazing walks, plus tempting you to dip in the ocean down at Seahaven Cove for some cold-water swimming. Zenya here will be in charge of our gong and breathwork classes, plus moonlight mantras which we hope will open up some soul searching and meaningful conversations. There is a leaflet with all of the classes and times in your yurts, so don't worry about remembering all of this. Plus, there is a map of the local area and plan of the site here. My mobile is on there, too, should you not be able to find anyone to ask.'

'Sounds like a blessed army camp if you ask me,' Vodka Man snorted. The other four guests all gave him a look. He harrumphed. 'Sorry, sorry. Let's just say I'm not here of my own free will and leave it at that for now, shall we?' The man's deep voice boomed.

'Jesus,' Zenya whispered in earshot of Rita and Teo.

'Zenya and Teo will be taking your luggage up to your yurts, so goodbye for now, you two.' The pair left with a smile and a wave.

Rita cleared her throat. 'Gosh, I feel like I'm going on a bit.'

'No, it's great you are so organised,' a thin, bespectacled woman in her early thirties added quietly.

'Fabulous.' Rita smiled at the encouragement. 'So, bear with me while I rattle through the rest.' She checked her notes. 'Oh yes... The six...' Kelly kicked her gently. 'I mean, seven areas you need to be aware of are as follows: High Meadow, where your yurts are positioned. I don't think even the most cynical person would be able to complain at the view up there.' She didn't dare catch Vodka Man's eye. 'The Singing Tree, located near to where your yurts are positioned, is a beautiful old sycamore under which you can get some shade and rest and meditate. Here, which is the Snack Shack where we will serve cold lunches and hot dinners. Breakfast will be a hamper full of Cornish goodies, plus a healthy option and various beverages. It will be left outside your door at seven a.m. every morning with the choice of eating alone or on the picnic tables up there.'

'I take it there will be coffee?' Vodka Man shouted out.

'Yes, and I can promise it won't be instant.' Rita gritted her teeth. 'All food served at the retreat will be vegetarian, with no alcohol provided. But for those of you who can't bear the thought of no fish, meat, or booze then there's a great pub called the Winking Pilchard, plus other eateries down in the bay which is a short bus or car ride down the hill. And for which I have discount vouchers.'

'The Winking fucking Pilchard. Fucking genius,' Vodka Man announced, causing everyone to hesitantly laugh.

'What about vegans?' an overweight girl with purple hair and a septum piercing piped up, her phone held high, as she filmed the proceedings.

'All *kale* the vegans,' the distractor boomed. Everybody ignored him.

'And, sorry... I don't know all your names yet...' Rita addressed Vegan Girl.

'Lola,' she replied, pressing a stop to her recording.

Rita's voice remained calm but firm. 'I'd rather you didn't film now. I think it's important we respect guests' space. Some people might not want to be on camera. After all, I can imagine a few of you are here to take a break from the madness that is social media.'

Lola lowered her phone with a small, theatrical pout.

'Thank you.' Rita reinstated her smile. 'And of course, we have you vegans covered.' But inwardly, she cringed at her own blatant lie, realising that some guests would almost certainly expect vegan options. She was sure Zenya had the cooking skills to manage it, but Rita wasn't about to start stocking every milk alternative on the supermarket shelf or catering to every fad diet going. Plain old cow's milk had always been enough for her and her family.

'I didn't want this to feel like some kind of wellness prison,' Rita noted. 'No juice-only regimes here. What's the fun in that?' She smiled and caught the eye of a laid-back-looking man with straight, shoulder-length mousy hair, annoyingly perfect teeth and sunglasses. He gave her a slow nod and a little half smile, as though the comment was meant just for him. Rita felt a flicker of heat rise in her cheeks – for heaven's sake, was she actually blushing? *Get a grip, woman.*

She cleared her throat. 'Back to buildings of note. The Splash Stop is in the annexe next to the farmhouse, with a shower, bath, and proper loo. There is also an outside toilet, shower of sorts and sink in the outbuildings down by the orchard, signposted "Number Two".' Another small ripple of laughter. 'The Serenity Barn, adjoining this building, really is our peaceful go-to space and where most of the sessions will be held. The Orchard is where we will run yoga sessions if the weather holds like it has been. Or you may simply want to read or chill there. There's a resort guide book in each yurt that covers all of this, plus local walks, restaurants, bus times and timetables, cinema listings, everything you might need for Seahaven Bay. I'm sure you'll have loads of questions, but for now, I'll let you go and settle into your new home for the month of July.' Rita looked to Kelly, who mouthed, 'Guest slot.'

'Oh, yes and at the Seahaven Bay Retreat we like to mix it up a bit and have a special monthly guest slot, details of which I will enlighten you with during your stay.'

Having delivered the guests' luggage to their yurts, Zenya and Teo rushed into place at the back of the tent. 'Up to you if you'd like to walk up to High Meadow. It's around half a mile from what I'm calling Yurt Avenue. Zenya here is happy to show you the way. Or Teo will be outside in the Land Rover if you'd prefer to get your bones rattled.' People began to stand. 'Oh, and one more important thing. Zenya, Teo and I will be under the Singing Tree at six p.m. tonight where the plan is a really informal meet and greet circle, where you can ask as many questions as you like. We'd love to see some of you, ideally all of you, there.'

As the guests slowly filed out of the marquee into the steaming July afternoon, a soft buzz of anticipation hung in the air. Four of the guests followed Zenya on foot towards the High Meadow, chatting quietly, whilst Vodka Man, to Teo's complete confusion, heaved himself into the Land Rover, shouting, 'To the High Meadow, lad, and don't spare the horses.'

Rita stood outside the marquee with the afternoon sunshine warming her shoulders, Kelly by her side, now laughing aloud.

'Bloody hell, Reet, can we open some wine now, please?'

Rita smiled, emotion catching in her throat. 'You can. I want to stay sober until at least after the meet and greet. Weirdly, in all the preparation for this retreat I never thought about *who* might book onto it; I didn't realise quite what having five different personalities under one roof might bring to the proceedings.'

Kelly smirked. 'Well, we know someone who won't be staying sober. Hilarious. I can't wait to hear his story. And who's the guest slot for July?'

Rita laughed. 'I've no idea but I'm sure something will come to me.'

They made their way inside the cool farmhouse. This was it, a new beginning, a new venture. The Seahaven Bay Retreat was officially open, and Rita Jory could finally release some of her money worries and, hopefully, begin to grasp a new lease of life.

TWENTY-THREE

By six o'clock, the late sun was slanting golden through the branches of the Singing Tree, a slight breeze setting the wind chimes on their dance of heavenly tinkling. The grass was warm, the bees were heading back to their hives, and Teo had just finished arranging some hay bales in a wonky semicircle.

Rita stood at the front, her nerves disguised beneath a cheery smile. Zenya sat, legs crossed and barefoot, in the grass. Teo leaned against the trunk.

Rita was happy to see all the new retreat guests were gathered, each clutching a biodegradable welcome cup filled with more of the fizz from earlier.

'Welcome, everyone,' Rita said brightly. 'I hope you've settled into your new temporary homes – they have a pretty amazing view, won't you agree?' Nobody said anything. Zenya and Teo shared a quick 'brace yourself' glance. 'You've officially survived your first few hours at Seahaven Bay Retreat, so well done. Tonight, as we are such a small group, I thought we'd do a gentle welcome circle under the Singing Tree. My personal favourite place to just be.'

A few hesitant glances passed amongst the group.

'Optional but encouraged,' Zenya said, standing up.

Rita continued, 'We'd love for you to introduce yourselves –

just your name, maybe why you're here, or what you hope to get from the retreat. Or you can say nothing at all.'

A woman perched confidently on a hay bale in a cheetah-print kaftan and gold wedges, her thick blonde hair curled to perfection, didn't wait for permission.

'I'll go first. I'm Annie. Fifty-nine. Former cabin crew where I spent thirty years serving tea at thirty thousand feet while avoiding turbulence and terrible pick-up lines. Not much has changed. Serial dater. Serial heartbreaker. And seriously terrible at Tinder. I'm hoping to find inner peace or a man with a decent pension and a bad heart. Either will do.'

Zenya nodded graciously, as if the extroverted Annie had just announced she was here to study philosophy.

'Well, don't be looking at me with pound signs in your eyes,' Vodka Man quipped.

'I do have some standards,' Annie spat back.

Everybody was now smirking.

Next to Annie was Lola, looking glorious in lemon yoga pants, smelling of patchouli oil, her purple hair in a single plait this time. She beamed enthusiastically. 'Hi! I'm Lola. I'm twenty-five, a Virgo sun, Pisces moon, and I run a plant-based wellness brand called Vibe & Thrive on Instagram.'

She paused for dramatic effect, expecting recognition. She wasn't deterred when it didn't come. 'I've just come off a five-day liquid chlorophyll cleanse and I'm hoping to spiritually realign, emotionally detox, and maybe lose the last stone that's clinging to my aura.'

Vodka Man groaned audibly and then luckily only in Teo's direction, whispered, 'To her fat arse, she means.'

All heads turned to the middle-aged man with a pot belly, red nose, and perfectly coiffed silver-grey hair with tidy matching beard. He was slouched with a suspiciously large reusable water bottle between his legs and a scowl miserable enough to turn the weather.

'I'm Michael,' he muttered. 'Divorced. Divorce lawyer. Old

enough to know better. Recently detoxed from own marriage and now actively retoxing with spirits and I don't mean the ethereal kind. There will be no singing. Or tree-hugging. And don't even think of sticking a blessed herbal enema anywhere near any of my orifices.'

Lola blinked. 'Maybe that is exactly what you need. I think you might be holding a whole lot of stagnant energy.'

Rita, realising this probably would be the only thing Michael would be holding on to, quickly intervened. 'Well, welcome, Michael, and let's hope we can release some of it in other ways, eh?'

Michael muttered and took another swig from his potent water bottle.

Next came the chiselled-featured long-haired, good-teeth man. He wore dark sunglasses even in the shade and hadn't spoken much since arriving. He pulled them down slightly now, revealing tired, kind eyes.

'Call me Paul. Here to write music and escape the industry and the world for a bit.'

He gave a lazy shrug. Rita felt her stomach flutter as his gaze lingered on her just a fraction too long. He carried a sexy arrogance that made her pulse quicken. What was going on with her? She hadn't seen Jago for a while, but out of sight had not meant out of mind. Something had stirred within her, and she wasn't sure how to navigate her feelings. She shifted slightly, self-conscious, and cursed herself for noticing Paul's unnerving charm. Annie eyed him with interest and the others looked like they were trying to place him. Then came the awkward pause. All eyes shifted to the small, mousy woman on the end who had been pretending to be part of the tree trunk.

She cleared her throat nervously.

'I'm Emily.' She was almost inaudible. 'An accountant. Thirty-three. I didn't... really want to come, but my company thought I needed "a reset". I'm um... here for the peace and to read books. So, if I don't say much, it's not personal. It's just... me.'

Everyone softened a little at that. Even Michael.

Rita clapped her hands gently. 'Thank you all for sharing. Or not sharing. Either way, you're here, and that's the main thing. Dinner is at seven thirty, a delicious vegetable chilli, with ingredients straight from the farmhouse garden, and Zenya will be doing a moon stretch class in the orchard afterwards. Optional but good for the glutes.'

'And the gut,' Zenya added.

'Not after a blessed chilli,' Michael added.

Teo raised his mug. 'And remember, if you hear bells at night, it's just the Singing Tree. Or maybe the goats.'

'Or your conscience,' Paul added dryly with a smirk, catching Rita's eye.

Lola gasped excitedly. 'Do we get to meet the goats?'

And just like that, under the rustling branches of the Singing Tree, the group began to take its first wobbly step towards becoming something more than strangers. Or at least, an eclectic mixture of characters who might survive a month with limited Wi-Fi.

TWENTY-FOUR

Rita, knowing that she had promised to get the breakfast baskets up to the yurts by seven sharp, set her alarm for five thirty, had a quick shower, and went downstairs to make herself a coffee. Betty had kindly said that as she and her Derek were up baking from 3 a.m. anyway, one of them would drop the cool bags at the end of the farm drive daily to save Rita coming down the hill. Another reason for getting up early was to be nosy and see if any of the guests had joined Teo for his first trek, yoga and swim session at Seahaven Cove. Once they had found some kind of routine, she told herself she would get Teo to do a private session with her. Just the short ten minutes of relaxation that he had shared in the orchard certainly had certainly made her feel lighter – until Jago had arrived, that was.

'*Hola, chica.*' A sleepy Teo arrived, grabbing a coffee for himself and hunting for the Land Rover keys in the pot on the kitchen side. It had been a no-brainer for Rita to get him insured on Archie's vehicle. She had found out that her cheerful yoga instructor was fine to drive with his Spanish licence and had said as long as she didn't need it for guests, he could use it at his leisure, too, which had delighted him.

'Let us see if anyone has got out of bed, shall we?' Rita said aloud, nursing her coffee and spying out of the window. She was not only delighted to see that Lola, Paul and Annie had made it down from the High Meadow but also at how polite and proficient Teo was in greeting them all.

Seahaven Bay boasted two beaches: a long, expansive sandy stretch loved by surfers, and Seahaven Cove, a small, quiet inlet so hidden even satnavs struggled to find its small car park. The cove, a favourite of early morning swimmers, was framed by tall, weathered cliffs streaked with wild gorse and heather. Unlike the sandy beach, here there were only smooth grey pebbles, flattened and polished by time and weather. Reaching the cove required a half-mile walk along a wooded path that opened onto a flat grassy area with a breathtaking view of the horizon. From there, rugged steps had to be carefully negotiated to reach the peaceful, seaweed-strewn beach below. It was a perfect scenario and setting for a short hike, yoga and swim session.

'Wow, this is amazing,' Paul breathed, as the four of them stepped out of the wooded path and were hit by the full force of the view ahead, the vast sweep of ocean and stunning enclosed beach unfolding beneath the grassy hillock they were now standing on.

Annie, puffing like a steam train, raised an eyebrow. 'I take it you've never been to Cornwall before, then, Paul?'

The long-haired musician gave a tired grin. 'Nah, never. Been on my list but never made it, until now. I've travelled the world but seen nothing quite like this.' He paused, letting the sea air fill his lungs. 'Different kind of vibe.'

'Should I know who you are?' Annie had already been trying to take a sly photo which she could put into Google images as soon as the phone signal was good enough.

Paul smiled wryly. 'Probably not. I'm more of a background

kind of guy. And that was the old me; I'm here now. OK. Just Paul. And I'd like you to get to know me as just Paul the person, OK?'

'Bet. Gotcha,' Annie replied, rocking her expensive designer tracksuit. She reached in her rucksack for her mat and a bottle of water.

Lola, with her purple hair in two pigtails, tight black yoga pants enhancing her very round bottom and a BEETS NOT BEEF-branded T-shirt, screwed her face up at Annie's attempt to get down with the kids.

'So did you see the others this morning?' Teo enquired, choosing a spot as near to the cliff edge as he dared to lay down his yoga mat without causing a landslide. The others followed.

'Thank God Michael was snoring like a warthog,' Lola added. 'Far too early to face a drunken, misogynistic pig.'

'Yo. That's harsh, lady,' Paul piped up. 'Hurt people, hurt people and all that.'

Eager to defuse the situation, Teo ushered everyone to sit down cross-legged on their mats.

'OK, let's find some peace in this beautiful setting, shall we? Take one huge breath in, hold for four seconds, and let it out for *ocho*... eight... eight, I mean.'

As the salty sea breeze carried the waves crashing against the shore and gulls screeched their approval of the warm day ahead, Teo Serrano looked completely in his element.

'OK, *amigos*,' he continued, his white grin highlighted by his tanned skin. 'This morning, we move, breathe, and move some more. Vinyasa. Flow like the sea, *sí*?'

The trio shifted to attention, their eyes on him as he brought his hands to heart centre.

'Big inhale... reach to the sky,' he instructed, rising with the breath. 'Exhale... fold forward. Let go of the weight you are carrying.'

They moved through sun salutations, each transition smooth, almost dance-like. Teo flowed with them, his voice steady and encouraging. The sounds and view of the ocean lowering their heart rates without them having to try.

'Don't worry if you wobble,' he called out. 'Life is wobbly. Yoga helps us to ride the ups and downs.'

Annie laughed and threw herself off balance.

Teo stepped between mats, gently adjusting Lola's stance, offering a quiet '*Perfecto*' to Paul. The Spaniard's calming energy was magnetic.

As the class reached its final downward dog, Teo smiled and said, 'Now we rest. You have earned it. Let the breath do the work and then we go down to the *playa* to swim.'

So far, so good, Rita thought as she made her way up to the High Meadow in her trusty Jimny. She had been delighted that the breakfast hamper execution had worked like clockwork, with Derek delivering them exactly on time and the contents looking and smelling better than she had imagined

'I won't be long, girls,' she shouted from the car window to the goats and chickens, already impatient for their breakfast.

Quietly pulling up a few metres from the yurts, she was just unloading the cool bags when she was startled by a massive '*ATCHOO!*'

She smiled to herself. Everything about Michael Stone was loud, even his sneeze.

Tiptoeing past the spot where the eruption had come from, she heard a zip being pulled open. Michael appeared, blinking like a mole, his silver-grey hair now reminiscent of Doc Brown stepping out of his DeLorean.

He croaked, 'Breakfast in bed. How delightful.'

Rita gave him a measured glance.

He looked sheepish. 'I'm rather hoping there's at least a three-strike rule here.'

Rita put his breakfast hamper down in front of his yurt and smiled. 'I'd best get the bouncers in, then.'

'Look, I'm sorry.' Rita could tell that Michael meant it. 'I was loud, probably rude. Not exactly the ideal guest in your little slice of paradise.'

Rita continued placing the hampers outside the other yurts. 'I appreciate that, but I think it's the others you want to be saying sorry to, not me.'

He put his hand to his messy hair and raised his voice. 'Ironic that a fuc— I mean, flipping divorce lawyer gets divorced. It would have been all right if she hadn't been one too.'

'Ouch.' Rita smiled, coming back over to Michael as he was easing himself onto one of the deckchairs outside.

'Moved back in with my daughter, who very quickly realised that was a terrible idea. Told me to come here. Sort myself out. Stop drinking so much. Stop being such a cu— I mean... mess.'

'To be clear, we're not a health retreat, as such, Michael.'

'And I'm not an alcoholic as such, Rita. Just lost my way a bit, you know.' Rita noticed the sadness in his yes.

Rita bit her lip. 'I kind of do, yes.'

It was tragic, Rita thought, in this now-frantic world, how little people knew about each other. Everyone so busy with their own their lives, rarely stopping to ask what might be going on underneath. She made a vow to do more asking.

She looked to the view out over Seahaven Point. Gulls' cries carrying on the salt-tinged breeze. Below, the sea murmured against the base of the cliffs, its surface glittering with kisses of sunlight. Kitesurfers danced on the waves in the far-off bay, and a fishing boat bobbed lazily near the horizon.

'This really is a spectacular spot.' Michael stared out at the ocean vista in front of him, too.

'I know. I'm incredibly lucky, and Michael...' Rita smiled warmly. 'I'm sure you won't be the last person to arrive here in bits.'

He stuck out his bottom lip. 'Your observation is oddly comforting. Like a TripAdvisor review for the emotionally rock bottom.'

'Sorry, too much?' Rita asked, worried that she might have upset him.

'You're asking *me* that question?' Michael grinned, causing them both to laugh.

Rita was just about to get in the Jimny and head down to feed the goats and hens when Emily appeared from under the Singing Tree, book in hand.

'I've left your breakfast hamper outside,' Rita offered quietly.

Emily smiled shyly. 'Thank you... and for this.' She held the book up. 'I love *Rebecca*. Second time for me. Have you read it?' Rita nodded. Emily's eyes were bright. 'It's so haunting, isn't it? It made me think about how sometimes we're trapped by the shadows of what came before us, even when we're trying to start over.'

'I guess sometimes we just have to find the courage to let the light in and move forward.' Rita surprised herself with her own insight.

'Thank you,' Emily whispered.

'Right, these animals won't feed themselves. *Bon appétit*,' Rita shouted as she sprang into the jeep.

TWENTY-FIVE

Rita sat near the back of the bus, her bag on her lap, fingers absently tapping a rhythm against the strap. She was on her way down to the bay to pay Betty for this week's hampers and also to pop into Sail Away to see Jude about the future retreat reads.

As the number seven trundled past the drive that led up to Hawthorn Acre, something caught her eye. She turned instinctively toward the window. There, at the farm gate, stood Jago. Tall, dark and as handsome as ever with Meg, his trusty sheepdog, at his feet. And beside him, laughing, head thrown back, was a young man leaning against a gleaming silver Porsche. Rita's stomach lurched. It looked just like her Thom, who was beginning to look more like her Archie each day. A double whammy of confusion.

She blinked hard and looked again. The bus was already turning the corner, trees swallowing the view. Her forehead furrowed in confusion. No, it couldn't have been. Thom hadn't had anything to do with the Jenkens, *ever*. And surely he would have said if he was coming to Seahaven. But the confident way he was standing... The way he threw his head back when he laughed, just like his father had done before him. It seemed so familiar it made her throat tighten.

You're tired, she told herself, shaking her head gently. *Too much going on. You're seeing things.*

But as the bus approached the harbour, a quiet unease settled in her gut.

Jude was busy serving a customer when Rita pushed open the door to her favourite bookshop. Needing a second to quieten her restless mind, she went to the back of the shop, got herself an espresso from the fancy coffee machine, sat on one of the Lloyd Loom chairs and took in the busy Tuesday morning view of the harbour. A fishing boat chugged steadily out towards the open ocean, its engine humming low and purposeful. Nearby, a Seahaven Bay Tours boat was being hosed down by the crew, sunlight catching the spray as they readied it for a day of trips along the coast.

'You OK, Rita?' Jude asked politely as if he had noticed the lack of her usual zesty energy. 'It's not like you to stop and stare.'

She nodded too fast. 'Yes. No. Oh, it's probably nothing. I just thought I saw someone earlier, but it couldn't have been him.'

Jude didn't ask. Instead, with folded arms, he leaned against the bookshelves and began to recite to her.

'Why do you make me leave the house
And think for a breath it is you I see
At the end of the alley of bending boughs
Where so often at dusk you used to be;
Till in darkening dankness
The yawning blankness
Of the perspective sickens me!'

A tear began to roll down Rita's cheek. '"The Going".'

Jude nodded. 'One of Hardy's finest, in my humble opinion. All that loss and yearning for his first wife, whom he met down here in Cornwall, actually.'

'I don't know much about his real life.' Rita downed her espresso.

'He was a tortured character like most of our literary greats.'

Rita sighed deeply. 'I must have a read-up.'

Jude joined her in the adjacent chair. 'Grief, regret, memory... it never follows the rules, does it? Pops up when you least expect it. It's not just the person we mourn, sometimes. It's the could-have-beens, too.'

'Tell me to bugger off if you want to, but who did you lose, Jude?' Rita asked gently.

'Long-term boyfriend left me for someone else.' He took a breath. 'It had been going downhill for a while, but I ignored it.' He wobbled. 'Smashed my heart in two, so I ran away and on arriving here and having time to be introspective, I realised I'd spent so long chasing crumbs of affection, I'd forgotten what it felt like to simply be at peace with myself. No drama. No longing. Just... stillness. And then look what happened... I took over Sail Away and followed my real passion.'

'Well, it suits you, sir.' Rita smiled. 'The stillness and of course this wonderful bookshop.'

Jude grinned. 'I was thinking maybe a selection of Thomas Hardy for next week's books. I aim to focus on authors and poets with some kind of tenuous connection to Cornwall. Do you think poetry would work?'

'I think the guests should think themselves lucky they are getting such an added luxury. I've decided on two books for a month's stay and any less than that, just the one.'

'That's fine by me.' Jude smiled. 'I really appreciate the business, thank you.'

Rita took a sip of coffee. 'And Hardy is perfect. It might do some of them good to delve into the mind of a man who emphasises that whatever emotional weight we place on the moment, nature is unmoved. That it is bigger than any of us.'

'You're one cool woman, do you know that, Rita Jory?'

Rita blushed. Jude grinned as she stood up and threw her cardboard cup in the bin. 'Thanks, Jude.'

'No, *thank* you. You're a good soul, Rita, and the retreat is a wonderful idea. I saw a flyer the other day that said to watch this space regarding opening up some of the classes to everyone. A cute Spanish guy was handing them out...'

'That's Teo. I think he might have said the same about you too.' Rita winked.

'Oof, OK,' Jude replied camply, and laughed.

'Drop me a message.' She handed the bookseller one of her newly printed resort cards. 'And I'll send over the finished schedule. Half-price sessions for you, of course.'

Jude frowned and shook his head. 'Rita, that's not the way to run a business. But allowing me to provide the retreat books at cost price, then, is.' He held out his hand. 'Deal.'

'Deal.' Rita grinned.

She walked towards the door and looked back. 'And Jude, it would be such a waste if you didn't let somebody else in one day, you know.'

Jude gulped. 'Don't be going all Tennyson on me now.'

A few moments later, Rita pushed open the door to Jilly's Pilates studio and eyed the nearest Reformer machine like it was a creature that might bite her.

At the noise of the bell, Jilly swept in from the back in her Lycra uniform, hair tied tightly back, make-up flawless.

'I knew you couldn't resist coming back.' Jilly laughed. 'Let's have a go at your pelvic floor today, see if you like that.'

'I actually only popped in to see if you'd be willing to offer a small discount on your classes for my wellness groups. Thought it would give me a broader treatment range to offer, plus bring you some extra business.'

'Ah, that'd be boss, thanks! Of course, I can do that, anything to help you out and keep the wolves from our doors. Now come on, get on your back, girl.'

Rita, already in her fitness gear from running around at the retreat earlier, lay back on one of the Reformer machines as Jilly adjusted a strap with expert flair.

'Now, pop your feet here... and no farting. The acoustics in here are savage.' Jilly laughed at her own coarseness.

Rita laughed too. 'It's my biggest fear.'

With Jilly's help, Rita cautiously put her legs in the straps, flinching as the springs creaked.

Jilly went into teaching voice. 'Right. Breathe in... lift your hips... and engage that fanny floor like you're holding in a secret.'

Rita burst out laughing but gave it a go. Her limbs trembled almost immediately. 'Jesus, I can feel muscles I never knew I had.'

'That's the idea,' Jilly said with a wink. 'You'll be shagging like you're at a hen party in Benidorm in no time.'

'God, it's been a long time since I did that.'

'I know you're still grieving but...' Jilly raised an eyebrow, 'sex is incredibly good for you, gets the blood flowing, boosts your mood, and if nothing else burns a good few calories.'

Rita laughed again. 'Jilly Cooper. You're incorrigible.'

'Just like my namesake, well, her characters, at least. I say watch *Rivals* and start channelling Sarah Stratton... the ultimate man-eater. Now, how are you feeling today? Mrs Munroe tells me your guests have arrived.'

'So, I guess you know their hair colour, what they had for breakfast and possibly what time they are visiting Number Two, my toilet block.'

'Genuis.' Jilly laughed as Rita continued to lift her hips gently up and down.

'I'm good, actually, thanks for asking. Having a focus has taken my mind off Archie, to be honest. And the missing will.'

'Ah. One of those.' Jilly released the straps. 'My next class is not for half an hour. Come and have a coffee with me.'

Rita followed Jilly over to the fitness balls at the reception desk, and took a seat, perching carefully as Jilly handed her a cup of coffee.

'Sit tall, hold that pelvis. Wherever you are, just do it. You will thank me in the future, I promise you.' Jilly took a sip from her own mug.

Rita balanced awkwardly.

'Can I just say, Rita, that what you say to me is what you say *to me*. I never gossip. Living with a con for the whole of my married life, it was more than my life was worth.' She sighed deeply.

Rita took a drink of her coffee. 'I respect that and it's kind of why I wanted to mention the will, I guess.'

'Do you think there's some kind of foul play then?' Jilly asked matter-of-factly.

'I don't know but it does seem a bit dodgy, don't you think?' Rita's brow furrowed.

'Tell me more about Archie. What happened that night? If you don't mind, babe.'

Rita's knees wobbled, and not just from the workout. 'It wasn't the cliff' – Rita took a noisy breath – 'or the car – that's what everyone says to make it sound dramatic. Grace Kelly romantic almost. But it wasn't. Not really.'

Jilly elegantly crossed her legs. 'Go on.'

'He had a blowout,' Rita said quietly. 'Lost control. The car went over. That's what the coroner said. But everyone hears *sports car*, *cliff* and thinks he did a Thelma and Louise, like your husband. Sorry, sorry. That was insensitive of me.'

Jilly's expression didn't change, but her hand reached out, resting lightly on Rita's leg. 'People are twats.'

Rita gave a dry laugh. 'It was a terrible day. We'd rowed about garlic bread earlier that evening. Can you believe that? He wanted it with lasagne; I told him he would have go the big Tesco himself and get it as I couldn't be bothered to make it. I had a French stick. I should have made some myself.'

'Oh, Rita. That's just life. We all argue.'

'I know, I know, but we don't all lose our husbands after a row, do we?' Rita felt her anxiety rising. 'Anyway, after dinner he went out to check on the cows as usual and when he came back he was properly angry about something. He grabbed the keys to his new convertible. Said driving with the roof off along the cliff path would sort him out, clear his head.' Rita made a funny little squeaking noise.

They sat in silence for a moment. Then Rita blurted, 'His last words to me were, "Next time, I will take you." In fact, as he was going out the door, he made a point of coming back and kissing my forehead and said it: "Next time, I will take you."'

Jilly was welling up herself now. 'Shit, that's shit.'

'It's not shit, it's beautiful.' Rita suddenly stood up, clanking her mug on the reception desk as she did so. 'I've only just remembered him saying and doing that. He wasn't angry at me, Jilly. He wasn't angry at me at all. Or he wouldn't have said or done that, would he?' She slowed her voice right down. 'Thank you. Thank you so much. I always thought it was maybe my fault, that I caused him to be in such a mood and...'

'He had a blowout, Rita,' Jilly said softly. 'There was nothing you could have done. And sometimes, we only hear what we want to hear and remember what we want to remember. Our brains are clever things.'

Jilly stood up and grabbed a cloth to rub down the Reformer machine they had just been using.

'You know what I miss the most?' Rita mused. 'The way he made his own tea. Clanking around, with his big hands, opening the tea caddy, smashing the kettle down. Two sugars, strong, then mine, squeezing out the bag with a weird kind of gentleness. Stirring it gently as if it really mattered.'

'I get that. My Dave was a sod, but he could make a cracking brew. He may have had fingers in many bad pies, but he used to warm the mugs with hot water first, like he was prepping them for royalty.'

'Yeah.' Rita nodded, smiling through wet eyes. 'It's the little things, isn't it?'

'It's *always* the little things.' Jilly noticed one of the women booked onto her next class walking up the hill. 'Right. That's enough trauma for one day. You did well, girl. On all counts.'

Rita grabbed her bag. 'Do I owe you anything?'

'Widows' rate.' Jilly winked. 'Which is the same as mates' rates, i.e. friendship costs nothing and you only wiggled around for a few minutes!'

'Aw. Thank you again. For everything.'

'Ah, you're all right, girl.'

Rita turned around when she got to the door. 'So, are you OK to create some discount leaflets, then?'

'Sure, I'll mail them to you. And Rita, have a think about it. Enemies, lovers, long-lost family... wills have a knack for stirring up a right old hornets' nest and bringing the worms crawling right out of the woodwork.'

TWENTY-SIX

Rita arrived home to find Henry the labrador stretched out to double his size on the courtyard, eyes closed tight, sunning himself. He barked his approval at her return.

'Come on, boy, let's make some tea.' She looked across to the barn. It was Zenya's gong and breathwork class this morning for those who fancied it. Craning to catch any signs of life from the retreat, all she heard was the soft, gossipy chattering of the chickens.

A few days into the retreat and she'd noticed Paul and Emily taking the bus down to the harbour together. Zenya had already struck up a routine and had instructed those who wanted her to provide lunch or dinner should text her once they'd decided on their plans for the day. Which was not only good for her but also for Rita, so as not to waste either food or money. Paul liked to help Rita lay the table or sit and chat over a cup of tea in breaks between sessions. He had also taken great delight in telling her that he had signed up to a surfing course – something he'd always wanted to do but never had the time or the guts to do until now.

Paul wasn't the only one enjoying himself; Emily had told her that she was in love with the window seat at Sail Away. If Jude hadn't been gay, Rita was certain the pair of them would be a match made in heaven. But when had the path of true love ever been that straightforward? And who was she to judge what might work? She'd been only twenty when she met Archie, with just two previous lovers, if you could even call them that. The first had been a blurry encounter after Kelly, ever the cheerleader of bad ideas, had encouraged her to go back to her then-boyfriend's flat with his mate 'just for a laugh'. Rita still wasn't entirely sure who she'd ended up with, her only recollection, Malibu, lava lamps, a futon, and an awkward trip to the chemist for cystitis medicine two days later. The second was a two-year relationship with Danny Barlow, whom she met at sixth form college and her first proper love, which ended so traumatically she'd declared over Sunday roast that she'd never recover and was destined to be a tragic singleton for the rest of her life. Her kind, long-suffering parents had assured her that time would heal everything. Two years later, she met Archie and they'd been right.

God, she missed them all. Far more than the chickens missed Nigel, that was for certain.

She sat down at the kitchen table, opened her laptop and, taking a slow sip of tea, first updated her resort spreadsheet by reducing the book costs. She squinted slightly to make out some of the figures clearly, and groaned. Kelly had said that she'd had to get her reading glasses at forty-five. Rita, thinking that wearing glasses was the first unmistakable sign of creeping decrepitude, had decided she would wait until she couldn't read the headline on a newspaper on a service station forecourt.

She also worked out a plan to pay off her existing credit cards in a way that minimised interest while still leaving enough spare cash to upgrade one of the outbuildings into a decent toilet and shower space, hopefully before the end of the year.

Although running month-long retreats had seemed easier in terms of fewer check-ins and yurt turnarounds, she figured that shorter retreats were ultimately more lucrative, plus she would allow herself a few days' grace between them. She updated her social media to reflect the new offering.

Work done, her thoughts drifted to the worries that work had kept at bay. She hadn't had time to search for the will again and certainly wasn't going to ask Hilda anything about it, not when she was being so cruel about Jago's intentions. Even Sennen had been slightly secretive on the phone the other day and if it was Thom who she had seen earlier, what was he doing chatting to Jago?

As to Jilly's comment about enemies, lovers and family, she wished her brain would block this too. The thought of Archie having had an affair when he was with her was too much for her to bear. No, that was a ludicrous thought; she would have known. They had loved each other deeply. Yes, there were enemies in the Jenken camp, but she didn't know the whys or wherefores and as for family, theirs was small. Hilda's siblings had passed now, and with Rita being an only child, it was just herself, Thomas, Sennen and Hilda who currently carried the Jory name. Again, Hilda would have been the first to tell her if there was any kind of family scandal, wouldn't she?

Just as the pressure in her head started to subside, a sudden, thunderous roar created another. She looked out on the courtyard to see a sleek silver Porsche screech up, with dust swirling like a storm behind it.

Thomas Jory jumped out, his usual cocky grin flickering with something unreadable. His likeness to Archie caused a lump to form in her throat. Walking outside, she gulped then forced a smile to her lips.

'Hi, darling, what a lovely surprise!'

Thom's hair was cropped quite short, showing off his striking blue eyes – eyes that had never been short of admirers. He stood a solid six feet and two inches tall and with his broad shoulders could easily pass as a rugby player. He shared the same auburn hair as his sister, and to this day, Rita hadn't quite worked out where it had come from as Archie was dark and she was light brown, albeit with a slight red tinge in a certain light.

He was smartly dressed in a crisp navy blazer over a tailored white shirt, paired with dark jeans. There was an effortless charm about him. It was no wonder he was doing so well in IT sales, Rita thought. He had not only the gift of the gab but also a sharp mind that could read a room in seconds, knowing exactly when to listen and when to close the deal. He approached his mother with a weak smile.

'Hi, Mum, I've got a conference in St Austell with work, combined with a team-building event – surfing, rock climbing, kayaking, et cetera, I think it is. Thankfully, before the kids break up or traffic would have been hell. So, I couldn't not come and see my old ma, now could I?'

'Less of the "old", thanks.' Rita felt a yearning to hug her one and only son, but Thom had never been that twin. Only when he had wanted something.

'I was just about to make a late lunch. Come on in; I'll fix something for us.'

Beneath the dappled shade of the orchard trees, Rita and Thom sat down opposite each other on the picnic bench, tucking into the crusty sourdough rolls filled with grilled Mediterranean vegetables and mozzarella that Zenya had left in the fridge, neatly wrapped in cling film and marked with an 'R' – a small gesture that never failed to make Rita smile. It had been a long time since she had felt truly looked after by anyone.

Dessert was a bowl of fresh strawberries from the retreat garden, topped with a generous dollop of clotted cream. Rita had opened a bottle of fizzy water and Thomas had nicked one of Teo's zero-alcohol Estrella Galicia beers from the fridge, which Rita made a mental note to replace.

As they ate, Thom's gaze flicked down and he noticed something odd. 'Mum... your necklace. The one Dad gave you?'

'I looked for it.' She faltered. 'But... nothing. It's gone.'

Thom frowned. 'I thought for a moment you'd decided to stop wearing it.'

'No, darling.' Rita put her hand on his. 'I lost it in the goat pen in the spring. My only thought' – a rueful smile tugged at Rita's lips despite the frustration – 'is that one of the goats got hold of it. And if that's the case, there's no way I'm looking for it now.' Rita poured herself a glass of water. 'So, it's been months since you've rung, or even replied to a message. You're good? Work all right? Any new girlfriends to mention?'

'I'm fine, Mum, thank you. I'm flying at work, hence the new car, and as for girlfriends, that's too big a topic over a short lunch. Let's just say I haven't found the one yet, but I'm having a lot of fun looking.' He grinned the same lopsided grin as his father.

'Sennen said she spoke to you the other day?'

'Yes. Not really a newsflash, though, that is, is it? She is my twin sister after all. Shame about her and Alex; he was a good bloke, and you know how needy Sennen can be.'

Rita shook her head. 'Shouldn't you be on her side?'

Thom reverted to the bolshy teenager she had both loved and struggled with in equal measure. 'All's fair in love and war and all that, and I'm just being honest.'

'So, what have you been up to this morning, then?' Rita pressed.

'Driving here.' Thom took a drink straight from his beer bottle.

Rita felt an urge of something she wasn't quite sure of rising within her. And then it was out. 'I madly thought I saw you a few hours ago... at Hawthorn Acre... talking to Jago.'

Thom paused, took another sip of beer, and remained silent.

'Did I?' Rita reiterated, almost frightened of what she might hear.

'Yes.' Thom was abrupt. 'Sorry, yes, Mum. He was herding his sheep up the road; a couple broke free. I had to stop. We had a very brief chat, then I went down to the surf beach, had a swim, got an ice cream from the kiosk, just like I used to.' He screwed his face up at her. 'What is this anyway, the Spanish Inquisition?' Thom laughed, but it was clear that he was not feeling it inside. 'We just had a brief chat, me and Jago, that's all. He's not exactly a friend, is he? I mean, I'm still seething you sold Dad's cows and tractor to him.'

'Our cows, Thom. And you know I had to.'

'I still can't believe that Dad left you in debt, Mum. That wasn't his style.'

'I know it wasn't, darling.' Rita sighed deeply. 'There's something else I need to ask you.'

Thom replied before she could finish her sentence. 'About the will, you mean?'

Rita was open-mouthed. Thom made a groaning noise. 'Oops. Don't say anything to her, please, but Granny Jory told me... well, she asked if I knew anything about it.'

'And do you?' Rita did her best to keep her voice level.

'No, I don't. I find it hard to believe that Dad didn't tell you if there was one. Maybe Granny Jory has just got confused. You know what she's like.'

Sharp as a tack was what Granny Jory was like, Rita thought, feeling angry that she had got her son involved. In a back-handed positive way, at least it proved that Hilda didn't know where the will was either.

'I think you should just forget about it, Mum, and also stop playing at this retreat lark. I mean, you've got no experience of running a business, let alone a wellness retreat.'

Rita felt tears spring to her eyes. 'I ran this farm like clockwork for years, as well as bringing up you kids, so how dare you say that. And what else am I supposed to do, tell me that, Thomas.'

'It's not a farm now anymore, is it, really. You've got a few old goats and chickens; the crops are long gone. The land is wasted. I think you should sell up. Stop all this nonsense. And as we are being so...' Thom made inverted commas in the sky, '"honest" with each other, that is exactly what I told Sennen I thought you should do the other night on the phone.'

'No, no way. The farm is my home. Our home.'

'It's huge, Mum; you're rattling around in it all on your own. It's ridiculous.'

'I'm not now. Teo has moved into the annexe and Zenya is a true confidante.'

'What, that homeless hippy in the field Sennen told me about.'

'Thomas!' Rita shouted so loudly, her son actually stopped in his tracks with a look of shock. She clenched her jaw, trying to hold it together. 'What is this really all about?'

'Jago Jenken would buy it, I know he would. You told me he paid over the odds for the other stuff, so why not the farm? You could still stay in Seahaven Bay and get yourself a little cottage and probably wouldn't need to ever work again. Do nothing. You know it makes sense.'

Rita blew out a huge breath and looked to the sky to stop her tears from falling.

'I don't like to see you upset. Come here.' Thom went to hug his mother, who instinctively pushed him away.

'I know your game, Thomas Jory.' Rita's voice was cracking. 'I'm forty-five, with hopefully a long life ahead of me and I don't just want to do nothing. For the first time in a long time, I'm feeling some kind of happiness, some sense of achievement. So, don't you dare come at me saying what *you* think is right, because to be honest, I'm not listening anymore.' Anger was now doing the talking and wouldn't shut up. 'You swan in here, after only seeing you three times since your father passed, and start throwing this around. Maybe you should've spent more time thinking about how I've been feeling and getting through that instead.' Rita threw out her arm and pointed towards his car. 'Get to St Austell, Thomas. Enjoy your work jolly.' Unable to hold it together any longer, tears burst from Rita – tears of anger, grief, confusion all tangled together. She clumsily got out from the picnic bench and ran at full pelt towards the farmhouse.

Thom casually walked behind her, got in his car, and sped off the drive, causing gravel to fly up and leave a cloud of dust in his wake, and covering Teo, who was just walking towards the barn to prepare it for his sunset yoga class later.

On seeing Rita opening the front door in a state of snot and sobbing, he rushed to follow her in, coughing and brushing down his peeling NAMASTE T-shirt as he went. Henry, sleeping in his bed by the Aga, opened one eye and shut it again.

'Oh, my beautiful Rita, not again.' Taking her in his arms, he hugged her tightly, her head resting against his firm chest, speaking in Spanish in a soothing voice until her tears had subsided and her breath was at a normal pitch. She pulled away, leaving remnants of eyeliner and mascara on his top. Her face was contorted in anguish. She let out a huge hitch of breath.

Teo pulled her towards him again and almost comically gripped her to his chest. 'Who is this terrible person, who has hurt you so badly? Tell me.'

For fear of suffocation by tanned and firm pectorals (but what a way to go!), Rita pulled herself away again and moved across to the sink. She shook her head slowly, a strange mix of shame and sorrow tangled in her chest, making her hesitate to respond. It was as if admitting that it had been her own son who had hurt her so badly was a failure on her part, a crack in the foundation she'd tried so hard to keep intact with and without Archie. Like it might be a betrayal, not just of him but of herself.

'My son, Thomas,' she blubbed. 'He wants me to sell up.'

'Oh. OK.' Teo's voice wobbled slightly. He then took a breath, held the tops of both of her shoulders and looked right at her with his soft, molten brown eyes. 'Whatever it is, we'll figure it out. Death and money does strange things to people. You're not on your own, OK?' He nodded. Keeping close eye contact, he repeated, 'OK?'

He continued to nod until Rita eventually whispered a watery, 'OK.'

TWENTY-EIGHT

'Hold on, Kel. I'm taking you into the Den,' Rita shouted into her phone speaker whilst grabbing her mobile and mug of tea from the kitchen counter. She settled into the window seat, cradling the warm drink in her hands, and gazed out over the cliffs ahead.

Kelly sounded animated, as usual. 'Just wondered how all the fun at the farm was going.'

'Well, Camilla's pregnant, a fox has dug up Nigel and Teo's just reversed into the Snack Shack.'

They both started laughing involuntarily. Rita composed herself. 'I have a scorned divorce lawyer, a millennial vegan, a voluptuous man-eater, a wolf in mouse's clothing and a disillusioned but hot rock star as retreat guests, but aside from that I'm fine.'

'Stop.' Kel laughed again. 'Have you ever considered stand-up?'

'"I'm Still Standing" should be my theme tune at the moment.'

'Aw, what's up, chicken?'

Rita took a huge breath. 'Thom came to see me.'

'Wow, the prodigal son returns. What did he want?'

'You know it... he wants me to sell the farm. Thinks I'm playing at being a businessperson.'

'And how would he gain from that, unless he is genuinely looking out for you?' Kelly said in a measured tone.

'Oh, I don't know. But I'm loving doing this, Kel. I haven't felt this sense of purpose for a long time.'

'So don't let him bully you.'

Rita blinked hard. 'Archie used to get his way a lot, too, didn't he?'

Kel's voice was softer. 'Yes, he did, Reet. We are programmed to remember the good times, don't forget that.'

'Are you all right? Ron behaving himself?'

'Don't get me started. He just did a lap of the garden shouting, "Winner!" as he got Wordle in two goes.'

'I think you'd miss him if he wasn't there.'

'Maybe, but only because I'd have no one to correct my grammar.'

'Right, I'd better get on. Thanks for checking in.' Rita finished off her tea.

'Before you go, any more notes in the tree? You know I'm living vicariously through your mystery note leaver.'

'No, the last one was, "If you don't know what to do, do nothing and the answer will come to you."'

'Hmm. Strange. Any ideas what that could mean?'

'I guess I'm still waiting for the answer to come to me, whatever it may be.' Rita laughed and stood. 'I'd better go and oversee Stan and Teo getting the Snack Shack back in order... and make sure Nigel is resting in peace.'

Kelly groaned. 'Don't mention the cock!'

Rita noticed the beautiful vase of flowers on the coffee table and her thoughts drifted back to the kiss. What if Hilda was right? What if her son and Jago were in cahoots, trying to force her into selling the farm? Surely her judgement couldn't be that off. But then again, if money was involved, Jilly and Teo were right. She'd seen how it could turn people into vultures. Even the ones you thought you knew. She reached for her washing basket from the utility room and headed outside.

Rita unpegged clothes from the washing line that Teo had kindly strung up in her private walled garden, tucked neatly out of sight of the guests. Her mind was racing as she shook out T-shirts with unnecessary force then threw them untidily into her ancient plastic washing basket. The breeze had picked up, flapping at the sheets still pegged on the line, and with every tug of fabric, her frustration bubbled higher.

'Same as me, domesticity never did come easy to you, did it?' Hilda's voice drifted from the garden gate as she stepped through it, wearing black leggings and a pink T-shirt to match her trainers. 'Before I met Archie's father, I was more used to sending out laundry from a boutique hotel in Florence than folding it myself in a Cornish garden.'

Rita didn't turn. 'If you've come to lecture me again, don't bother. I've had enough this week already.'

'Yes, I saw the marquee took a hit.'

Rita replied tersely. 'It's hardly a firm structure and just a scratch on the Land Rover's bumper so all is well, thank you, Hilda.'

Hilda came to her daughter-in-law's side. 'I came to help you bring the washing in. Not to have a go at you.'

'Fine. But I'm still annoyed with you.'

'Is this about Jago Jenken or the will?'

'Of course it's about the will and yes... Jago too! Why would you mention that in front of Thom? I don't want him to think I can't cope or worry him unnecessarily.'

Hilda folded a tea towel and threw it in the basket. 'I just wanted to see how he'd react. You're acting like you can trust everyone, even with the financial mess Archie left you in. And whether you believe it or not, Rita, I've got your back.'

'I have to be able to trust my own son, surely.' Rita sighed. 'Or what kind of mother does that make me?'

'But can you?' Hilda's voice remained level.

That stung more than Rita cared to admit. She looked away. 'What, you think he may have hidden the will. But why?'

'I don't know. But he might be influenced. By someone who knows how to twist things to their advantage.'

That did it. Rita's spine stiffened. 'Right.'

She dumped the rest of the washing into the basket and left it on the grass. 'Thanks for the help, Hilda, but I've got something to sort out.'

'Rita, act in haste, repent at leisure!' the old lady called out.

But Hilda's words were lost on the breeze, and Rita was already marching across the courtyard, reaching in her pocket for her keys and flinging open the door to the Suzuki with enough force to rattle the window. Her short drive to Hawthorn Acre was a blur of red mist and furious thoughts.

When she pulled up in a cloud of dust, Jago was in the yard, shirtsleeves rolled up, bent over a tractor engine.

'Jago Jenken,' she shouted, slamming the door and marching towards him. 'We need to talk.'

Oblivious of the fury afoot, Stan raised his hand at her from the hay barn.

Jago straightened slowly, his emerald-green eyes showing a smattering of amusement. 'Well, this is an unexpected pleasure. Shall we take it inside?'

'No, I'm fine just here.' Rita felt like she could barely breathe. 'Did you really think that I would sit and stare whilst you and my son stitch me up over selling the farm?'

He flinched. 'That's not fair.'

'No, what's not fair is you playing me like a fool. The yurts, the flowers, the kiss. Was any of it genuine or was it merely a strategy to blur my judgement?'

He stepped forward, calm but assertive. 'Rita, I haven't

planned anything. I've never conspired with Thom. In fact, I like you...'

'But he was here yesterday.'

'He was at the gate, yes. For ten minutes. A couple of sheep wandered; he had to stop.' Jago paused. 'Shocked me how much he looked like Archie, actually...' His voice trailed off. 'I barely know the lad.'

'That's exactly what he said to me, to the word,' Rita huffed. 'Almost like you practised it together.' Then without thought she said, 'No wonder you're single if you're this bloody devious.'

She took a breath, realising she had maybe overstepped the mark, and more.

Jago's expression darkened in an instant. When he finally spoke, his tone was icy. 'Don't speak of things you know nothing about.' The handsome farmer held her gaze. 'I've been nothing but kind to you. And here you are allowing your cloak of grief to cover you in misery and think everyone is out to get you.' He dropped the tractor bonnet with a sharp clunk.

As he looked down at her with a sadness that said more than words, Rita stared right at him. Everything she'd been feeling, anger, attraction, confusion, had fused into something unmanageable. They were close now. Too close. Her heart pounded with the same fury that had driven her here.

Jago broke the tension. 'You've got that handsome Spanish chap now who seems really handy, so I'm happy for you to have use of Stan for the rest of the month. Then, I think for both our sakes, it's better if we keep away from each other, just like we used to.'

'Fine!' Rita said far too loudly, flouncing towards the Jimny.

Jago, visibly upset, started walking back to the farmhouse. Then he turned and shouted, 'I'm not a liar.'

Rita turned the radio on full blast and drove her little Jimny as fast as it would go. She drove away from Hawthorn Acre and Jago Jenken, away from Seahaven Bay and all the muddle it had come to represent. With the windows down and the wind in her hair, she followed the scenic coastal road towards the headland of Seahaven Point.

When she reached the bend in the road where Archie had met his tragic end, she instinctively slowed down. Her chest tightened. The sobs came suddenly, deep, gasping sobs for Archie, for the mess with Thomas, for herself and the endless, wearying failure to trust anyone completely. She was angry, grieving, lost, all the painful emotions she'd tried to outrun now rushing in to catch her. Realising she couldn't see properly through the tears, she continued slowly to the tourist car park at the top of the point and parked up close to the bench with its enviable position of facing straight out to sea.

She was surprised, and quietly relieved, to find the car park almost empty for a July day. Granted, the kids hadn't broken up for the summer holidays yet, but even so it was glorious out. Sliding on her sunglasses to hide her now-puffy eyes, she wandered over to the little kiosk and bought a coffee from the handsome, tanned bloke manning the counter. Then she made her way to the bench and sat down, grateful for the quiet she could no longer find at the top of the High Meadow. The view was perfect: a hard, clean horizon cutting the cloudless sky and blue-green sea in two. Slowly, she began to melt into herself. The rage, the chaos, the full-body emotional storm of the past hour started to ease off. She tipped her head back to catch the warmth of the sun and for a while she just sat there, breathing shallow and ragged, Jago's words ringing in her ears.

... for both our sakes, it's better if we keep away from each other.

The words echoed, sharp and certain, yet somehow still refused to land fully. They hovered in the air, not quite believable, not quite dismissible. The tears came again, and this time she let them fall freely. She hated this feeling. Hated being so exposed, so peeled-back. But most of all, she hated the confusion. The impossible tangle of anger, affection, sadness, and something far more complicated that she hadn't dared name.

And goodness knows how she would have reacted if she'd seen Jago, who had pulled quietly into the car park just moments after her, watching from a distance as she sat down, safe, coffee in hand. And then, with a clenched jaw, he drove away without her noticing.

TWENTY-NINE

Rita had always thought that the waves crashing onto the beach sounded different at night. Softer, somehow. As if the ocean was letting its shoulders drop after a long day, too.

A full moon hung above the dark ocean at Seahaven Bay's surf beach. Its silvery light spilled onto the sea, casting a shimmery path that stretched all the way to the shore, as if inviting you to step out and walk across the waves. Stars were dotted above like tiny pinpricks in black velvet, each one flickering as if delivering a secret message from the cosmos. The tide whispered close to the fire pit Zenya had dug earlier that evening, and the soft crunch of bare feet on sand signalled the arrival of her small moonlit crew wearing the head torches that Rita had asked Teo to put in each yurt that afternoon.

'All right, soul seekers,' Zenya said warmly, spreading out the last of the battered beach blankets and flicking her torch off. 'Welcome to the first ever midnight moonlight mantras. No phones, no expectations. Just stars, snacks, a slurp of Sauvignon and possibly profound revelations.'

'Just the one glass for me!' Michael announced loudly. 'I can't be being a complete drunken tosser again and risk you all leaving me out here in the dark, now can I?'

'Well done,' Rita said encouragingly, having realised quite quickly that her no alcohol ruling had been shortsighted and might even put off some prospective guests. She wanted the retreat to be a place for freedom and choice, not one bound by rigid rules.

'One bottle, he probably means,' Lola said to the sky.

Rita and Teo sat on either side of their warrior queen, offering moral support. Truth be told, Rita needed some of that herself after her scrap with Jago. She still felt a bit sick from it all, a bit rattled, raw.

Realising none of them were wanting to abstain from alcohol for a whole month, the group had decided to bring wine. Even Emily had thrown up her hand when they'd taken a vote earlier that day. As Teo had driven them all down to the beach, Rita was also inclined to drown her sorrows.

Michael dropped his camping chair into the sand with a grunt, held up a packet of marshmallows like a peace offering. 'Do these count as soul food?'

Emily giggled. 'Only if your soul's made of glucose and self-loathing.'

Michael snorted. 'Darling girl, even Satan would move out of my head if he was living with my thoughts.'

Annie, already cocooned in a Rupert the Bear onesie and two blankets, peered up at the sky. 'Is that the Bear? I'm sure I can see the Bear.'

Zenya looked hard at the sky. 'Yes. Ursa Major – the Great Bear. Well done, that woman.'

'She looks like a blessed great grizzly bear in what she's wearing,' Michael whispered to Paul, who couldn't help but laugh.

'What star sign are you?' Emily asked Annie, squinting thoughtfully at the constellations.

'Whichever one is shit at relationships, I guess. My birthday is March thirteenth.'

'Pisces.' Zenya nodded gently. 'I'm one, too. Definitely got the creative side, still learning the romance bit.'

Annie grunted. 'It's fish, isn't it? Probably why men keep slipping through my fingers.' She took a huge slug of wine from her paper cup.

'I thought there would be more stars on a clear night like this,' Rita added, leaning back onto her blanket. Paul, who had moved to be nearer the sea, flopped down beside her, cracking open a can of lager. He laughed. 'Maybe they are just a little shy with all these weirdos staring up at them.' Rita felt his presence strangely comforting.

Zenya produced a Tupperware of something homemade and vegan. 'Moonballs. Oats, dates, almonds, sprinkle of hope and a touch of luck. Help yourself.'

Michael leaned in. 'I'm just saying, if anyone starts chanting or howling, you'll find me lying in the dunes over there.' Then, on seeing somebody walking right towards them completely in the dark, he jumped. Zenya lifted her torch to see who it was. There was Jude, the quiet and unassuming bookseller, puffing on a vape.

'Aw, you made it. I'm so pleased.' Rita smiled warmly and threw him a spare blanket. 'Get yourself warm and help yourself to a drink.'

Jude caught the blanket with a slow, confident smile, the firelight flickering in his glasses. 'Thanks, I'll gladly take you up on that.'

Rita noticed Teo's gaze flicked to Jude, a slow, deliberate glance that lingered just a beat too long before he looked away. The handsome Spaniard pretended to be focused on the fire, but the sparkle in his eyes said otherwise. She felt a naughty little thrill that the evening was already proving more interesting than she'd dared hope.

Zenya sat cross-legged on her blanket, a glow stick looped around her wrist.

'OK, you lovely lot. Let's do a check-in. Nothing heavy. Just say something silly or true or both. One small thing the moon should know about you tonight.'

She nodded at Michael first.

He puffed out his cheeks. 'Christ, really! OK...' He laughed.

'The moon should know I once cried during *Paddington* 2 and blamed it on hay fever. Will that do?'

'Good, good,' Zenya encouraged. 'We are very bear-themed tonight, aren't we, but keep them coming.'

Lola followed. 'I keep googling "how to tell if you're going through a spiritual awakening" but all the quizzes say I'm just dehydrated.'

Paul raised a hand as if in school. 'I have fourteen unfinished tracks, am father to a kid I hardly ever see and make a mean lasagne.'

Emily, her mousy brown hair pushed back with a bright flowery headband, deadpanned, 'I have killed seven housemates, I mean houseplants, in as many weeks. I was dating a narcissist and I'm not ready to talk about it yet.'

Annie chipped in. 'I was once on a first date and accidentally set fire to a napkin while trying to be seductive with a candle. Took his whole beard off. I never saw him again.'

Zenya laughed and pressed a hand to her chest. 'See? This is exactly what the moon wants. Vulnerability wrapped in nonsense.'

The crackling of the tiny driftwood fire was hypnotising. As Rita refilled everyone's cups, Zenya leaned back on her elbows, looked to the stars, then cleared her throat.

'All right, now that we've exposed our secrets to the sky and established that you're all either emotionally unstable, arsonists or plant killers' – everyone tittered – 'let's just do one more thing before you head back to the comfort of your yurts.'

She passed around mica-flecked stones she'd collected earlier. Holding one up, she instructed, 'This is just a little symbol, for whatever you want to let go of tonight. You don't have to say it aloud unless you want to.'

There was a quiet rustling as they all got their thoughts together; even Michael was still paying attention.

'Think of something. A thought you keep going back to. A hope you've been afraid to name. Something you're tired of carrying. Give it to the night.'

For a moment, no one spoke.

Then Jude's voice, low and steady. 'I want to stop pretending I'm content with solitude. Yes, I enjoy the peace, but... it's not always enough.'

Teo put his hand to his heart, stuck out his bottom lip and threw Jude a comforting smile.

Michael stirred beside him, tossing his stone gently from one hand to the other. 'I want to believe I'm not past it. Past starting again, I mean. Maybe even finding love.'

Lola grinned but her eyes were glassy. 'I want to stop apologising for taking up space. Emotionally, physically, all of it. So I'm a fat vegan; get over it.'

'I want to finish some of what I've started,' Paul said suddenly. 'Even if it's crap. Even if no one listens to it but me.'

Emily gave a dramatic sigh. 'I want to try and rekindle my passion for painting.'

Annie sniffed and wiped her nose on her onesie. 'I want men to take me seriously. See what's beneath all this bravado.'

Teo then spoke, his voice slower, more thoughtful than usual. 'Leaving the world of horse racing was so hard. I miss the rush. I miss the adulation. I want to settle somewhere. And within myself.'

'Rita?' Zenya asked gently.

Rita took a deep breath. 'Grief isn't something you get over. It's something you carry until one day, it just doesn't feel so heavy. I think... I'm ready to put some of it down now.'

The group fell into a brief, respectful silence.

Zenya closed her eyes for a moment, letting the words settle. Then she lifted her stone and tossed it into the sea. One by one, they followed suit, quiet splashes marking wishes and worries being carried off by the tide.

Rita sat for a while then, as the others got up to go, began packing up. Paul joined her, helping gather the glasses. 'Looks like it's just me and you.' Paul yawned as the others made their way sleepily to the beach car park for Teo to drive them back in the

Land Rover. 'Can I come back with you in the jeep? I don't think I can bear any more of the woo-woo stuff.'

'How do you know I call it that?' Rita laughed.

'I didn't. I call it the same.' Paul grinned.

Rita picked up a couple of stray blankets and made sure that the fire was fully out.

'Here.' He took the blankets off her, walked towards one of the dunes and placed them gently down on the sand. 'Are you in a hurry to get back, Rita?'

'I do need to be up at six to get your breakfasts to the yurts.'

'I'm sure nobody will be up early tomorrow.' Paul handed her a beer.

Rita smiled, feeling a little thrill at his tone, and took the beer. She shivered, and Paul gently pulled a blanket around her, his hand brushing hers for just a second.

'It's so beautiful out here.' Rita's voice softened as she looked at him. 'The beach at night... really is a magical place. I can't believe I've lived here all this time and never done this.'

'It's beautiful. The ideal place to escape to.' Paul's perfect smile caught the moonlight, and Rita felt her heart skip at the romance of it all.

She opened the beer and edged closer to him, catching the warmth of his arm. They sat in companionable silence, listening to the waves, and then Rita asked, 'So what are you escaping from?'

'A few things. I used to be... someone.'

Rita turned slightly, meeting his gaze, curious. She felt an undeniable pull toward him, and just a little reckless this evening. 'Don't be silly. You still are.'

He gave a wry smile. 'I mean... *famous*. Drummer in a band that once headlined Glastonbury. Lost my way after that. Too many tours, too many pills. Got my girlfriend pregnant. She left. Can't say I blamed her. I was a mess.' Rita didn't speak. Just listened. 'I like it that no one here knows who I am. Because nobody needs to. Because I've been thinking about it and what does fame even mean, really? A name in lights that flickers.

Applause that fades. A million strangers who think they know you and want to judge you. But no one really knows anyone, other than themselves. Do they?'

He turned to her then, something honest and unguarded in his face. 'In fact, I love that you know me as I am now. Plain old Paul Best. Not Rex Wilder, the guy on the cover of *Rolling Stone* magazine.'

Rita gave a half smile, eyes soft. 'Plain's not the word I'd use.' She wrapped her arms around her knees and rested her chin on them. 'You said you wanted to write again?'

'Yeah. It's been a struggle lately. My life's been like one big chord playing off-key.' Paul looked sad for a second.

'I didn't think that drummers were usually the writers.'

'Yeah, I never did conform.' Paul took a sip of his beer. 'And I do play all sorts of instruments. It's the drums that I love most, though.'

Rita took a drink. 'And why the struggle, do you think?'

'I'm not sure... usually when I'm in a funk words come tumbling out of me. And if my heart is breaking or I'm on a come-down, I could write a flipping sonnet.'

'Maybe what people need right now is something a bit more upbeat? Could you try that, at least?'

'All I know is that when the time is right the answer and the words will come to me.'

'Oh, OK! That's weird.' Her thoughts broke through.

'In what way?' Paul looked puzzled.

'Oh, it's nothing.' Rita took another drink.

Paul shrugged and looked at her again, more directly this time. 'And what would you write, Rita?' He paused. 'If nobody was watching.'

'Wow, that's quite a question. Is it too cliché to say a new beginning with a happy ending.'

He looked at her, really looked, and put his hand on her knee. 'This great retreat of yours is an epic new beginning; you've set it up beautifully.'

Rita felt like she was going to cry.

Paul glanced at her and seeing the tears in her eyes said, 'You wear your sadness like a familiar cardigan, one you keep meaning to throw out, but somehow always end up slipping back into.'

Her breath caught just slightly; she turned and caught Paul's soulful gaze.

A vision of Jago crossed her mind... *for both our sakes, it's better if we keep away from each other.* Fuck him, fuck Archie, fuck everything!

'Well...' she stuttered. 'Maybe I'm ready to take it off.' The alcohol had loosened her, as if someone had taken over her conscience and she really didn't care. 'But... fraternising with the guests... it's a bit like a doctor sleeping with their patients, isn't it?'

Paul laughed, warm and genuine. 'Then you're the best-looking doctor I've ever had an...' He paused and smiled with a grin. 'An... appointment with.'

'Flattery will get you an extra croissant in the morning,' Rita flirted.

'I'm sure we can do better than that.' He let his fingers brush hers. She felt the warmth of his touch, like a tiny spark, unexpected and real.

She pulled her hand back gently, not coldly.

'I can't,' she whispered, almost to herself. 'At least... I keep telling myself I can't.' She gave him a sideways look, half apologetic. 'I'm not looking for anything with anyone. Or maybe I am. I don't know. God, I don't know.'

Paul nodded slowly, eyes fixed on the horizon. 'And as for happy endings, isn't all of our life really just a series of events that start and finish? Hellos, goodbyes... and in the middle if we're lucky, a few good bits.' He paused. 'Nothing is permanent in this life, Rita. Let's just ride the good bits, eh? Because face it, all we have is the now and we are a long time pushing up daisies.'

Rita didn't answer straight away. But this time, when his hand found hers again, she let it stay. Tilting her chin gently to face him, Paul whispered, 'Do you mind?'

Rita shook her head. The kiss was simple yet charged. It wasn't fireworks or grand declarations, just the soft press of lips between two human beings on a deserted beach.

Slowly, their bodies drew closer, the world narrowing until there was only the rhythm of breathing and the gentle brush of skin on skin. Fingers traced tentative paths along arms and backs, learning the map of one another, careful, reverent.

It wasn't messy or desperate like the passion Jilly joked about, with none of the wild abandon of a Sarah Stratton in *Rivals*. It wasn't the confusion of Jago Jenken and everything he represented. No, this was something quieter, something deeper.

Moving together with an unexpected ease of familiarity, Paul's hands cupped Rita's face, thumbs brushing over her cheekbones as he kissed her again, longer this time, softer, the kind of kiss that says *I'm here* without needing words.

And in this one magical moment, Rita let go.

Let go of Jago saying he didn't want to see her again, of her own son not believing in her, and of the unsettled feelings stirred by Archie's missing will. Let go of the past, the pain and the fear that had held her back for so long.

And as the waves whispered along the sand, she gave herself permission to explore another's body, and to be explored, until, with a soft cry of long-held yearning, Rita's body spilled over in quiet surrender.

As the tears began to fall, Paul pulled her into his arms, pressing a soft kiss to her forehead. Then, as if in rhythm with the ebbing tide, he began to rock her, whispering, 'I've got you, babe.'

Above, a lone seagull cried out.

THIRTY

Rita was dreaming of being on the Pyramid Stage at Glastonbury with a microphone in one hand and a red rose in the other singing a duet with a tall, dark-haired man wearing a red and black lumberjack shirt. The audience were all cockerels who looked like Nigel, and she annoyingly couldn't make out the face of who she was duetting with, as they had sunglasses that literally covered their whole face. She was just about to pull off his disguise when her alarm pierced the fantasy like an out-of-tune bass guitar.

Groaning, she rolled over and patted blindly for her phone: 5.56 a.m. Four whole minutes before she needed to be vertical. She stole them all, plus a sneaky fifth, then heaved herself up and out of bed, with her eyes squinting like a reluctant mole emerging from its hole.

Remembering what had happened with Paul the night before, she groaned again and messaged Kelly ordering her to ring her as soon as she got her message. Then she made her way to the bathroom. Before Rita had even a chance to open the toothpaste, the sleepy voice of her best mate greeted her.

'You all right, Reet?'

'Fine, fine. But let's just say, last night I gave one of the guests a bit more wellness than I probably should have done.'

Kelly laughed, then made an oof noise. 'Oh my God, I know my Ron ain't no oil painting, but I can't imagine that big beer belly bashing against mine. Reet!'

Rita laughed. 'Oh my God, it wasn't Michael.'

'Sunglasses Man? You lucky dog. He's hot!'

Rita made a screeching noise. 'On the beach, like a harlot. We didn't like... go the whole way but it was enough to make me realise that I do miss *it* and I've still got *it*.'

'I can't even tell you how jealous I am. How was his cock?'

'So weird touching a different one after all these years, but it was lovely; he was lovely... just gentle and considerate.'

'Enough now. The envy is real but joking aside, how are you feeling, mate? That's a big step.'

'Is it too soon, do you think? I just worry people might judge... like I'm moving on too fast.'

'No one knows but me, do they?'

'No, of course not.'

'Then keep it that way. People will always have opinions and probably those who've never been through what you've been through would be the most vocal. But at the end of the day, you're the one living with this. If it brought you a moment of peace, then it was the right time.'

'Aw, thanks, mate. I cried afterwards.' Rita let out a low moan. 'So embarrassing!'

'I would have done, too, tears of complete joy after not having had it for so long.' They both laughed. Kel softened. 'Sorry, Reet. I'm not downplaying this. How did he react when you did that?'

'Just hugged me tighter. He is so the perfect free spirit for this to have happened with.'

'Good, I'm glad. So glad, in fact, I was worried that, in the words of the Mad Hatter, you were losing your muchness and it sounds very much like your muchness is well and truly on its way back.'

Rita's mind flicked to Jago for a moment, but she quickly shoved the thought aside. Some things were better left unsaid, for now. Her loins had stirred at Paul's attention, a guilty thrill she couldn't quite shake. But in all its confusion, she feared her heart was yearning for Jago Jenken.

She checked her watch. 'Shit, I need to get a move on, breakfasts to be delivered and all that. Thanks for being there, Kel.'

'Always here with an ear.'

Kel hung up.

The air was cool, the sort of July morning that whispered promises of heat later. Pulling on her hoodie and wellies, because the dew soaked everything, Rita padded across the courtyard followed by an ambling Henry.

Bless Zenya, she must have gone up to the main gate earlier as the breakfast hampers were lined up by the front door, all ready to be delivered to the yurts. Loading them into the Jimny, she drove up next to the food store, grabbed a sack of grain, then parked up by the chickens.

'Morning, your majesties,' she called to the goats as she passed the pen. Henry set about sniffing and doing his business. 'I'll just do the feathery ladies first.' She made a mental note to ring the vet, just to check Camilla was still doing OK. And really, she should have told Jago that his Cedric was almost certainly the father... but 'should' was a funny old word, one she often disregarded until a 'would' or a 'will' finally pushed it out of the way.

The chickens were already chattering at the coop door. Rita scattered grain and smiled at their eagerness to run free. 'There you go, ladies. Keep laying those golden eggs like you have been.' Mavis gave a sassy cluck in reply.

As Rita approached the goat pen, she spotted Emily kneeling on the dewy grass, dressed in cut-off jeans and a plain grey jumper, watching Camilla graze. At the sound of footsteps, Camilla lifted her head, and within seconds, the whole herd sprang to life, jostling and climbing over each other in a chaotic dash to be first in line for breakfast. Startled, Emily scrambled to her feet and brushed the damp patches from her knees.

'I'm not overfeeding her. She's due early to mid-August, I think.' Rita nodded towards Camilla. 'Stubborn as hell, this one, and loves to escape. This'll be her third pregnancy.'

Emily smiled faintly, watching the white goat snuffle down some apple.

'She looks so... calm,' Emily murmured. 'Like she knows she's safe.'

'She is.' Rita felt a surge of pride. 'My girls get the best of everything here.'

Emily was quiet for a minute, her eyes tracking the round rise and fall of the goat's belly.

'Did you enjoy last night? The moon and stars and all that malarkey.' Rita filled the last of the goats' tins.

'Yes. It was lovely.' Emily smiled. 'It's a funny old group. Like some weird dysfunctional family, but I fit in... so that's OK.'

'That's good, then,' Rita said plainly, not wanting to pass judgement on anyone.

'I was pregnant once.' Emily released a big freeing breath.

Rita didn't move, just stayed still beside her, listening.

'Last year. It was unexpected. I showed him the test and he just... blinked. Said, "That's not part of the plan, Em." And I knew. I knew the way someone knows a storm's coming before the clouds roll in. You know.' She swallowed. 'I tried to be OK with it. Bought vitamins. Told myself he'd come around. But I think the baby knew. Knew it wasn't wanted.'

Rita turned, eyes wet but unwavering. 'No, Emily. Don't you dare think that.'

Emily bit her lip. 'I lost it at eleven weeks. Just... gone. And I couldn't help thinking... maybe it was my fault. Maybe I wasn't enough. Or maybe it didn't want *me*, either.'

Rita took Emily's hand in hers and squeezed it.

'Listen to me.' Her voice was low and steady. 'They hang on if they want to stay. But sometimes they just don't. Sometimes it's not about us. It's about timing. About their little soul not being ready yet.'

Emily let the tears fall now, unbothered by the mess of it. 'But I wanted it. Even when I didn't think I did. I did.'

'He or she would have known that. That little spark, that flicker of love. It wouldn't have gone unnoticed.'

They stood in silence until Camilla let out a long, irritated bleat.

Emily laughed through her tears. 'She's judging me, isn't she?'

'I think she's saying you're stronger than you think.'

Emily wiped her face with the sleeve of her jumper. 'You always say the right thing, Rita; you're so lovely.'

'I just say what I needed someone to say to me once.' Rita pushed down her own tears at remembering the miscarriage she had had, a year after the twins had been born. She had had feelings of not knowing how she would cope with three under two, had blamed herself for that tiny flicker of doubt. 'So, are you still with your partner, Emily?'

'No, thankfully, and also I have no job, either. I quit two weeks ago. I lied the other day. Taking a sabbatical for "creative recharging" sounded far sexier than "completely unravelling emotionally". Sorry, Rita, you must have a million things to do. I'm going to go back to my yurt.'

'No, walk with me back to the farmhouse. Here, carry this if you don't mind.' Rita handed her the egg basket.

'He never hit me. Not with fists. But the other kind, you know?' Emily blurted. 'The kind that makes you feel like you're made of shells like these and everything you say is a mistake.'

'Emily, I'm so sorry. You really have been through it, haven't you?'

'I think I forgot who I was... and then I came here. The quiet. The sea. The yoga with strangers. It's like... layers are peeling off. And underneath, there's still someone worth saving. I just need to pick up a paintbrush now.'

'Well, there's a few outbuildings that could do with whitewashing.' Rita grinned, feeling a sense of peace herself that the retreat was not only helping her but others, too, just as she had hoped for.

Emily laughed. 'I'd happily do that. But I meant messy, abstract stuff. I used to lose hours in it. It was like dreaming with my eyes open.'

'What happened?'

'He used to call it "my little hobby". Said it was "cute". Said it was a shame I never really had the "talent" to show it to others. I stopped.'

Rita's face darkened. 'He sounds like a proper arse.'

'He was and I miss it.' Emily sighed. 'But every time I think about trying again, I freeze. Like I'm scared I've lost it.'

At that moment, with a crunch of gravel, Stan pulled up in front of them in his Land Rover and lowered his window. He smiled at Rita and acknowledged Emily with a nod. 'Have you got a minute, Mrs Jory?'

'I'm going to head back,' Emily intuitively chipped in, placing the basket on the doorstep. 'Thanks for listening, Rita.' Looking lighter in her step, Emily walked towards the High Meadow.

'You all right, Stan?' It wasn't like the farmhand to appear this early unannounced.

'I'm good, thanks. Just wanted to say, him up there.' He nodded his head in the direction of Hawthorn Acre. 'Well, he may have said I can't be doing stuff for you when August turns, but what I do in my own time ain't nobody's business.' He produced a battered tin from the passenger seat. 'Mrs Bodkin's carrot cake, I know how much you love it.'

'Thanks, Stan. I appreciate it.' Rita deposited the cake in the kitchen, then wandered back across the yard to the barn, key ready in hand. The yoga class wasn't for another hour, but she liked to let the morning air freshen the place. The back doors groaned open. A shaft of sunlight cut through the gloom, catching the dust motes like glitter in a snow globe. And then that magnificent, breathtaking vista up and over the fields and down to the cliffs and beaches yonder.

How lovely that Emily felt she could confide in her; she had been so candid, and it made her realise that mums came in all guises. Rita's thoughts then turned to Sennen, whom she realised she hadn't spoken to in a while and made a mental note to call her.

Thinking back to last night, to her and Paul, making out like teenagers on the beach, she felt a fluttery feeling go through her, like a shiver. It wasn't just the act itself; it was the way it made her forget, even if just for a few seconds, the mess that was Jago Jenken.

She'd never been this confused about anyone before. With Jago, everything felt tangled. But Paul? Paul was simple. Real. Like breathing fresh air after being underwater too long. Calm waters, to Jago's stormy and tortured soul, who caused her to feel passion and tension with equal parts longing and frustration.

Whatever it was with the laid-back musician, it had been fun and maybe having a little bit of fun moving forward wasn't such a terrible thing after all. She surprised herself with how relaxed she was being about it. For the first time, she had had sexual relations with a man who wasn't Archie. She had thought that it would be a lot harder to do. That she would have felt a guilt or some kind of angst. But no, it had felt good. And guest or no guest, she wouldn't be averse to doing it again.

Rita paused, took a huge breath as she looked down the barn and over the sea view. Peaceful. Then. Thump! She struggled to realise where the sound was coming from. Another thump, followed by an unmistakable rustle of hay. Looking up to the hay loft with its gaudy curtains pulled untidily across, she narrowed her eyes. A curtain twitched.

Rita walked over slowly. 'Please don't be a rat,' she whispered. 'Or worse, a big fox.'

A head popped out.

'Jesus Christ!' Rita nearly jumped out of her skin.

'*Tranquila*, Rita, it is just me,' Teo said croakily, his black hair sticking up at odd angles.

Rita blinked. 'What are you doing up there? Please don't say Hilda has chucked you out.'

Another groan, this one deeper toned, came from the hay loft.

Teo's eyes widened in panic. 'Don't look! Don't look, OK? I... I didn't mean to... it just sort of happened.'

Rita began to laugh. 'I'm not your mother. What you do in your private life is your business.'

Jude's head popped out next to Teo. Rita almost didn't recognise him, his face looked so different without his glasses on.

'I've seen nothing.' She comically put both her hands over her eyes. 'For a moment I thought it might be Annie,' Rita joshed.

Teo made a retching action. The bookseller looked worried. 'You won't tell anyone, will you?'

'Tell anyone, what?' She winked.

'Thank you,' Jude said. 'The Seahaven Bay Facebook Gossip Group would dine out on this one for years. BOOKSELLER FOUND FORNICATING IN HAYLOFT WITH FITNESS INSTRUCTOR FOURTEEN YEARS HIS JUNIOR. I'd better go home and get ready to open the shop.'

'I give you a lift.' Teo popped his head back behind the curtain.

Rita stepped back into the soft morning light, stretching her arms wide and letting out a long, hearty yawn. The air now hung heavy with the promise of rain, thick and electric.

As she climbed into the Jimny to drive the breakfasts up to the yurts, she did something she hadn't done in ages: she sang along to the radio. She felt light, happy. And she liked it that Teo and Jude felt happy too. They could all just live and let live. Last night was proof that life really could turn on a sixpence. And maybe, just maybe, Zenya's moon mantras weren't quite as woo-woo as she'd thought. After all, Jude's wish on a star had definitely come true. Well, at least it had last night.

Rita was already back in the barn in her yoga gear when Teo returned to run his session. 'Glad we've set up in here today, first day of rain in a long time.' Rita moved a stray cushion onto a milk churn.

'Yes, *perfecto*. Let's see how many leave their yurts after a late night and now this weather. I did go up earlier and see if anyone wanted a lift down, but I got no response.'

'So, Teo. Now I am fully party to your love life.' The handsome Spaniard grinned. 'I realise I don't really know much about you at all. If you don't mind me asking, where do you come from? What is your story?'

Teo gave a shy smile and ran a hand through his tousled dark hair. 'It's what you English call a mongrel, I think. I'm half English, mostly Spanish. My mother, she is a spirited woman from Sevilla. Met an Englishman, a fleeting romance, a summer fling. She never saw him again.'

Rita's eyes widened. 'So, you never knew your father?'

Teo looked a little unsettled as he shook his head furiously. 'No. No. My mother raised me in Sevilla on her own. She is *bajita*.' He put his hand to neck level. 'Just under five foot, like your Hilda, but has a fire within that lights up a room. I think I must have inherited most of me from her. Her passion, her temper, her kind-ness, and love for life.'

'She sounds incredible.' Rita smiled.

'*Sí, sí*. She is.' Teo nodded, his gaze distant. 'She taught me to embrace every *momento*, to find joy in the *pequeño*. Small, small, I mean. Even when times were tough after my *accidente*, she never let me feel the weight of the world. Instead, suggested I retrain in something that made me as happy, or nearly anyway.'

'I'm so happy that you did.' Rita's eyes twinkled.

'It was Mamá who suggested Cornwall actually. Said it was one place in England that I should visit. Wrote a list of places I could surf, one of them being here.'

'She has good taste, your mother, clearly. It's funny...' Rita mused, 'how our past shapes us, even the parts we don't know.'

Teo looked at her, his eyes thoughtful. 'Yes. But it's also about what we choose to do with it. Our past is a foundation, but we build the rest. All I know, right at this moment, is that it feels right being here in Seahaven Bay.'

'I'm glad, because it feels right having you here.' Rita squeezed his arm.

'I know it sounds a bit... and I use your words here... woo-woo, but this place... it has a pull, doesn't it? Maybe Zenya has lured us all here to find ourselves or someone else, maybe in my case.'

'It certainly seems like magic is happening for a few people.' Rita laughed softly.

Teo looked coy for a moment. 'Rita. I know it must be hard to talk about but please now that I have shared, can you tell me a little bit about your husband, your Archie.'

'Well, he had a light in his eye too. Everybody loved Archie. He was fun and would do anything to help anyone in trouble. He was fiercely passionate about us.' Rita put her hand to her heart. 'He, too, had a temper; I used to hide and read in the hayloft sometimes, wait until it had blown over, but he was a fair man.'

Teo was listening intently. 'He sound like a good man.'

Rita nodded. 'He had his moments, like we all do. He'd disappear sometimes when things got a bit rough on the farm. I only learned recently from Stan that he'd sit under the Singing Tree and think. Just like I used to and still do, sometimes. Whenever he could find time for a beer with his mates in the Winking Pilchard, he would, and despite his mother not always being the easiest of women, he looked after her really well, especially after his dad died. Hence me taking on that mantle now.'

'Hilda – her barking is worse than her biting, is that what you say?'

'Nearly.' Rita laughed and before she could correct him, Teo's face dropped.

'And your son? Maybe his biting is worse than his barking.'

Rita took a deep breath and shook her head. 'Let's do some yoga, shall we?'

Rita felt a sense of relief when Paul didn't walk into the barn the morning after their unexpected encounter. It wasn't that she regretted what had happened; she didn't. But the uncertainty of how they'd both react upon seeing each other again made her hesitant. And the thought of anyone else discovering what they had done was something she wanted to avoid. Imagine that in her first online retreat reviews. *Great stay, the owner is a complete harlot. Just give her a glass of wine, a can of beer and place her under a starry sky and she's all yours.*

Annie, Michael and Lola were already sprawled across the floor of the barn, their yoga mats unfurled as the moist sea breeze gently ruffled their edges. The rain wasn't strong enough to have to shut the barn doors – in fact, it felt lovely to have a warm breeze flowing through their space of tranquillity.

Teo, dressed in relaxed linen trousers and a loose white vest, moved with the quiet confidence of someone completely at home in his own body. Maybe because somebody had been completely at home with his, the night before, Rita cheekily thought.

'*Buenos días*, everyone.' He rolled his shoulders. 'I hope you enjoyed your time on the beach last night. This morning, I welcome you to Hatha yoga. Today, we go slow. We breathe. We stretch. We feel amazing, *sí?*'

'As long as old blue eyes himself here doesn't keep breaking into song,' Annie announced, putting one hand into her tight yoga top and rearranging her huge breasts. 'If I hear "Fly Me to the Moon" one more time, well...' Rita was sure she was actually directing her comments with affection towards Michael. 'He nearly got a croissant through his flap this morning.'

Lola screwed her face up. 'Please tell me that's not a euphemism.' Everyone laughed.

Michael woke up. 'Let this poor old bastard feel happy for one minute, at least, can you? Last night was the first time I've enjoyed myself for a long time.'

Lola giggled. 'And at least it was in tune.'

'Thank you, Lola,' Michael replied, looking to Annie, who smothered him in baby air kisses.

Teo continued, his voice warm and steady. 'In Hatha, we balance, sun and moon, strength and softness. No need to rush. This is not a race. We are not on our horses,' he added with a wink toward Rita, who was at the back about to join in, and smiled back warmly in return.

He stepped onto his own mat. 'So... we start simple. Sit tall. Close your eyes. Inhale... exhale... forget the to-do list, forget the phone, forget the singing.'

Teo smiled to himself as he stood up and looked around at everybody doing as they were told, serene looks on their faces.

'This place,' he whispered when he was alongside Rita, 'is almost better than the racetrack.'

Michael and Lola walked out of the barn, shaking out limbs and laughing about who would be the most sore tomorrow. An unlikely friendship, Rita thought, especially considering how much the young woman had despised the filter-free lawyer at first. Annie lingered by the door, rubbing her shoulder with a thoughtful expression. 'Hey, Rita?'

Rita stopped from tidying away the yoga mats. 'You all right, Annie?'

'I'm great, thanks. I just wondered, if it's not too much trouble, would you... maybe show me where the Reformer Studio is one day? I think I'd like to try it properly. Get a bit fitter, you know.' Her big personality seemed smaller somehow.

Rita smiled. 'Of course I will. I've been avoiding doing a full session, actually. We'll go together.'

THIRTY-ONE

Rita jumped at the gentle tap on the kitchen window, turned off the iron and went to the front door. Zenya smiled as she bustled through the kitchen doorway, a basket of freshly picked herbs and vegetables tucked under one arm.

'I thought I'd put together a special menu tonight.' Rita noted her flawless skin tanned from the glorious weather they had been having prior to today's rain. Her salt-stiff plaits were knotted with lavender stems. 'The guests have been here a whole week now; feels like they deserve something a bit more celebratory. Something fresh, seasonal, and from the garden. If that's OK with you, of course.' She laid the basket on the kitchen table, spilling out glossy courgettes, ruby-red tomatoes, fragrant basil and a handful of wild berries.

'Great idea. I'm not offering alcohol on a whim. We can use up the leftover elderflower fizz. I need to keep eye on our profits.'

'They'll probably be knackered after last night anyway. I saw Paul creeping back up with his head torch on way after the others.'

'Oh, did you?' Rita replied breezily.

'You like him, don't you?' Zenya smiled, catching Rita's eye knowingly. Rita flushed and busied herself at the sink.

Zenya switched topics, 'I'm thinking a roasted veg tart like I did at Hilda's the other night, and for pudding, a raspberry crumble topped with coconut cream. Light, tasty and perfect for this time of year.'

'You're amazing, Zenya, that's what you are.' Rita wiped her hands on a tea towel.

'I wish to be,' Zenya replied coyly, her cheeks now colouring. 'Being around you... it's like having the big sister I always hoped for. Someone strong and kind who doesn't pretend to have it all figured out but just keeps going anyway.' Rita swallowed as Zenya's voice softened. 'I never really had that. A person who makes you feel like you matter. So, thank you, Rita. For letting me in.'

'I'm glad,' Rita whispered, herself welling up. She folded the ironing board. 'You'd better text the rabble and see how many want to come down and eat.'

Later that evening, Rita was just getting ready to head over to the Snack Shack when she heard the crunch of tyres on the gravel courtyard. She looked out of her bedroom window expecting to see Teo back from the harbour in the Land Rover. But bold as brass in the trailer behind Jago's tractor, standing squarely and smugly atop a bale of hay, was Camilla.

Jago looked up to give a casual nod as he passed, barely slow-ing, causing Rita to take a sharp intake of breath, her heart suddenly beating an unwelcome symphony.

Camilla gave out a loud, offended, 'Maaaaa-aaaahh!'

As Rita appeared at the front door, Camilla then let out a low, theatrical bleat.

Jago shouted back over the engine. 'I daren't argue with a lady in her condition!'

Rita raised an eyebrow. 'I'm not even sure if we can get Cedric to pay the kid's maintenance. I think she's been pregnant more times than she's escaped, this little harlot.'

'Maybe she's a romantic. Falls in love every spring and regrets it by autumn.'

Rita could tell by Jago's face just how much he regretted that comment. They shared a look, brief, loaded. Jago cleared his throat. 'I'd have got Stan to bring her back, but he had to leave early today.'

'It's fine. Thank you.' Just the presence of this man unsettled her. It was like the air around her was suddenly charged with electricity. He made her feel alive in a way only Archie had done before him.

'Would you like me to take her up to her pen?' Jago smiled with his eyes, that easy warmth that both comforted and confused her.

'Yes, amazing. The guests are coming down for dinner soon; I'd better help Zenya.' Rita was itching to escape the invisible pull that made her heart race, and her thoughts spin out of control. She needed space, room to breathe.

She shut the front door behind her, the latch clicking a little harder than intended. As she walked towards the Snack Shack, Jago's voice carried after her, low, almost uncertain. 'My mum used to say to me that between what is said and not meant, and what is meant and not said, we can lose so much.'

Rita paused for the briefest of moments, eyes fixed ahead. But she didn't turn. He was the one who had said it was better if they kept away from each other. She said nothing, just kept walking, her ears open but whatever Jago Jenken wanted to say next never came.

THIRTY-TWO

Lola knocked gently, then wandered into the farmhouse kitchen, her purple hair scraped into a messy bun, an oversized charity-shop T-shirt hanging loosely over yoga shorts. Her face was light pink from being in the outdoors for so long. She paused in the doorway, nose twitching as she caught the scent of something unfamiliar, her colourful water bottle clutched in one hand. 'Is that *actual* coffee I smell?' she asked, mock horror on her face. 'As in, non-fair-trade, non-locally sourced, possibly rainforest-murdering coffee?' She laughed.

Zenya, busy making some raspberry jam from the fruit-laden plants in the vegetable patch, raised an eyebrow. Rita, who was checking supplies in the fridge, grinned. 'You know it's organic and shade-grown, thank you very much. I don't even have to recycle the guilt anymore, thanks to you.'

Lola let out a faux dramatic sigh of relief and crossed to one of the bench seats in the marquee. 'I was after some water, actually. I ran out from my breakfast pack.'

Rita went to hand her a plastic bottle out of the fridge and then quickly retracted it. 'Oops. I am getting better, Lola, thanks to you. I kind of wish there were more adverts telling us what we shouldn't be buying packaging wise and how exactly to recycle everything.'

'It's not bloody brain surgery,' the young woman replied flippantly.

'I know, I know but we get set in our recycling ways, don't we?' Rita took Lola's bottle. 'I'm more than happy to fill it but just so you know the outhouse sink is mains and drinkable. Next time you come, if you want to, that is, there will be more facilities out there for you. Better showers et cetera, too.'

Lola sighed, shoulders dropping. 'I must sound like cracked record, but I've been reading a lot lately. And watching, like, *really* watching, the nature documentaries, and I can't stop thinking about it. I know people get mad at the climate protestors, but like, what if we've already screwed it all up? What if it's too late? Rising temperatures, mass extinctions, rainforests destroyed, plastic in the reefs, the Arctic ice melting. It's all happening so fast.'

Rita softened. 'I know. It's overwhelming when you do pay attention.'

'David Attenborough is in his nineties and still fighting.' Lola's voice was now thick with emotion. 'He should be swinging in a hammock, relaxing in the sunshine, not begging us to stop destroying our planet.'

'I have a weird crush on him,' Zenya piped up, pushing a teaspoon of jam across a saucer to check it had set. 'He's *amazing*. A beautiful, brilliant force helping us to listen and understand. And sadly, most people are too busy or ignorant to care.'

Rita looked to Lola. 'But *you* care. You're influencing people in real ways, not just some face forcing us to buy the next best wrinkle cream or to take some expensive collagen shots that the promoters would probably never even consider touching their own lips.'

'Maybe I need to rethink. Maybe it's not about having thousands of followers.' Lola took another drink. 'Perhaps I/we should be convincing one person at a time to bring their own coffee cup or switch to shampoo bars and asking them to pass it on. We don't have time to get this wrong, Rita. And sometimes it feels like everyone's still asleep.'

Rita nodded slowly. 'Well, I shall do my bit to make this place as sustainable as possible.'

'Hear, hear,' Zenya added, putting jars in the Aga to sterilise.

With Zenya now busy in the Snack Shack and Lola away to the bus stop for a trip down to the harbour, Rita had just sat down to enjoy her second cup of coffee at the kitchen table, when the back door creaked open and Jude poked his head round.

'Morning.' The bookseller sounded tentative. 'Sorry to barge in, Rita, but do you know where Teo is? We've arranged to lunch in the orchard.'

'Have you now.' Rita smirked. 'Did you try the annexe? I saw him come back from a run earlier; maybe he's showering.'

'Ah, I didn't think.'

'So, if it's not too nosy, how's it going?' Rita took a sip of coffee.

Jude gave her a look. 'Well, we are still at the talking-into-the-early-hours-of-the-morning stage. I've been walking around like the happiest of zombies all week.'

'Aw, I love this for you both...' She stuck out her bottom lip. 'And I'd forgotten how amazing new love is.'

'Well, I'm not sure if it's love yet.' Jude winked. 'But there's a healthy dose of lust going on.'

Rita felt sad for a moment, and Jude clocked the change in her expression. 'You'll find it again, Rita. You're far too beautiful for someone not to fall for you... someone who won't be able to bear being anywhere but by your side.'

'You should write a book.' Rita laughed.

'Or next best thing, become a bookseller, eh?' Jude pushed his glasses back up his nose and grinned. They both noticed Teo walking across the courtyard.

'Go to your boy.' Rita smiled.

'*To love again, I felt my heart consenting.*' Jude declared dramatically.

'Who wrote that?'

'I just made it up.' Jude grinned, blowing her a theatrical kiss. As he headed for the front door, he was completely unaware of how deeply that quote had struck a chord with her, too.

THIRTY-THREE

The next day, the rain had stopped, making way for another beautiful summer morning. Rita quietly placed the last breakfast hamper against Michael's yurt then crept across the top of the field to the Singing Tree. The morning was still. Not silent, however, with gulls wheeling overhead and the soft rushing of the tide far below.

Something about the other night on the beach had helped her to find her inner boho. Had made her dig out clothes that she had always felt she wanted to be wearing but hadn't felt confident enough lately to do so. Wearing a loose, tiered maxi skirt in a rich rust-red, a soft cream vest showing just a flash of midriff and a floppy sunhat, she could easily have come straight from the Glastonbury Festival. Sitting on Archie's bench with a sigh, her eyes drifted out to sea, and she let herself think of Jago. Of the way he'd looked at her yesterday. Of the kindness in his eyes, and the hurt and the danger of sorts.

Then, inevitably, she thought of Paul, and despite the sheer wildness on her part, how tender the whole encounter had been. She also realised that she hadn't spoken to Sennen in a while, or Kelly for that matter. And then Thom, whose name landed like a stone in her gut. Her boy. Her beautiful, distant, furious boy. Her dear old dad had always said if she had a tantrum to think about 'what the matter was really'. Because nine times out of ten it wasn't what she had been kicking off about. 'Thom, what is it?' she said aloud as if the tree would have the answer for her.

A tear slipped down her cheek before she could stop it. She brushed it away with the heel of her hand, half annoyed with herself. But it didn't stop the ache. She leaned back and closed her eyes for a moment, letting the sea breeze lift her hair and the faint rustle of the Singing Tree whisper above her. Somewhere in the wind, she could almost hear Archie's voice, quiet, knowing, full of that dry old humour. Another tear fell. Just then, a white feather floated lazily through the air, dancing its way to the ground and landing at her feet, right by the entrance to the old cubby hole.

Heart skipping, she bent forward, slipped her hand inside, and, groping blindly, her fingers brushed against folded paper. With a small gasp, she pulled it free.

Another note. Neatly typed. Familiar.

Her hands trembled as she unfolded it.

When the time is right, you will start looking

'Who are you? What do you want?' she shouted, her voice cracking as she shoved the note into her pocket. Tears began to stream down her face. Whoever it was, she thought, they were trying to tell her something, something she needed to hear. It *had* to be Hilda. She was the only one who seemed to have been looking out for her lately, in her own Hilda way. But maybe it was time to stop wondering who and why and start listening to what the notes were saying instead. Because whoever was leaving them wasn't just doing it for fun.

She was aware of someone approaching, soft footsteps on the earth. 'Rita?' Paul's voice was low, gentle.

She startled, and turned to greet him, wiping hurriedly at her cheeks. 'Hello,' she said through a watery smile.

'Hello, you.' Paul's eyes crinkled with mischief. His faded band

T-shirt and a pair of tatty cargo shorts that hung low on his hips, revealing just a hint of tattoo ink curling around one thigh, made him look effortlessly cool.

'You're here for your peace and quiet, not a hysterical woman breaking all of the above.'

'We're all human,' Paul soothed. 'And you were far from hysterical the other night.' He smirked, then softly said, 'I can't even imagine how difficult it must have been for you, being with someone new.'

Rita sniffed loudly. 'And you made it so easy, thank you.'

'Sometimes us humans just need to feel things. If we don't feel sadness or anger or fear or love or hate or any other feeling I can't think of at the moment' – Paul smiled – 'then how boring would life be. Get it out, lady, I say.'

'And *what* about us?' She swallowed, then began to gabble. 'I'm worried, worried that if I don't take things further, I'll upset you. I don't want to make it weird between us, either, and I don't think I want a relationship. And I think you're amazing and...'

Paul put his hand to his chest and gave her a slow, reassuring smile.

Rita sighed. 'I'm so naïve with relationships. All I've known is Archie for the past twenty-five years.'

'And how lovely is that?' Paul added, squeezing her hand tightly. 'Rita, the other night, it was a beautiful moment in time. No expectations, no strings attached. Like I said on the beach. Just that moment. Pure and simple.'

He reached out, brushing a loose strand of hair behind her ear. 'You're a gorgeous person, Rita. But that doesn't mean I want a relationship with you either. That night, I'll never forget it. And I hope you don't either. I'd like it to be the start of many happy moments for you. And I'm pretty stoked to be able to say I was your first.' He smirked.

Rita laughed. Paul sighed deeply. 'You... this place... have helped me so much, you know. It's released something in me, too.

Encouraged me to start writing a song. Even got the guitar out the other night; we all had a sing-along.'

'No way!' Rita sniffed, her eyes still glistening from the tears.

'Yes, way. And I intend to finish it. And I'm not saying any more, but I think you'll like it.'

Rita exhaled, a fragile smile breaking through. She looked out to the timeless expanse of ocean, then back at Paul, feeling a warmth she hadn't expected.

'I love that fact! And as for that night, it will be a moment to hold on to whenever I feel like I'm falling.'

'Exactly that.' Paul nodded, squeezing her hand gently. 'But let's hope there won't be too much more of that, eh?' He lifted her hand and kissed it. 'It's just so peaceful here, isn't it.'

Then, *ATCHOO!*

They both jumped. Paul glanced toward the sound and grinned. 'Well, it was. Before Michael's sneeze just declared war on tranquillity.'

Rita laughed out loud.

'That's better, sweet cheeks.' Paul grinned.

Rita yawned loudly. 'Right, I'd better see what Annie's doing. I'm taking her down to the harbour to show her the delights of Reformer Pilates.'

'Good luck with that.' Paul chuckled. 'I'm sticking to a deckchair and Thomas Hardy today, I think.'

A smiling Rita stood up. 'You're the best, Paul Best.'

Paul gave a mock bow. 'Quite simply.'

THIRTY-FOUR

The Seahaven Bay Reformer Pilates studio smelled deliciously of Jilly's grapefruit perfume when Rita pushed open its door, swiftly followed by Annie, wearing tight yoga pants and a huge baggy T-shirt with Minnie Mouse on it.

Jilly had the back doors wide open, letting in the sea breeze and the occasional squawk of a furious gull who'd been denied someone's half-eaten pasty.

'Right, ladies!' Jilly clapped her hands. 'Shoes off, dignity optional. Let's stretch our souls and our hamstrings, shall we?'

Rita nudged a nervous Annie forward. 'Come on, it'll be good for your back. And our moods.'

'I don't trust a woman in full make-up who can touch her toes,' Annie muttered, pulling her T-shirt down over her wobbly bits.

'Oi.' Jilly overheard, as always. 'This woman in full make-up can not only touch her toes, love, but once got cramp whilst doing a reverse cowgirl and still managed to fake an orgasm. So, less lip, more lunge.'

'I'm loving that studio rule.' Annie laughed.

Rita shook her head. 'Not sure I am.'

The pair mounted the Reformer machines awkwardly. Jilly

expertly adjusted springs and straps, while Rita attempted to look graceful and Annie looked like she was preparing for childbirth.

After forty-five minutes, Annie's hair had burst free from its scrunchie, and she was sweating in places she'd forgotten existed. 'Why do people pay good money to feel like a hog trussed up for roasting?' She panted and strained against the foot bar.

Jilly lay back on her machine and opened her legs in a V, so wide she could've done semaphore.

'Ooh, I can do this one all right.' Annie laughed, widening her legs as far as she dared. 'Although it's been a while.'

Jilly laughed. 'I hear you, sister, and ignore the pain; Pilates is just so good for your back and your core. You're on the final exercise now – pelvic curls. Heels up on the foot bar. You will thank me next time you sneeze and don't wet yourself.'

'Don't make me laugh,' Rita added. 'Or I might actually wet myself now.'

They were silent for a few minutes, aside from a few cracks, exhales and the occasional muttered swear.

Then, unexpectedly, Annie said, 'Do you think we let men get away with too much?'

Jilly paused mid-pelvic curl.

'I mean' – Annie's voice wobbled – 'I'm on the dating apps, you know. The last one, Sean, his name was. Couldn't even plan a date. Just kept saying he was *busy*, but not too busy to ask if I'd send him a nude photo. We hadn't even exchanged last names. And what did I do, took over an hour getting in a position where the tits looked big, the stomach looked passable, and turning my ankle on the high heels that I've only ever worn once to a day racing at Royal Ascot.'

'Bloody hell,' Rita sighed. 'I'm so out of the dating game, I can't even imagine going into it like that.'

'It's worse than awful.' Annie lay back flat on the machine, talking to the ceiling. 'I told him to piss off, eventually. But I still felt... used, I guess? Dating is so difficult, right now with men offering such low effort with high expectation.'

Jilly slowly rolled up from her machine, suddenly serious.

'Sweetheart, I've been there. It's a minefield. And let me tell you something, it's not just the men taking the piss. It's us letting them, too. Because we think if we ask for more, they'll leg it.'

Annie blinked. 'So, what do you do?'

Jilly piped up. 'I've gone the opposite way. I laugh in their faces if they ask me that and delete. It's called self-respect, darling. You're allowed to want the picnic, not just the crumbs, you know.'

Annie sat up and gave a sheepish shrug. 'I always go for the young ones, too. Late twenties, floppy hair, confused about their career but confident in bed. Which is great at the time, but... not for the future, I realise that.'

Rita gave a little laugh. 'For what it's worth, from someone who is so far removed from it all, you don't need a boy who's still working out who he is, Annie. You need a gentleman. Someone who's been there, done that, and still opens doors for you. Someone who knows the value of peace and kindness.'

Annie let out a breath, her lip wobbling again. 'God. That sounds... normal... and nice.'

Jilly stood up. 'It's called being treated properly. And don't let anyone convince you that asking for that makes you high maintenance. Right, stand up and stretch, and then we're done.'

'Yes! Even just suggest a coffee without asking what bra size I am.' Annie stood up and tutted. 'I've been so foolish.' Annie's eyes filled with tears. Rita eased herself off the machine, copied Jilly's stretch and then squeezed her shoulder.

'You don't owe anyone a performance in exchange for their respect. That's one thing my Archie was, respectful.' Rita was thoughtful.

Annie was kind. 'I'm so sorry for your loss, Rita.'

Rita offered a small smile, brave but bruised. 'We get up, and we go again.'

She glanced over at Jilly, who met her eyes with quiet understanding.

Annie was on a roll now. 'I guess I just thought... maybe if I were less picky, or less intense, I know I can be bold and mouthy but underneath that's not completely me.'

'No,' Rita cut in. 'Don't shrink yourself for someone who can't even send a proper message, never mind handle your heart.'

Jilly starting tidying papers on the reception desk and sighed. 'Yes. Ask more. Want more. Be more annoying if that's what it takes. Because the ones who get scared off by that? They were never going to show up when it mattered, anyway. My old ma used to say, "Wait until they are banging your door down and then you'll know. The rest of 'em, they just ain't that into you."'

Annie reached for her purse. 'You should charge more than you do for all this added therapy.'

Jilly cackled. 'Great idea! It's thirty quid if you well up, thirty-five for a jaw-dropping revelation and forty for a full-on sob.'

THIRTY-FIVE

The next morning Rita was washing up her breakfast things furiously in the kitchen sink, her bashing and crashing disturbing Henry enough for him to retreat to the Den. On the kitchen table behind her lay a cream envelope, its contents strewn where she had thrown them down in frustration.

Zenya appeared in the doorway, her cheeks pink from a morning trek to Seahaven Cove with Teo and the group.

'Morning, how's it going?' She grabbed herself an apple from the fruit bowl and took a huge bite.

Without a word, Rita turned around, wiped her hands on a tea towel, and pointed to the table.

Zenya put her apple down on the envelope, then picked up a letter, typed on stiff white paper, headed in bold with CRIPPS & HAVERING SOLICITORS.

'He's trying to force me out, Zen. Out of my home. Archie's not been gone a year, and my own son is circling like a greedy vulture waiting for pickings.'

'Shit, Rita. I'm so sorry.'

Rita sat down, eyes brimming.

Zenya lifted the letter, reading aloud with a frown.

'Re: *Estate of the late Mr Archibald Jory* (*Deceased*)

'Dear Mrs Jory,

'We write on behalf of our client, Mr Thomas Jory, a beneficiary under the rules of intestacy in the estate of the late Mr Archibald Jory.

'It has come to our attention that the primary asset of the deceased's estate, namely Seahaven Farm, has not been valued or listed for sale. We are instructed to request that you undertake an independent valuation within fourteen days of this letter, with a view to initiating a sale, so that all legal beneficiaries may receive their rightful share.

'We must remind you of your duty as a representative of the estate to act in the best interests of all beneficiaries and to avoid any appearance of self-dealing or undue delay.

'Should no satisfactory action be taken, our client reserves the right to pursue legal remedies to ensure a fair distribution of the estate.'

She set it down gently, then looked Rita dead in the eye.

'I'm no expert here, but I think it's a scare tactic, Rita. Nothing more. You owned this jointly with Archie, right?'

Rita nodded.

'I've got an idea. How about you talk to Michael. He'll know the score and it'll be free and a quick response, at least.'

'Oh, Zenya, I don't know what I'd do without you.'

'I'm like a walking emergency kit, me,' Zenya quipped as she headed to the door.

Once alone, Rita sat at the kitchen table, the solicitor's letter trembling in her hands like a living thing, sharp, cold and accusing. This wasn't just paper and ink. It was Thom's voice turned to ice, a final verdict that slammed down between them, driving a cruel wedge where love once lived.

Her chest felt like it was being crushed, the weight far heavier than anger or frustration. It was grief. Confusion.

Betrayal. A knot twisting deep inside, squeezing tighter with every heartbeat.

Why? Why would Thom do this? Her boy, her baby, whose dreams she'd cradled like fragile glass. And now, instead of a call, a conversation, he'd sent the lawyers. Like she was a stranger.

Her heart was broken, not just because he'd taken this step, but because it felt like a signal she'd missed. Had she failed to hear him? To reach him as a mother? Was this letter a desperate plea for years of feeling unloved?

She couldn't bear the thought. Thom had never been as open with his feelings as Sennen, but she'd always held them both close, equally, fiercely.

And yet, beneath the wreckage of hurt and confusion, a stubborn pulse of love still beat strongly. He was her only son and she couldn't find it in her heart to shut the door on him. Not yet. She needed to understand what storm had driven him to this bitter shore.

Slowly, trembling, she folded the letter, a quiet defiance blooming inside her. Because love, she finally knew, wasn't just about holding tight when everything was calm. Sometimes, it was about holding on when the very ground beneath you threatened to crumble.

Michael sat under the Singing Tree, on the bench that bore Archie's name, collar turned up against the sea breeze, the Hardy poetry book resting on his knee. He was looking out aimlessly to where the sky met the sea.

Rita approached quietly, clutching the solicitor's letter in her hand. She had debated interrupting one of her guest's moments of peace, but the weight in her chest had grown heavier by the hour. She needed answers.

'Mind if I join you?'

'Of course not.' He tapped the bench beside him.

She hesitated, then held up the letter. 'I wouldn't normally bother a guest, and you can tell me to bugger off, but... I just wondered if you could have a quick look at something for me. Not now, but soon...'

'It'll cost you.' He smiled and took the letter, reading it slowly.

After a few seconds he said, 'Firstly, I'm so sorry for your loss.'

'Thank you. It's been a few months now, so...'

He looked up, his expression kind. 'So what? You've covered it well, my dear. And kudos to you for running this retreat so superbly.'

Rita felt a small warmth inside.

'Do you mind if I ask?' Michael said, folding the letter carefully. 'Is the farmhouse in your name now?'

'It was always in both our names, but I haven't changed it to mine alone yet. I thought maybe that happened automatically.'

Michael shook his head. 'Then this letter is nonsense. Empty posturing.'

Rita let out a breath she hadn't realised she was holding.

'I thought so. But it rattled me. Thom, that's my son, he's always been hungry for more. Even as a kid. Wanted the biggest slice of cake, had the loudest voice at the table.'

Michael handed back the letter. 'He may rattle, but he can't bite, not legally. The house is yours. And unless there are significant assets solely in your husband's name, there may be nothing left for him to claim once the bills are paid. Is there a will?'

Rita swallowed. 'That's the worst part, Michael. The solicitor who was supposed to be holding the will... they've lost it. We can't find it anywhere.'

Michael's face darkened. 'Lost it? That's not just careless, that's ridiculous. It's actually breaking the law. A will can't just disappear like that without serious consequences. You need to get to the bottom of this immediately.'

Rita nodded, feeling the knot tighten in her chest.

'So, does that mean Thom might have a case?' she asked quietly.

'Potentially,' Michael said slowly, with a grimace. 'If he feels he's been unfairly treated, he could make a claim against the estate, or even against you, depending on the assets. The law allows children to challenge a will, but it's not automatic. He'd have to prove his case. But with the will missing, things get more complicated.'

'Even if the house is in my name?'

'Correct. Ownership is important, but courts look at the entire estate's fairness. He might still try.'

Rita stood up. 'There *has to be* a solution. And I'm so sorry for disturbing your peace, Michael. You came here to escape the world, and I've dragged you into mine.' She smiled weakly. 'But you've helped me so much.'

Michael smiled back. 'That's what I'm realising it's all about. It's not *The Michael Stone Show*. This place is magical, really is. And Hardy was a great writer. Someone I might never have discovered without you.'

He raised his arm dramatically. 'And I quote: "Happiness was but the occasional episode in a general drama of pain."'

Rita smiled. 'Look at you, getting all literary.'

She tucked the letter back in the envelope. 'Yes, we have to cling to the good bits. I'm slowly learning that too.'

At that moment, Annie appeared in a vibrant red kaftan, her hair wrapped in a flowery turban.

'Ooh, whose good bits have I permission to cling on to?' She winked at Michael, who flushed slightly. He laughed and shook his head at her vivaciousness.

He stood. 'This too shall pass, dear Rita. And if you need anything else whilst I'm here, please ask. But what you need to do, pronto, is find that blessed will and hold that irresponsible solicitor accountable.'

'Thank you.' Rita swallowed hard and fingered the recent tree note in her pocket. Maybe it *was* time to start looking.

THIRTY-SIX

Rita was strolling back down the High Meadow towards the farmhouse when her mobile rang. Delighted that it was Sennen, she answered immediately.

'Darling, are you OK?' Always conscious not to be the needy mother, she just stopped herself from saying that she missed her checking in on her so often now.

'Just so busy, but the money is flying in so that's very nice. Weddings by Sennen will be going international at this rate.' The young woman laughed.

'I'm so pleased, darling, and you sound happy?'

'I am, Mum, don't worry about me. I've had a couple of dates with one of the photographers I use. So, Alex who? He can do one. Are you OK? How's it all going?'

'It's all going well. A fun group and they all seem to be enjoying it. I've had a couple of confirmed bookings for next month too. I've decided to run shorter retreats. A month is bit intensive, to be honest.'

'I did think that, but I know you needed the money, so I let it lie. Thom told me he'd popped in.'

Rita's voice flattened. 'Yes, yes he did.'

'You don't sound very enthused.'

'He wants me to sell the farm, Sen, and I don't want to.'

'That again – don't listen to him. You know what he's like.'

'Shit!' Rita suddenly exclaimed as she looked down towards the house.

'What is it, Mum?'

'Sorry, darling, but talk of the devil, that brother of yours has just pulled into the courtyard.'

'Oh. Oh yes, he's on his way back from his work thing, I think.'

'Sen, has he ever mentioned anything about your father's will to you?'

'No, why?'

'It's nothing... I'd better go. Love you, darling. Talk when you can and when you get a bit of a break come down and let me wait on you.'

'What, like last time?' Sennen laughed. 'When you were so hungover I had to cook breakfast, and your best mate killed Nigel.'

'Be gone with you.' Rita was laughing now too.

'Twice in one week and it's not even my birthday.' Rita tried to keep her voice level as she handed over a steaming mug of coffee to her only son.

'I felt I couldn't travel home without popping in.'

'Event go well?' Realising that big talk would be distressing for her, Rita continued with the small until she was ready to take the plunge.

As Thom took a sip of coffee and sat back in his chair she felt a pang go right through her heart. Not just because he was the spit of her Archie but because she couldn't believe the way he was treating her right now.

Here was the boy/man she had nurtured and cherished through endless nappies, two schools, braces, exam nerves and first love heartache. The boy/man whose bad dreams she had kissed away and who she'd sat up all night with in A&E when he had broken his leg playing rugby. Where had this person in front of her come from? She definitely hadn't brought him up to be this kind of unfeeling monster.

Thom ran his hands through his short hair. 'I take it you got the letter.' Rita remained silent. Thom sighed. 'Look, I'm not trying to be the bad guy here, Mum. But the farm needs to be valued. It's only fair. You can't just hold on to it like it's not part of Dad's estate. You know how this works.'

Rita was curt. 'Yes, I do, actually. I've had a bit of legal advice. Proper legal advice.'

Thom hesitated. 'Who from?'

'One of my guests.' She extended the truth slightly. 'He's spent thirty years sorting out messes like this.'

Thom's jaw shifted. She could almost hear the gears turning, recalculating his position.

He spat back without thought. 'Well, that's... fine, but he... he wasn't Dad's solicitor.'

'No, but he understands the law. And here's the truth, Thom. The farm was in both our names as joint tenants. That means when your dad died, it passed to me automatically. It's mine now. Not part of the estate. End of story.'

'I know that. But what about the rest of it? You can't just ignore...'

'There's nothing else to ignore. The savings are gone, spent on funeral costs, keeping this place afloat and the ridiculous financial mess your father left me in.'

'What about the money from the sale of the cows and the tractor?'

'Thom... it's gone. I have the house and now the money coming in from the retreat. That's it. Please don't do this to me.' She coughed to push back her rising emotion.

'So, you're saying there's nothing, *nada*, not one penny left for me and Sennen?'

At the mention of her daughter's name, Rita felt a surge of fear that Sennen may be involved too. She hadn't given anything away when they had just spoken. No, surely that wasn't the case, for that would destroy her totally. 'Not from the estate, Thom. No.'

He stared at her, stunned, not by the answer, but by the fact she'd dared give it so directly.

'But Mum, you haven't even seen Dad's will. This isn't fair.' Thom's handsome face suddenly turned ugly.

'It's not about fair.' Rita's voice softened. 'You sent a solicitor's letter thinking it would scare me. It did. But I've spent too long keeping this place going with or without your father... so to be pushed out of it now, well, it ain't happening, sunshine.'

A long silence.

'You could still sell,' Thom muttered. 'Like I said before, live somewhere smaller. Easier. You're not getting any younger, Mum. You'd have no money worries then, be set for life. You could split what was over with me and Sen and then everything would be sorted.'

Rita stood slowly. 'I may not be getting younger, but I am getting stronger by the day, yes.'

Thom suddenly looked awkward. And then out it came with a whoosh. 'What if the will says something different?'

A red mist came over Rita, the same steaming fury she had felt towards Jago days previously.

'What do you mean?' Rita felt the temperature in the room suddenly lower, her voice coming out in a low growl. 'Thom, is there something you know that I don't? Are you broke? Are you worried that you're not going to be left with any money? Don't worry, I'm not intending to remarry any time soon. What is it? What is wrong with you?'

Her tall, handsome boy stood up and with what Rita thought looked like tears in his eyes reached for his car keys. 'Maybe there was more to Dad than any of us knew, that's all.'

Rita frowned. 'Thom? You can't say that and not expand on it. You know where the will is, don't you? This is what this is all about. It has to be.'

He didn't answer.

Rita was now shouting. 'Thom, have you seen your father's will?'

Thom cracked. 'NO! NO, I fucking haven't, but one of us needs to.'

'What do you mean by that?' Rita screeched as Thom headed for the door.

Again, no answer, instead, he just huffed, and walked out, leaving the door as wide open as the crack that had just split straight through the centre of Rita's heart.

THIRTY-SEVEN

Rita's sharp knock echoed through the unusually quiet annexe. Normally, the place would be alive with the tinny theme tune of *Six Feet Under* or the murmur of her mother-in-law commenting loudly on the acting in it. Today, though, there was only silence, thick, still, and faintly unsettling.

Hilda opened the door, cigarette poised between two fingers, the thin smoke curling lazily upwards. Her black funeral suit clung tightly to her tiny figure, and her hair, tied neatly in a perfect bun, made her look like an aged Audrey Hepburn.

Knowing Rita wasn't here for a friendly chat, the old woman took a drag, exhaled through pursed lips, then after checking her watch, ushered Rita to sit at the table in the kitchenette. 'I have twenty-three minutes precisely until I need to leave. It's going to be a good one today. Myrtle Tregowan was the perfect snob and highly likely to have arranged her own wake down to the last vol-au-vent.'

Rita swallowed hard. 'I need you to tell me the truth, Hilda. None of this bullshit insinuation lark. Did Archie ever say anything, anything at all, about his will?'

Hilda flicked ash into a chipped saucer, fingers trembling ever so slightly. Her eyes, usually sharp with judgement, now shimmered with something softer, regret, maybe even sorrow.

'I promised my son I would never ever tell a soul.'

'I don't think he'll hear you now, do you?' Rita tried to push down her rising anger. 'Tell a soul what?'

'God rest his dear soul.' Hilda crossed her chest. 'But I suppose it's too late now for secrets. I saw your face as our Thomas just left, and, as much as you may dispute this, I can't bear to see you in so much pain.'

Rita's heart was pounding through her chest. Jilly's words rushed through her mind. *Enemies, lovers, long-lost family... wills have a knack for stirring up a right old hornets' nest.* Maybe she should stop Hilda now, walk right out of the door before her world was about to be blown apart by something else she wasn't ready to deal with.

'You may even know already. I don't know what went on in the marital home.'

Rita realised that Hilda was backtracking, and that whatever was about to reach the light of day from within her wasn't going to just be the revelation of Archie's lottery numbers.

'I don't think he ever told you, did he?'

'No!' Rita whined. 'Jesus, no. *What*, tell me!'

'There's, there was... someone else.'

Rita felt panic rising fast, threatening to overwhelm her. She let out a small, shaky squeak from deep in her throat and drew in as much air as she could to steady herself.

'He didn't cheat on you,' Hilda said quickly. 'Never... not as far as I know, anyway.'

Rita drew in a deep gulp of air.

Hilda grimaced. 'But there was a child.'

Even the room seemed to hold its breath at this shocking revelation.

'What are you talking about, Hilda? As in he had a child I didn't know about? No, no, you're delusional.' Rita shot to her feet.

Hilda looked uncharacteristically lost for words. She glanced at her watch.

'You can't leave me in the middle of this,' Rita said through gritted teeth.

Hilda stubbed out her cigarette, and with a trembling hand lit another, and fired off a quick text from her mobile. She exhaled slowly. It was the first time Rita had ever seen her mother-in-law so rattled. And somehow, that unsettled her more than anything else.

Rita gripped the edge of the sink, grounding herself.

'So that's why the will's gone, isn't it?' Rita blurted. 'He changed it. And now someone has made it disappear.' She poured herself a mug of water and drank it down in one long swallow. 'And if it's not Thom... and it's not you... then who the hell is it?'

Hilda reached for her handbag, her fingers trembling slightly. She glanced at her watch again. A long, measured exhale, followed by a toot from a smart Mercedes pulling up outside the annexe door.

'Oh, thank God.' Hilda's relief was palpable. 'That'll be Eric.'

'Eric?' Rita wrinkled her nose.

'Yes, Eric... a new...' Hilda paused, trying to decide what Eric actually was. 'A new friend of mine. Met him by a graveside the other day.' She reached for her bag. 'We might just make it in time for the vol-au-vents, if we hurry.'

With a rattling cough and already halfway to the door, Hilda turned. 'As much as you don't think it, I think the world of you, Rita. I can't tell you how, just yet, but I am going to sort this mess out once and for all.'

And with a waft of Chanel No. 5, cigarette smoke and Fisherman's Friend lozenges, Hilda Jory, part battle-axe, part guardian angel, swept out.

As Rita walked back over to the farmhouse, each crunch of gravel seemed to measure out a thought she didn't want to have. Her mind clawed for something to hold on to. A reason. A denial. But all she could hear was Hilda's voice, quiet and steady, repeating the words that had just detonated in her life.

There was a child.

If Archie had known, if he'd loved that child even half as much as she suspected... then what had she been all those years? The main act? The interval? A safe harbour he left when the wind changed?

Had every time he said he was going to some agricultural show been a lie? Every call he took outside, every faraway look over dinner, had that been someone else's bedtime story, someone else's tiny pair of arms around his neck?

The thought made her dizzy. She pushed open the front door, eyes burning.

Who was the mother? Where were they now? Did she or the kid know about her? Or worse, did they not even know she existed?

A low wind rattled the farm's old weathervane, Rita thinking its rusty creak sounding today like laughter. Mocking her for the absurdity that she hadn't had an inkling that her husband had been a father of three!

She stepped inside, her trainers leaving a faint trail of dust on the flagstone floor, the weight of Hilda's words pressing down with every step.

There was a child.

And as she sat down at the kitchen table, head in hands, every memory of Archie suddenly felt like a puzzle she didn't have all the pieces for. The question was, were the missing fragments lost... or simply waiting to be uncovered in places she'd never thought to look?

THIRTY-EIGHT

'I still can't believe Archie's got another bleedin' ankle-biter,' Kelly relayed through the handset and a mouthful of toast.

Resting her feet in the Den's window seat and with her mobile on speaker, Rita glanced out to see Teo running a yoga class at the top of the orchard and Zenya on hands and knees, weeding a bed in the fruit and vegetable garden.

'I can't either. This is serious shit, though, Kel. I mean, he's hidden a child from me for all these years. It's actually quite unbelievable, knowing what a softie he was with our two.' Her thoughts turned to the way he used to laugh with Thom when he was little, crouched down at eye level, pulling faces until they were both breathless. And the way he had played prince to Sennen's princesses, telling her that he would always protect her, however old she was.

Kelly reverted to serious mode. 'How was Hilda when she told you about it?'

'She was a mixture of relief and regret to release the burden of such a huge secret, I think. I can see why she didn't tell me, though. She was not only covering for Archie, but I do believe she didn't want to upset me. She's not a bad old girl, really. I mean, she loaned me the money to get started on the retreat.'

'Probably because she knew why you were broke in the first place. Archie was sending the kid or the mother cash?'

'God, yes, what a mess but money never went missing before, I'm sure. It's all been recent, this, or I would have known, surely I would have known.' Rita put her head in her hands, struggling to make sense of it all.

Kelly sneezed loudly. 'Maybe he led a double life; you see that on the TV.'

'Kel! No, don't say things like that.'

'Sorry, sorry and no way. Archie wouldn't do that.' Kelly backtracked.

'It's just all very odd. I'm still processing it.' Rita took a deep breath and remembered she hadn't updated Kelly on the latest on the will. 'But on a positive, the solicitor has called me in for a meeting later this week, so I'm assuming the will has been found and all *may* be revealed.' Rita stood up, stretched, and let out a big yawn. 'This is all so exhausting.'

'Are you happy to find out everything, do you think?'

'Yes, I want to know every sordid little detail.'

'Really?'

'Of course I do. I need the whole story. I have to know if he had an affair or not, because if he didn't, the child would be an adult by now. And whoever they are, they're still half of Archie and possibly the key to the missing will.'

'I wonder if they live in Seahaven Bay?' Kelly was serious now.

'Part of me hopes so. The Seahaven Bay Facebook Gossip Group might have to disband out of sheer ineffectiveness.'

Kelly laughed. 'But the will might not give you the answers or worse still it could open up a can of worms.'

'And that's the chance I've got to take.' Rita ruffled Henry's ears as he nuzzled up to say hello.

'I'm quite jealous, really. If only my Ron was half as exciting to have kept such a clandestine secret for all those years.'

Rita couldn't help but laugh. 'Oh, Kel, what would I do without you?'

'Joking aside, are you all right, Reet? And are you sure you don't want me to come down and stay?'

'No, I feel surprisingly calm. And it's comforting having Michael here, to be honest. I haven't told him about "the child", but he said to see him again if I wanted to talk to him about anything.'

'That's nice. He's turned out not as bad as we first thought, then.'

'No, he's a decent bloke. And a hugely different man sober.'

'He did have a lovely face; it was just the belly that put me off.'

'That's very shallow of you,' Rita said in mock seriousness.

'Especially as mine is nearly the same size.' Kelly laughed. 'I keep having inappropriate dreams about Pete the Pilchard – maybe he could solve my sex drought. I reckon he'd be really filthy.'

'I can see you as a buxom landlady.'

'Oh no. I'd never leave my Ron... I adore him. It's just his meat and two veg have turned vegan. He is the epitome of a wet lettuce in the bedroom and ironically that's all I'm asking for.'

Rita's shoulders were rocking. 'When did you get so disgusting?'

Kelly guffawed. 'I know, vile, right. I blame an all-girls' school. Anway, Reet. Any more fellatio on the beach or is the musician too busy writing you a love song?'

Rita groaned. 'No, that was a one-off and it's a busy old week here at the Seahaven Bay Retreat, I'll have you know. I will be saying goodbye to them all soon. And as much as I have enjoyed having them, I cannot wait to have a bit of time to myself before the next one, to be honest.'

'Are Zenya and Teo going to stick around in between?'

'Yes, I think so, they are so happy with food and board, and I just pay them for their time, so it works nicely. Stan is being an angel too.'

Kelly softened. 'You are so loved, Reet, and I meant to ask, how is the delicious Jago? You haven't mentioned him for a while.' Kelly paused, then, rising a decibel, 'Oof! Can you just imagine what *that* sex on a stick could do for you on the beach? You'd need resuscitating by the coastguard.'

At the mention of Jago, Rita felt slightly sick. 'Right, I'd better get on, I have work to do. I need to set up the art class and a final moonlight mantra before they all head home. Zenya is cooking a proper last night feast for them too.'

'They'll be eating your profits with all your generosity and an art class?' Kelly laughed. 'Love you, mate.'

'Yes. I promised a monthly guest and activity and I've found somebody very cool to run it. Love you back, mate, and I will need you here to keep me sane, soon.'

'When you light the fuse on the inheritance fireworks, you mean?'

'Let's hope it's not that bad.'

'Keep me posted, Reet. Remember... I'm always here with an ear.'

THIRTY-NINE

Glanna Pascoe, Seahaven Bay's visiting artist and bohemian beauty, stood with her back to the amazing view in the barn in her usual attire: a linen smock streaked with every colour of the rainbow, gold hoop earrings, a red lip and battered Doc Martens. Her cropped blonde hair was perfectly cut and at her feet lay Banksy, her graceful whippet. All slender limbs, soft black fur, and liquid eyes that held the kind of wisdom most people didn't inherit until their last decade. He blinked slowly at the gathered group staring at him and his owner, the very embodiment of calm resignation that he was about to be subjected to a lot more scrutiny.

Glanna had driven over from the south coast town of Hartmouth that morning, where she still ran her art gallery in Ferry Lane Market. Though she rarely mentioned it, rumour had it that a very well-known film star once bought three of her trademark rainbow paintings after her exhibiting alongside famous Cornish artist Isaac Benson.

After Rita had welcomed Glanna to the group, the attractive artist cleared her throat and smiled widely. 'Welcome, everybody: reluctant artists, wannabe artists or maybe we have a Rembrandt amongst us. I just wanted to say a few words before we start.'

She was quiet for a second before she began her soliloquy.

'Why does art matter? I find it's not just about learning to paint or draw pretty pictures. It's about reconnecting with a part of us that can get lost in all the noise and the mess of life. Art gives us a way to breathe, to feel, and sometimes to heal. It reminds us that creativity and hope live inside us, even when things are tough.'

'Hallelujah,' Michael shouted out. Amazingly, there wasn't a murmur from anyone else.

'So, whether it's an object, or an animal or just a splash of colour on a page, every stroke is a little act of courage. And here, in this space, we can all be brave together.'

Rita saw Emily take a huge breath, then, as Glanna clapped her hands to start the class, she noticed that despite her wedding ring, Paul was checking the artist out with an intensity that was hard to miss. For a moment, she expected to feel something, jealousy maybe, or that familiar twinge of being overlooked. But nothing came. Just a quiet, unexpected sense of peace.

She wasn't bothered. And more than that, she was glad that she wasn't.

Becoming aware of her own wedding ring, she began twisting it, the gold warm from her skin. Ten months. Was that long enough to start letting go? She had already let herself go a little bit on the beach with Paul and the feelings she had for Jago, although confusing, were far from chaste.

She didn't feel ready to take it off, not exactly, but she also wasn't sure what she was still waiting for. Some sign? Some thunderbolt moment of permission? She knew that grief didn't come with a checklist and "till death us do part", that oft-recited wedding vow, had not made much sense to her before, but today, with everything that was going on, it glaringly did.

She turned the ring once more, slowly, then let her hand fall back into her lap. Not right now. But maybe soon.

Glanna remained upbeat. 'Rita did think it might be fun for us to try and paint one of her goats.' The artist gave Rita a sly wink. 'But our oblong-eyed models really weren't in the mood.' A slight titter from the audience, who were all sitting in the barn on milking stools with easels incorporating a paint tray in front of them – Zenya included, as she had told Rita how much she enjoyed learning a new skill.

Glanna had asked Rita, quietly but firmly, if they could keep the session alcohol-free. 'Just a preference,' she'd added with a gentle smile. So Zenya had prepared a mocktail punch for the break, which was cooling in the fridge, and had named it a 'Picasso Punch': a delicious blend of mango, pink grapefruit and pomegranate juices, brightened with fresh lime and mint, finished with a splash of the sparkling elderflower fizz that Rita still had buckets of.

'Today, you'll be painting the noble, tragic, underappreciated muse of my life.' She gestured grandly to the floor. 'My Banksy.'

As if on cue, Banksy gave a long-suffering sigh.

Michael squinted at him. 'He looks like a furry croissant. How am I meant to paint *that*?'

'Have you ever seen a furry black croissant?' Lola asked, immediately regretting that question as the whole group fell about in peals of laughter.

'If he plays his cards right,' Annie added to a response of complete silence.

'I've put his jewel-encrusted collar on today,' Glanna explained, 'so you'll get a bit of contrast against his fur. Now, what you first need to do is draw the outline of our subject in the gridded art card on your easels in pencil, then afterwards rub out the lines with the eraser provided. It's a bit like painting with numbers really. I want you all to come away with something you can frame and keep, whether it be for your toilet, or someone else's.'

Rita smiled, pleased with her choice of artist. Jude had heard about Glanna through Isaac Benson, whose paintings he adored. Glanna wasn't expensive either; she had said as long as her gallery got some promotion, she loved doing events like these. Now a fairly famous artist, she enjoyed keeping things real and giving back by sharing her skills.

Annie tilted her head. 'Is it wrong that I want legs like those? The dog's, not the artist. I mean, look at them.'

Paul, chewing the end of his brush, said solemnly, 'I think he's embodying the fragility of the modern male.'

Lola screwed up her nose. 'Fragile? Do women even want fragile men? Perleese. I'd take a furry croissant over a sensitive snowflake any day, and that's coming from a lesbian who's already had enough drama to keep a soap opera in plot for at least a year.'

Emily sat quietly at the edge of the group, sketching furiously. When her eyes met Rita's, she gave a small, grateful smile, one that said she knew this whole mad class had probably been arranged just for her. A lump rose in Rita's throat. For Emily, this wasn't just about painting, it was proof that art still had a place in her troubled life. That *she* still had a place.

And in that one watery look, Rita suddenly understood just how much this retreat meant, not only to her, but to everyone who had crossed its threshold... and everyone to come.

FORTY

Seahaven Bay's surf beach was bathed in light by the full moon suspended in the ink-black sky. Its glow spilled across the ocean in a glistening ribbon, while waves murmured gently as they curled onto the shore. A warm, salt-laced summer breeze drifted in, carrying the unmistakable scent of the sea.

The fire pit Rita had built crackled softly as the hush of approaching footsteps drifted over the sand. Head torches bobbed like curious fireflies in formation as her moonlit crew arrived.

'Welcome to moonlight mantras,' Zenya declared, raising her glass of fizz to the starlit sky. 'And for our very last one, Earth's lantern is a full one at its best.'

Annie tilted her head to the sky, her thick blonde curls catching the moonlight. 'Has anyone ever wondered who the Man in the Moon actually is? Like... was he dumped up there for doing something awful? I've never read up on it, you know.'

Zenya smiled. 'There are a load of legends. Some say he was caught stealing firewood on a holy day and got booted up there as punishment. Others reckon he's just a lonely soul with a lamp and a long memory.'

Michael grinned. 'Annie, maybe he's your type. Aloof, distant, no emotional availability.'

'And absolutely no chance of texting back,' Annie sighed. 'Ideal, actually.'

Laughter bubbled around the fire pit as Michael placed his hand on Annie's, and they shared a warm smile. 'Well, whoever he is, he's shining his face off tonight.' Zenya took a sip of bubbles from her paper cup. 'Is that everyone?' Zenya looked to Rita, who nodded.

'Yes, just our five lovely guests, you, me and the wonderful Teo.'

'Yeah,' Teo piped up. 'Jude said he'd leave us to it tonight. He's catching up on his reading, deep in a new rom-com. He loves it. Said romantic comedy is a highly underrated genre and who am I to get in the way of his main passion.'

'OK, let's start then,' Zenya enthused. 'As usual, no phones, no expectations. Just stars, snacks, a slurp of champagne and hopefully some helpful revelations.'

'Don't all pass out.' Michael puffed out his chest. 'But I'm sticking to the zero beers tonight.'

Everybody gave a rousing cheer.

The group's newfound closeness was unmistakable as they lounged across sandy blankets, comfortable with each other in the way that only a month of shared hikes, honesty, mealtimes and the occasional shower queue could create.

'OK, you lovely lot. Let's do our check-in. Something silly or true or both. One small thing the moon should know about you tonight.'

Lola lifted her voice. 'I'll start. Before I came here, my entire life was TikTok transitions and trying to get the right aesthetic for my Insta grid. I spent more time filming my life than living it. I was *so* in it. So deep, I didn't realise how addicted I'd become. This place... helped me come up for air. Taught me it's OK not to be "on" all the time. That being present, in the real, messy, not-filtered world, is actually kind of beautiful, so thank you.'

'That's gorgeous.' Zenya took a long slow breath from her tummy. 'Let's all breathe that one out.'

A measured intake of breath and a raising of cups followed.

Rita took the champagne bottle from the cool bag, topping people up with a grin that masked how emotionally knackered she was feeling.

'I've written a song,' Paul piped up, clearing his throat. 'It's called "Retreat", and yes, Rita, it's all thanks to you.'

Rita, eyes brimming, put her hand to her heart. 'Paul, I don't know what to say and I can't wait to hear it.'

Emily raised her hand like a kid at school. 'So, uh... I'm not going back home. To the difficult life I had before. Sorry, all, but I told a little lie that work had sent me here. I'd actually quit.' Rita felt a swell of pride that the young woman had finally found the courage to share her truth with everyone. 'Glanna, you know the cool artist, well, she's asked me if I'd like to work for her in Ferry Lane Market, help with her exhibitions, and start painting again properly. And I said YES!'

Everybody cheered. Michael mock-clutched his chest. 'A new start, oh, how we love that.'

Annie giggled from beneath the blanket she was now sharing with the divorce lawyer. 'I've decided I'm done with fuckboys and younger men. Yes, I want a man with a pension, but he has to be funny, kind, steady, the kind who knows what it means to show up, and at least be able to boil an egg.'

Michael raised a knowing brow. 'I *do* make a marvellous eggs Benedict, my dear.'

They all erupted into laughter.

'Oh, God, it's my turn,' Michael groaned. 'I've learned how to listen. I've learned that alcohol doesn't make me happy. Quite the opposite, in fact. I've also learned that friendship comes in all shapes and sizes.' His voice wobbled. 'What have you done to me, Seahaven Bay Retreat!' He looked to his host. 'Whilst we are all together, I want to thank you, Rita, and your wonderful staff for making this month such a special one.'

'Hear, hear!' Annie shouted, swiftly followed by the others.

'Thank you. It's been a pleasure getting to know you all, but we're not done yet.' Rita looked to Zenya, who, smiling to herself, passed round a pouch of sea-polished pebbles, the moon catching on their smoothed surfaces.

'Same as before. Hold on to your stone. Whisper something to it or shout it if you want. Doesn't matter. But let it mean something. Something you may want to happen or something you are ready to leave behind.'

There was a hush as the group took a moment to think.

Michael was first. 'I'm sorry for being such a twat at the start. And middle. And occasionally last week. But I think I'm learning how not to be.'

Annie nodded solemnly. 'I want to believe I'm worth more than how men have treated me.'

Lola cradled her pebble. 'I want to be more present and stop trying to shrink myself. Not just physically. Emotionally too.'

Paul, softer than usual: 'I want to stop procrastinating, finish things. Even the hard things. Like beginning to have a relationship with my daughter.'

Emily whispered, 'I am starting to value myself and be brave enough to paint what I really feel.'

Zenya laid her pebble in the sand. 'I want to believe I belong. Not just here. Anywhere.'

Teo looked around at them all. 'My *mamá* once told me I had to visit this place. She said I'd understand why when I got here. And she was right. It felt like home the minute I met you, Rita.'

There was a brief silence. Zenya looked to Rita. 'You don't have to, if you don't want to.'

Finally, Rita spoke. 'I want to forgive and forget some of the things that are cropping up in my life. I want to trust again. To stop dragging old pain into new chapters. Just... let it go, with love, and finally move forward.'

Teo put his arm over Rita's shoulders as, one by one, they walked down to the shoreline and threw their stones into the sea.

Just then, Jude quietly appeared beside Teo, head torch on, and threw his stone to the ocean. Teo grinned and reached for his hand, their fingers lacing easily.

'I thought you were reading.'

'I was,' Jude murmured. 'But I didn't want to miss this chapter. I'm not lonely anymore.' His voice wobbled.

Teo bumped his shoulder gently. 'And I feel settled in myself...' He paused. 'I know, is crazy early, *sí*? But Jude Finch... I think I fall a little bit in love with you already.'

Jude blinked, his mouth opening just slightly, but before he could speak, a few soft guitar chords drifted across the sand.

Paul, sitting cross-legged by the fire, began to play. His fingers moved with quiet certainty. No one interrupted. No one needed to. The time was right. One by one, everyone sat back down by the fire and listened.

Paul's voice rose, low, smoky, hopeful somehow as he sang the heart out of his new ballad.

'I came here with pieces I'd hidden away
Old ghosts in my backpack, too heavy to stay
But the sea didn't ask me for reasons or proof
Just gave me the tide and a place to tell truth.'

He raised his voice as he reached the chorus.

'So, here's to the quiet, the brave and the broken
To words and hopes, now finally spoken
We found something real, in the salt and the sand
And I'm not who I was when I first came to land.'

Paul's voice hitched as he continued with the second verse.

'The nights felt like stories we wrote in the dark.
Each laugh lit a lantern, each tear left a mark
We're strangers no longer, not here, not tonight
We're stitched into starlight, and holding on tight.'

The group started swaying and moving in their own personal ways as the melody hit them. Then a few hums to the chorus.

'So, here's to the quiet, the brave and the broken,
To words and hopes now finally spoken.
We found something real, in the salt and the sand

And I'm not who I was when I first came to land.'
As the final chorus arrived everyone in the group joined in.
'So, here's to the quiet, the brave and the broken,
To words and hopes, now finally spoken.
We found something real, in the salt and the sand
And I'm not who I was when I first came to land
No, I'm not who I was... and I think I understand.'
As they made their way back to the car park, the hum of the chorus still soft on everyone's lips, Rita lingered a step behind. The moonlit sand stretched ahead, quietly lighting her path. For the first time in a long while, she felt ready to face what was unfolding around her. And maybe, just maybe, it was time to start making her hopes for the future come true.

FORTY-ONE

It was August and the retreat had fallen quiet. All the guests had gone back to their different lives, hopefully carrying with them a new sense of ease, or purpose, or at the very least a story worth telling. Suitcases had been wheeled over gravel, sleepy goodbyes exchanged, warm hugs given with the soft promise to return 'one day'.

The barn was empty, its wooden floors silent after days of chatter and laughter and the rhythmic hum of breath during yoga and Pilates.

Zenya, Stan and Teo were dotted across the grounds, emptying yurts, folding blankets, scrubbing floors, and checking gas bottles. Their movements were efficient but unhurried, the calm after the storm. Even the goats seemed mellow, sunning themselves lazily in their pen, whilst the chickens could never put an end to their squabbling.

Rita had been patiently waiting for this day. Because some things, like revisiting old grief and dealing with the mess that Archie had left her, were easier to deal with without an audience.

Dickens, Bryant and Feathers, an old-school solicitors' firm, was tucked away in one of the many back streets of Seahaven Bay. The polished wood and stacks of legal tomes lining the walls of the reception area gave the place an air of old-world gravitas. Rita felt like they should be in some fancy office in Holborn, not in a tourist town with seagulls cawing in the harbour below.

Rita had only ever been here once before, with Archie, when he had had some business to sort around the farm and the passing of his father. Just twenty, to Archie's thirty, she had been so naïve then.

Behind the reception desk sat a young woman who looked out of place amid the traditional surroundings. Chloe was barely out of her twenties herself, with sleek chestnut hair pulled into a loose bun and pretty tattoos peeking from beneath the sleeves of her smart blouse. Her perfectly manicured nails danced over the keyboard as Rita approached.

'Good morning.' Rita tried to keep her tone casual. 'I'm here to see Malcolm Feathers regarding my husband's will.' Chloe's fingers froze mid-keystroke. 'Rita Jory.'

For a moment, the young woman didn't look up, and when she finally did, her eyes were quick to dart away... too quick.

'One moment, please. I... I'll check if Mr Feathers is available,' she recited in shrill theatrical fashion whilst sending through a quick email to her boss.

Rita wasn't sure if she was just being paranoid, but she caught the flicker of something – unease? Surely not guilt.

Noting his reply on screen, Chloe plastered on a polite, practised smile. 'Please, take a seat; Mr Feathers will be with you shortly.'

A moment later, the door opened, and Malcolm Feathers appeared. He was in his late fifties, but looked far older, with silver-streaked hair neatly combed back and wire-rimmed glasses perched on his nose. His tailored suit fitted his slender frame impeccably, and his manner was calm, measured, everything you'd expect from a man who'd spent decades navigating wills and estates.

He held out a spindly hand for Rita to shake and then ushered her into his office.

'Sit, sit.' The solicitor waved a hand toward the leather chair across from his desk as he closed the door behind her. 'A drink of some sort?'

'No, no, I'm fine.' Rita's mouth felt like the desert, but she just wanted to get on with it. Find out what this man, the keeper of her husband's secrets, was about to tell her.

Malcolm opened the top drawer of his antique leather-topped bureau and pulled out a file. 'This isn't your husband's current will, but I do have some information for you, Rita.'

As he opened the file, Rita sat upright, her heart suddenly pounding in her chest like a frightened bird.

'Archie did make two amendments.' The solicitor's voice was careful. 'But all I know from Mr Bryant is that these were to make a change to the executor status and to make a small bequest to somebody he hadn't seen for a long time. Does that make sense?'

'Sense?' Rita felt tears prick her eyes. 'I didn't even know he'd made a will, Malcolm. And you'd think his wife should be the executor, surely?'

The solicitor cleared his throat. 'Archie called the morning he passed away and spoke to young Chloe here. He said the new executor, a family member, was going to pick up a copy of the will.'

Rita felt the blood drain from her face. 'Who was it?' Despite knowing the answer already, she had to hear him say it.

'Err... Rita. I... err...'

'Just say it.' Rita was getting tetchy. 'It was my son, Thomas Jory, wasn't it? It's fine. I kind of knew already.'

The solicitor looked awkward, shifting uneasily. 'I'm afraid it was a Monday. Chloe was on her own that day, with no one to ask, so she gave...' Malcolm Feathers paused. 'She gave... the family member... both copies. And, um... for some reason, we don't have an electronic copy either.'

Rita shook her head. The fact that her son had blatantly lied to her cut her like a knife. 'So, what you are saying is that my son now has both copies and somehow mysteriously everything else has been deleted from your computers – is that right?'

The solicitor stammered, unable to answer. Frustrated, Rita stood and marched to the reception desk. Chloe, who had been listening at the door, hurried back to her post.

Rita pulled up a photo of her red-headed son on her phone and thrust it toward Chloe. 'Look carefully. Was this the man who picked up my husband's will?'

The young woman looked terrified. 'I... I'd only just started working here. I don't really remember. He was handsome, like that, but I don't remember red hair and I think... I think he was older.'

'Well, try and bloody remember. Because whatever this will says, this is my future on the line, and I deserve to know where my husband's money is going.'

Malcolm rushed out, flustered. 'Mrs Jory, I realise this must be very disturbing for you, and I am truly sorry for this diabolical mix-up which I assure you we are going to get to the bottom of, but I think you should leave.'

Chloe, about to burst into tears, blurted, 'All I remember is that I think he said he was a brother; yes, that's right, it was Archie's brother.'

'His brother?' Rita was wide eyed. 'Are you really sure about this? Archie was an only child.'

Rita took the bend out of town like she was in *The Italian Job*, her little blue Suzuki Jimny growling in protest. She didn't care. Rage, heartbreak, and something dangerously close to hysteria were coiled tight in her chest, and the only thing that made sense was the sea.

She tore down the coast road, eyes misted, breath shallow, the radio babbling nonsense she couldn't hear. Every pothole rattled her bones, every gust of wind shoved at the car like it was trying to say, 'Turn back.' But she didn't. She wouldn't.

The weather had changed as quickly as the confusing news that Rita had just received. She pulled up at the beach, the same stretch of sand where, just weeks ago, she'd been wrapped in Paul's arms and buoyed by the laughter of her retreat friends. Now, the joy of that day felt like a distant dream.

The blue skies that once shimmered with promise had curdled into brooding grey. Rain began to fall, a soft patter at first, then harder, sharper, as if the heavens had lost patience, too. A low rumble of thunder rolled across the bay, followed by a jagged fork of lightning that tore the sky in two. She barely noticed the screeching of fretting seabirds above or the salty spray that stung her face.

Her fists clenched, nails digging into her palms, she walked along the wild and windy beach. Lies. Secrets. A brother? A will that vanished into thin air. Who the hell was Archie Jory? Because at this minute she didn't know. And as for Hilda, why on earth had she not told her that there was yet another Jory on the scene? Or was there? Everything was too bizarre for words. If this was true maybe Thomas had been telling her the truth when he'd said that he knew nothing about it. Then again, maybe he had thrown in the 'brother' card to hurl her off the scent.

She didn't know how long she walked, up and down the beach, the wind screaming in her ears, matching the chaos inside her. The grey waves crashed relentlessly onto the shore, breaking into foamy white like the fragile pieces of her shattered trust.

Rita stood facing the storm, the ocean's fury mirroring the turmoil within. Whatever it took, she would uncover the truth, she would find out who Archie's child was, who the woman he slept with was and no matter how deep the lies ran she would find out who this mystery 'brother' was too.

FORTY-TWO

Rita wrestled the key into the stiff old lock, rainwater dripping from her coat and pooling on the worn flagstones beneath her feet. The summer storm was still raging outside, wind howling through the outbuildings and the waves crashing against the cliffs below. Night had fallen earlier than expected, swallowed by thick, bruised clouds that clung low over the bay.

Inside, the farmhouse felt hollow. Even Henry didn't lift an eyelid from his Aga-fronted bed. Cold, damp air greeted her like a sigh. She kicked off her boots with a squelch, peeled her sodden coat from her shoulders, and left it in a heap by the door. Her jeans clung miserably to her thighs. Everything felt wrong. She felt wrong.

She didn't bother with the lights. All she wanted was to get into a deep, hot bath, a place to hide from the world where no one needed anything from her, not her thoughts, not her words, not her heart.

Before, when she'd spoken to Kelly, she'd managed to feel oddly calm about Archie's supposed mystery child. Detached. As though it had happened to someone else, in someone else's life. But now, back in the cold silence of the house that she and Archie had shared so many good times in, it hit her like a punch to the ribs.

The lies. The debt. The way he'd left her stranded in the middle of the financial storm he'd created. He hadn't even had the guts to tell her himself. Just let it all unravel around her while he vanished into the fog. What if Archie had a whole secret life she hadn't been part of, and he'd been stupid enough to think love was enough to fix it all?

She was halfway up the stairs when the knock came, sharp, impatient, too sudden to ignore.

She paused, heart thudding in that strange, hollow way it does when you're not sure who it might be.

Another knock. Firmer this time.

She sighed, padded back down, and opened the door.

Teo stood in the porch, rain speckled across his shoulders and cap. His cheeks were flushed, his expression unreadable.

'You look like a shipwreck,' he said gently, shutting out the storm.

'I feel like one.'

'I saw you come in; I was worried about you.'

'I was just going up for a bath, but sit... do you want a drink of something?'

'No, no, I go now. I'm staying at Jude's tonight for a change.'

'Zenya's away on a cookery course, too, isn't she?'

Teo nodded. 'Do you want me to stay so you are not all alone?' He really meant it, too. 'I can.'

'No, don't be silly. Enjoy the downtime with your fella, whilst we have no guests.'

Teo smiled gently. 'I was wanting to see if you were *bien* and to tell you that... well... it's Hilda. She no here, anymore. She gone.'

Rita frowned. 'Gone where?'

'No idea, but I could tell she wanted to escape without a word. Yesterday, some bloke picked her up in a black Mercedes. She had a suitcase with her.'

'A suitcase?' Rita's voice was weak.

'You probably know already... but when she saw me walking across the courtyard she seemed a little jumpy.'

Rita shook her head slowly. Her hair was still dripping. So were her lashes.

'I know nothing, as usual. She's such a dark old horse, that one. Did she say anything to you?' Rita screwed up her nose.

'*Nada*. Just jumped in the car like a woman half her age and off they went. I saw then she was smiling, so I shouldn't worry.'

Rita's face looked torn between a laugh and a cry.

Teo shifted his weight awkwardly, then looked at her with quiet concern.

'Do you want to talk to me, Rita?' he asked softly. 'I know there's something wrong.'

The kindness in his voice almost undid her. 'I'm just tired. It's been a bit stressful lately, you know.'

'Tomorrow, if you get a minute and the weather is calmer, let's go to the barn for a little Savasana together.'

'I'd love that.' Rita managed a half smile.

'Oh, *si, si*. I have something for you.' Teo pulled a crinkled plastic bag from under his coat. 'Me and Jude got carried away at Betty's. A ham hock roll and a cinnamon bun going spare.'

Rita swallowed hard and looked away, her eyes stinging. Oh, how she wished this beautiful, thoughtful young man could be the son she'd somehow lost along the way.

'You're such a good lad. Thank you, so much. And I could do with the sugar, to be honest.'

And as Teo made his way out to Archie's Land Rover, Rita realised it wasn't sugar she needed to get her back. It was the truth.

Rita lit a few candles around the bath, steam curling upwards, fogging the mirror. With a deep sigh, she slipped out of her towel. She had just put one foot into the soothing hot water, when a shriek split through the storm from outside. It was high, panicked. Then another. Definitely not human. Or one of the chickens.

She listened intently. Another shriek, then a furious bleating from the direction of the goat pen.

'Oh, for God's sake,' Rita groaned.

She grabbed her towel, went to the window, squinting through rain-spattered glass. The outdoor floodlight flickered on and off in the wind. Shapes moved in the chaos. A fox maybe? The bleating continued. Not stopping to think, she threw on whatever clothes she could find from the drying rack, then grabbed the old shotgun that Sennen had told her to get rid of.

As she charged downstairs, Henry raised an eyelid, then with a sleepy harrumph settled back down to sleep. Throwing on wellies and her favourite raincoat with the hood pulled up, she made her way out into the weather.

The wind punched her in the face, but undeterred, she ran, skidding over mud, and calling out to her beloved goats that she was on her way.

By the time she reached the goat pen, the torch string between her teeth, she knew it wasn't a fox. Of course, it was Camilla. So wrapped up in her own world of woe, she had forgotten it was near her due date. Feeling a huge pang of guilt for not being the dutiful goat mother she had always been, she dropped the gun and launched herself over the fence. Bribing the other three with treats she had in her coat pocket, she herded them into a separate part of the shed.

The distressed goat was down, belly heaving, eyes wild. Her cries were guttural, sharp, full of pain. She was in labour. And from the look of it, she was in trouble.

Rita fell to her knees.

'Oh, no. No, no, no, girl... I'm here now. I'm sorry, darling.'

Reaching for her phone with shaking fingers, she called the vet. No answer. Straight to voicemail! She left a quick message then tried to think who could help. Teo was with Jude, Zenya was on the vegan cookery course she had said she'd pay for, and even Hilda, who could have maybe helped to a degree, had buggered off with her suitcase somewhere.

In a panic now, she called Stan.

'Stan, it's Rita; Camilla's in labour. She's struggling.'

'Oh, love, you know I'd come, but I'm out for dinner, our anniversary. I'm an hour away. Have you called the vet?'

'Left a message.'

'Call Jago.'

'What?' Rita could barely hear him for the wind whistling around her ears.

'Call Jago. He'll know what to do.'

She stared at her phone. Rain streaked down her face. Her hair was stuck to her cheeks in strings. She hadn't spoken to Jago since everything unravelled. Since she'd started wondering if Archie had ever told her the truth about anything.

But Camilla was bleating again. Worse now. Urgent.

Rita wiped at her eyes with the back of her equally wet sleeve and pressed call.

The phone had barely rung twice before he answered.

Jago's voice, low and unmistakable, cut through the storm like a lifeline.

'It's Rita. I... I need help. Camilla's in labour and it's not going right. Teo's out. I can't reach the vet. Stan said to call you.'

He didn't ask questions. Didn't hesitate. Just a firm, 'I'm on my way.'

She hung up, heart hammering, and turned back to the pen.

Camilla was lying on her side now, legs kicking, her cries more desperate. Rita stroked the goat's flank, whispering sweet nothings she didn't believe herself, trying to remember everything Archie had taught her about breech births and calm energy and staying low to the ground.

Then came headlights, slicing through the rain like a miracle, and Jago's Defender came rumbling up the track, tyres spitting gravel and mud, its headlights sweeping across the barn as it slid to a stop. He was out before the engine even died, coat flapping behind him like a cape, boots already soaked through. Running at full pelt up to the goat pen.

He barely glanced at Rita as he dived into the pen. Crouching beside the goat, he pulled a pair of medical gloves from his pocket, quickly put them on, then pressed one hand gently to her side.

'She's trying. But something's off. It's OK, girl. I've got you. Try the vet again,' he demanded.

'Can you...?' Rita wailed, dialling the number and getting an engaged tone.

'I'll do what I can. But I'm going to need you. Can you get warm water and a couple of towels? Let's try and get her as comfortable as we can.'

Rita nodded, legs like jelly, and ran.

When she came back, soaked, with a bucket of steaming water and two old towels, Jago was already up to his elbow in goat.

He looked up briefly, his eyes locking with hers. 'I need you to talk to her. Keep her calm.'

Rita dropped to her knees beside him, stroking Camilla's head, murmuring her name over and over. The storm crashed around them, rain slamming at them like gravel.

It was over in a sudden, noisy rush. With one final cry, Camilla gave a mighty push, and out slid the tiny, slick form of a kid, a dirty white and trembling, ears twitching, the smallest flicker of life in the stormy chaos.

Jago moved with surprising gentleness, clearing the airways with a towel, rubbing the baby briskly until it let out its first thin, wavering bleat.

'It's a boy!' he shouted animatedly.

He placed the new life down for Camilla to lick clean, but before anyone could take a breath, her sides contracted again. Another push. A second kid, smaller, darker, slipped into Jago's waiting hands. 'Twins!'

Rita held her breath as he worked quickly, clearing the little one's nose and mouth, coaxing life into its limp limbs. Then, a second cry, softer, like an echo of the first.

'Another boy.' He popped the newborn down next to its

mother. Camilla turned, already licking them both with slow, rhythmic care.

Rita's hand came to her mouth. Her eyes, brimming with tears and rain, met Jago's.

'They're beautiful,' she whispered.

'You did good,' Jago murmured to Rita, as he pulled off his gloves. Camilla continued her nurturing, exhausted but calm.

For a moment, everything was still. Just the sound of wind, the bleats from the other goats, and the warmth of Jago's presence beside her.

She looked at him. He was close, so close, wet hair plastered to his forehead, eyes dark. He had a wild, untamed look, yet in that moment she understood how deeply he cared. 'Thank you so much. I don't know what I would have done without you, and I've been so remiss in looking after her through this pregnancy and...'

Jago reached for her cheek, fingers rough, warm. And without asking this time, kissed her. Slow and certain, like they had all the time in the word. She melted into him, into the press of his mouth, the solidness of his chest. She broke away, breathless. 'You said we shouldn't...'

'The heart does what the heart wants and all that,' Jago replied flippantly. 'And I can't stop thinking about you, Rita.'

'My head is so muddled.' Rita pushed the wet hair back off her face. 'And my heart...' She trailed off, pressing her palm to her chest like she was trying to still it. 'It doesn't know whether to run or stay. To fight for this or protect itself. I'm so confused.' She let out a shaky breath. 'And there's... something I need to tell you.'

'Go on.' Jago pulled her towards him as if he never wanted to let her go.

Rita took a huge breath. 'The will saga continues. According to Chloe Brimble at the solicitors', Archie has a brother.' Her voice trembled.

Jago's jaw tightened. She felt the shift in him, a subtle retreat.

She blinked. 'Oh my God.'

He grabbed his keys. Rita was wide eyed, her voice sharp with disbelief. 'You know who it is, don't you?'

He said nothing.

'Jago? Is that what this is?' She took a step closer. 'The Jenken–Jory feud? Is it to do with Archie's brother?'

The silence cracked. Not from Jago, but from above. A bright flash lit up the courtyard in stark white. Then low rumbles of thunder rolling across the sky, deep and growling.

Then headlights and a car pulling in, tyres crunching on the gravel. The vet stepped out, a headlamp strapped over his cap like a miner entering a cave.

'I have to go,' Jago announced. 'Tell the vet everything you saw. They should be all right now.'

'But Jago—' Rita felt her throat burning.

But he was already gone.

Rita stood there in the straw, the kids both making their first shaky steps, Camilla breathing steady beside them, the vet walking towards her with a massive apology at the ready.

And inside her chest, a dance of a million questions.

FORTY-THREE

It was only 10 p.m. but it felt way later. Rita paced the kitchen, still in her mismatched goat-birthing clothes, hair frizzed, body tired and aching, phone tucked under her chin.

'I know it sounds mad, Kel.' Rita flicked on the kettle. 'But it felt real. The kiss. Like he'd wanted to do it forever. And then the second I mentioned the brother. Bam. Shutters down. Gone.'

Kelly's voice crackled through the line, full of sympathy and suspicion in equal measure. 'So, what are you thinking?'

'I think he *knows* who it is. And whatever it is... it's big. Maybe it's to do with Thom? Maybe they're in on it, the whole farm thing. Maybe Jago's trying to get the land from me, and I'm just here like some kind of tragic widow he can get his evil way with... but you know when you know, don't you, Kel, and I kind of know it was real.'

'Whoa, whoa, slow down.' Kelly was laughing now, but kindly. 'You're tired. You're emotional. You've just delivered two goat kids and kissed possibly the hottest mysterious, emotionally unavailable farmer in Cornwall. You're entitled to spin out, but let's not start writing conspiracy thrillers yet. And like your old dad used to say, there has to be a sensible solution.'

Rita made a little groaning noise. 'I'm losing it, aren't I?'

'I think you've got a lot going on, and maybe you're seeing patterns that don't exist.'

Rita sighed. 'He looked at me like... like he *knew* something. And it wasn't good. I feel so betrayed. Why can't he just tell me?' Rita was about to say more when there was a knock at the front door. Sharp. Measured. Her heart jerked.

'I've got to go, Kel; someone's at the door.'

'Oh my God. Go! Go! Maybe it's him. It's late but message whatever time you like; I want to know what's going on. Take care, darling.'

Rita hung up and crossed the kitchen, tugging open the door to find Hilda on the doorstep, clutching a wheeled suitcase in one hand and an enormous handbag in the other.

'So, the traveller returns. I'm expecting you to tell me you've been to the Little White Chapel in Vegas.'

'God, no! You know I only go to funerals.'

Rita couldn't help but smile. Hilda reverted to serious. 'Anyway, there is someone I'd like you to meet.' From the darkness appeared a woman Rita hadn't seen before, but for some reason looked achingly familiar. She looked nervous but stood with quiet poise as Rita took her in, slightly confused as to what exactly was going on. The woman was short, with black hair swept into a loose bun streaked with silver at the temples. Her skin was sun-warmed and softly lined, especially around the eyes where laughter had clearly left its mark. She looked a similar age to Rita. There was a kind of timeless beauty to her, with her molten brown eyes and naturally turned-up lips.

Hilda's voice wasn't its usual bark. 'Rita, this is Carmen. She wants to talk to you.'

Carmen's lips trembled into the ghost of a smile. '*Hola*,' she said, shyly.

Rita stood aside. 'You'd better come in.' She flicked the kettle on. 'Tea?'

Carmen nodded. 'Can I use your toilet, please?'

Rita showed her the way then came back to the kitchen to face Hilda wide eyed.

'What the hell is going on?'

'I went to Spain for a day.' Hilda took a huge breath and looked in her handbag to check for cigarettes. 'All I had was a first name and a town. Bollocking mad, I know. But I had to.'

Rita frowned. 'Hilda, what the hell are you doing?'

Carmen stood in the kitchen doorway. 'It is OK, Hilda, I take this from here.'

Hilda put her arm on her daughter-in-law's. 'You have your answers now. Send Carmen back to the annexe when you've finished chatting. She's going to be staying for a couple of days.'

Carmen took a breath, and sat back down opposite Rita, whose heart was beating wildly. She felt she wasn't sure she could take any more drama tonight, but gripped her tea mug in anticipation.

'I met Archie. Millennium New Year's Eve. I was working as an au pair in Exeter. I was told that Seahaven Bay put on the best street party and fireworks display to see the year two thousand in, so that is where I came.' She looked down at her tea. 'I got pregnant. I never expected anything from him. Never tried to find him. I just went back home to Spain. That was my choice.'

Rita's breath caught. 'I met Archie in two thousand,' she said softly. 'In the summer.' She didn't know what she had expected to feel, anger? Jealousy? But it was the relief that he didn't cheat on her that was palpable.

'I didn't tell my son until he was older when he started asking questions. And by then, it felt too late. I managed to find out that Archie still lived in Seahaven Bay; I also found out that he had his own life and children with you, Rita.'

'I suppose you're here for the will,' Rita said resignedly.

Carmen shook her head firmly. 'No. No. Hilda – she talked to me. I know nothing about Archie's will. I never asked him for anything. Not a penny.'

Rita raised an eyebrow.

'My son, he travelled with his job. When he was twenty-one,

he contacted Archie without me knowing. Archie insisted he talk to me. Said he must make up for all the strife and worry I must have had being a single parent. He sent money,' Carmen admitted. 'Not loads but enough for my boy to go on his travels around Europe. He had an accident, you see.'

Tears were now running down Rita's cheeks. Suddenly, everything made sense. Why this woman looked so familiar. Why Teo had been overly caring. Her voice wavered. 'I know he did.'

'Being honest, I didn't want it to be just money. I wanted them to meet, in person. For my son to see the man, not just the gesture. We were going to meet him in Exeter. The week...' Carmen looked up to stop tears from forming. 'The week after he died.'

A silence fell over the room. Even Henry stirred slightly, as if sensing the weight of the sadness of it all. 'Just for a day,' Carmen said quietly. 'No more.' The pretty Spanish woman continued to well up. 'I maybe did it all wrong. But I did it the best way I thought.'

'And that's all we can do,' Rita replied kindly, looking at the woman in front of her and knowing why Archie had fallen for her, however briefly. Something shifted within her. Not judgement. Not sympathy. Just the understanding of grief in its many complicated forms.

She reached across the table and touched Carmen's hand. It was warm, shaking slightly.

'Well.' Rita's voice was hoarse with tiredness and emotion. 'You're here now.' Carmen nodded, unable to find the words. 'And Mateo is a credit to you.'

'Thank you. He wanted to see where his father came from. And when he told me he had got a job on your farm, I didn't know what to do. He loves you, Rita. The way he talks of you, his voice lilts. I said it wasn't a clever idea him being here, but he said you were so kind and the way you spoke about his father made him seem much closer to him. He is a good boy, my Teo. But I now feel so bad that he didn't tell you and now Hilda has made us confront this.'

Carmen stood up crossed the room, and, sitting next to Rita, took both her hands in hers. 'I am so sorry for our loss, but I am so happy for our gain.'

She looked up at the woman who had carried this truth alone for so long.

'I don't know what to do with this,' Rita whispered. 'And does Teo even know you are here?'

'Not yet and you don't have to do anything.' Carmen smiled.

'I can't believe he didn't say anything.' Rita sighed.

'Please don't be angry with him, Rita. He is a good boy.'

Rita screwed up her nose. 'Can I ask you how you found out about Archie's passing?'

Carmen nodded. 'His brother called me. He was distraught.'

FORTY-FOUR

Rita woke to her alarm. Five a.m. She groaned and turned over, then remembering she had two new kids, a nursing goat, an ex-lover and son of her husband on the farm to deal with, she sat up sleepy eyed and slowly got out of bed and dragged on joggers and a hoodie. Checking her phone for messages and realising she hadn't updated Kelly, she groaned again. Thinking her friend would understand the enormity of her late-night visitor, she fired off a quick text telling her there was drama, that she was OK, and she'd call her when she'd fed the animals. She'd just flicked the kettle on when there was a knock at the door. She checked her watch. Not even Zenya or Teo were on parade this early, especially as they had no guests at the moment.

It was Hilda.

'Bloody hell, Mother-in-law, did I just see a pig fly over the barn. You're rarely up in time for *Lorraine*, normally.' Rita reached for a second mug from the cupboard. She signalled to the table. 'You'd better sit down.'

Rita had never seen Hilda look quite this sincere as she sat opposite her at the kitchen table. She didn't even ask if she could have a cigarette, it was that serious. Her mother-in-law slurped her tea noisily. 'I suppose you want to know my part in this.'

Rita yawned. 'Just tell me everything, Hilda. I'm a big girl. I can take it.'

'Archie was drunk one night and blurted out he had a child. I never said a single word to him about it after that, or him to me. Then, months later, I think you must have been in London with Kelly, he turned up drunk here, broke down in tears. Told me about losing his father too young. The weight of the farm. And how much he loved you, so much that he was scared it would break you if you ever knew about the fact he'd had another child and not told you, sooner. I think the more it went on that he hadn't told you, he felt he couldn't open up.'

'We told each other everything,' Rita almost whispered. 'Or so I thought.'

Hida pushed a strand of silver hair back off her face. 'Look at how you've coped since his passing. You're strong. Stronger than he ever gave you credit for. He should've just told you, and then maybe we wouldn't all be going through this pain now.'

'So did you know it was Teo?'

'I had an inkling. Only because Archie let slip that her name was Carmen and she lived in the Triana neighbourhood of Seville. Her family run a company making flamenco costumes and that's how I found her. I didn't dare question the boy until I had the full story. I paid for her flight here as she was desperate to see Teo too. He didn't betray you, Rita.' She paused, eyes glistening now.

'Well, he did in the sense he didn't tell me, but at least he didn't cheat, I guess.'

'Exactly.' Hilda nodded. 'And to be fair to him, if Teo hadn't contacted him, he would never have known either. He also said he was going to write a will and put a provision in for his son, nothing major, just a gesture. Was going to say it was someone he used to work with, before you even met, so that you never would have questioned it.'

Rita stared at her, numb. 'So why didn't you tell me?'

'Because...' Hilda took a deep breath. 'Because the night of his accident, I said I thought he should tell you what was going on.

That he couldn't put something in his will that you knew nothing about; it was too much of a betrayal to you. And he got angry. Said it was his business, and he would tell you when the time was right.'

Hilda's chin wobbled. The silence between them thickened.

Rita shook her head. 'So *that's* why he came back to me so angry that night. Stupid sod. I don't know what he thought I would do or say, but we'd have got through it.'

Hilda's voice was hollow. 'It's my fault he died that night.'

Rita got up and ran around the kitchen table to hug her. 'No, no! It was an accident. There was nothing either of us could have done about it.'

Hilda jumped up. 'I'd better get back, before Carmen wakes.'

'Where is she sleeping?'

'In Teo's room. He stayed at Jude's last night. He will have a shock when he gets back.'

Rita ran her hands through her hair. 'Oh yes. It's all coming back now. Seems like a lifetime ago, but Camilla gave birth... I had no one to call... except Jago.'

'Oh. But all OK?'

'Yes, two beautiful baby boys.'

'Oh, the irony.' Hilda paused at the door. Her mouth twitching. 'No good will come of any of us mixing with a Jenken, though. You hear me.'

And then she was gone.

Rita tied her hair up in a scruffy bun and, despite the warmth of the August morning, she pulled on her wellies and slung a bucket of feed over one arm.

Mary, Elizabeth, and Anne bleated like mad the moment they saw her, crowding the gate as if demanding an update on Camilla.

'All right, all right!' Rita laughed. 'Honestly, you'd think I never fed you.'

Once all the aunties were fed, Rita jumped in the pen and

went over to the shed where all the drama had happened last night. The smaller kid, who was white and brown, looking drunk on his spindly legs, was suckling, tail wagging like a wind-up toy. Rita crouched down to check him. 'Look at you, you greedy little mister.' The other white one, the spit of his mother, was lying next to her, with bright eyes and what looked like a full little belly. Camilla stood calmly, one back leg slightly cocked, eyes half closed. Her sides rose and fell steadily and every so often, she turned her head and gave the nursing kid a gentle nudge with her nose, as if to say, *You're doing just fine, little one.*

Rita rested her chin on the top rail of the pen, watching them for a long moment. 'I need to name you, don't I?' She thought of the royal theme they'd used before, but somehow it didn't seem right for these two. Like it was the end of an era now. Hers and Archie's era. How he would have loved these little babies. These little twins.

Satisfied everyone was fed and accounted for, she made her way to the chicken coop. A wave of soft clucking and the faint smell of straw met her as she opened the door. The hens were already scratching about, fat and happy, kicking up wood shavings and bossing each other about like they always did.

'Morning, ladies. I trust you're all ruling the roost?' She collected the eggs, still warm in her palm, and whispered a small thank you like she always did. Then, leaving the bag of feed at the fence, maybe out of habit or maybe instinct, she wandered up the path towards the Singing Tree.

When she reached the bench, she ran her fingers over the carving, lovingly etched by Stan, then sat down. '*May You Always Hear the Sea*, Archie Jory,' Rita spoke aloud, then sighed deeply. 'I don't hate you,' she whispered, to no one and everyone. 'But bloody hell, Arch. You could've just told me.'

She looked out over the ocean, where the early morning light kissed the waves in their soft gold and turquoise shimmer. The horizon stretched wide and endless, a vast, calming expanse that somehow made her troubles feel both small and immense all at once.

It felt strange not having guests in the yurts. Like a canvas ghost town.

She had to admit that she had really enjoyed her time with a bunch of strangers. They had become friends of a sort. But exactly as Paul had said, life really was just a series of events that had a beginning and an end and in the middle, a few good bits. Realistically, she probably would never see any of them again, but in the now, it had been great, despite a few expected teething problems.

Paul had also opened her eyes, not just to new possibilities, but to herself. The way the musician had touched her, the slow, sure way he'd kissed her, like she was the only thing that mattered, had shaken something free inside her. It wasn't just desire. It was a quiet, steady knowing that maybe she could still feel alive again.

And then there was Jago. He made her feel alive, too, in a unique way. Like an unpredictable spark. When he was near, her heart raced, but so did the knot of questions she tried to ignore. The way he looked at her, like he was trying to steal her soul. The gentleness with which he had delivered Camilla's kids. The silent way he had helped her get the resort up and running without wanting anything in return. There was no question about it. She had to see him. Had to ask him what was going on. Because last night, when the conversation turned to Archie's brother, he had literally run away. That scared her. Scared her so much. But she had to know. Had to know why he pulled away when things got real, and why, despite it all, she couldn't stop thinking about him, as much as he said he couldn't stop thinking about her. Was it just the magnetic pull of lust or was it more than that? She was just reliving the kiss of last night when her thoughts were interrupted by the familiar sound of Archie's old Land Rover pulling up.

As she peered down Yurt Avenue, she saw Teo carefully getting out, two coffees in paper cups in hand and a carrier bag hung around his neck. He saw her and lifted a cup in greeting.

She sat back down as he climbed the hill. When he reached the bench, he didn't say a word, just handed her a coffee and sat beside her, pulling a cinnamon bun from the bag slung across his chest and giving it to her. A soft breeze stirred the branches overhead as Rita took a bite. She was exhausted, running on barely any sleep, and suddenly ravenous after the night she'd had.

'I thought I might never be brave enough.' His voice was barely above a whisper. 'So, it's a good job that Mamá is here.' Rita waited. 'I always wanted to know my father. But now I know he knew about me, and still didn't...' He broke off, teeth gritted. 'I don't know whether to be angry or just... sad now that I will never get to meet him.'

'I think both are allowed.' Rita squeezed the lad's knee.

'I keep wondering what I did wrong. If I hadn't been someone worthy of his time.' Teo sighed.

Rita turned to him sharply. 'Hey. No. Don't go there. This wasn't about you not being good enough. Archie didn't find out until you contacted him. And your mum told me you were going to meet him. Plus, he had us lot here to manage with the news. Which, granted, he did very badly.'

Teo blinked quickly.

'I loved him, you know.' Rita sighed and took a sip of her coffee. 'Still do, even now. And I hate him a bit, too, for keeping this from me. But I also know... he was a man with a big heart, and he thought he was protecting everyone.'

Rita reached over and laid her hand on his. 'You're not alone in this.' Her voice wavered. 'Whatever else he got wrong, he gave me you. And I'm not letting you go, Teo.'

His eyes filled, but he smiled through it. 'I don't know what my fiery Mamá would say about that.' They both laughed.

'Let me look at you.' She tilted his face towards her.

Teo blinked, surprised, but didn't resist. Beneath the dark hair and worried eyes, she saw Archie. Not just in the sharp angle of his jaw or the shape of his mouth, but in the way his eyes searched hers and the quiet strength he didn't know he had.

It hit her all at once, a thud of grief and wonder in her chest.

Archie was gone. But Teo was here. And somehow, impossibly, both of them were looking back at her.

'Don't get me wrong with my *mamá* and my *abuela*, I've always felt amazingly loved but also like a mistake. But being here, in the place where my father lived and breathed and doing what I love to do. Maybe I'm not.'

Rita reached for his hand. 'I don't think you realise quite how much you have supported me, and I also think you're exactly where you're meant to be now. You've never been on your own. OK?' Rita looked directly into his eyes. 'And you're not on your own, now. OK?'

Teo looked away, blinking hard, his jaw tightening as he fought for composure. But he didn't let go of her hand. Squeezed it as if his life depended on it.

'OK.' His voice was barely a whisper but then he began nodding furiously. 'OK.'

FORTY-FIVE

In the hazy blush of an August morning, the birds were having a right old singalong. They'd been at it since 4.30 a.m. when Rita had got up to have a pee, after tossing and turning in bed until eventually getting up at 5.30. Since the guests had left, she'd learned to embrace this time, when she knew she had an hour to herself to sit and have a cup of tea, go for a little walk, have some breakfast, and just breathe. Once the animals were fed, she would either go up to the Singing Tree or occasionally drive up to Seahaven Point and sit on *her* bench, just to watch the ebb and flow of the ocean on her favourite beach, where she would try to reset her heart and her constantly racing mind.

With Carmen on her way back to Seville, Rita felt she could relax again. It had been lovely to see how Teo interacted with his mother; they clearly had a strong bond. And despite the fact Archie had kept such a humongous secret from her, she felt so sad for him that he had not been able to meet the wonderful child they had created. But it had been Carmen's decision to keep her boy a secret and she had to respect the woman's reasons for that too. And if tragedy hadn't struck, the meeting would have taken place. And who knows, they could all have been one big happy blended family.

But the big black cloud of having to talk to Jago still hung over her. Part of her didn't want to face anything. Let the will hang in the ether. If Archie was leaving money to Teo then OK, she got it. She could see why Thom would be angry about this; but how would he have known in the first place? And did he know about the mystery brother, too? There were so many unanswered questions, and she felt that only one man knew all the answers.

Feeling like a healthy breakfast was required, she made her way to the vegetable garden in search of any remaining strawberries. Creeping past Zenya's tent, her footsteps muffled by dew-kissed grass, the air hummed with half-asleep bees and the scent of warm apples.

Zenya, who could hear a worm turn in the soil, responded instantly to the faint crunch of Rita's footstep; her tent zip whipped down and her head emerged, a long braid over one shoulder, yawning wildly.

'Oh. Hi, Rita.'

'Sorry, so sorry to disturb you. I just wondered if there were any strawberries left.'

'I can do better than that.' The pretty hippy whipped back inside her tent, then appeared holding a basket covered with a tea cloth.

'I come bearing carbs.' She lifted the cloth as if it were a metal cloche. 'Spelt and caraway. Good for your stomach. A Betty's Tearoom special.'

Rita beamed. 'Oh, sod being healthy, you're a saint. Do you have any butter?'

'No, but the Snack Shack fridge does.'

With the goats and chickens fed and Henry sniffing around nearby, the pair sat on fold-up chairs at the end of the orchard, taking in the view and munching on the rolls, butter and homemade raspberry jam, a fresh flask of coffee at their side.

'It really is just so idyllic here,' Zenya crooned. 'I pinch myself every day. Thank you so much for believing in me.'

Rita smiled. 'I never had a doubt.'

'Even when I crawled out looking like some kind of neolithic woman making my nettle tea the day you met me.'

'That made you even more employable.'

They both laughed.

'I can't believe I missed the goats being born, oh my God they are so sweet... and I'm so sorry I wasn't here to help you.'

'Don't be silly, I'm glad you have a life outside of here. We really must christen them.'

'Ha, yes.' Zenya smirked. 'I've been thinking about this. Something suitably nonsensical, like Billy Idol or Vincent van Goat.'

Rita shrieked. 'Oh my God. Genius! Billy and Vince for short, that's it... well done.'

Zenya eyed Rita for a moment, then poured them both a top-up from the flask. 'So, how are you feeling about the retreat? Now everyone's gone, I mean.'

Rita hesitated. 'Honestly? A bit... wrung-out.'

Zenya nodded. 'I can only think of it like after a music festival. The noise stops and suddenly your own thoughts get loud. I hear you.'

Rita exhaled, tearing a roll in half. 'It went well, though, didn't it? A proper mixed bunch but no one left early, and a couple hinted they may return.'

'You should be really proud.' Zenya nodded.

'I am. Proud of how far we've come already. But I keep thinking about what's next. How can we make it better? Is enough money coming in? All the worries of a new business. And I'd better shake myself as new guests are arriving in under three weeks.'

Zenya smiled. 'Don't fret. We are a team and we've got this.' She became animated. 'I checked the review page last night. Every single one of the last lot have left a glowing report.'

'Oh wow. I didn't even think to look; that's amazing. Um... what did Paul say?'

'I'll go and grab my phone – and something else I want to show you, hang on.' Zenya darted to her tent then ran back and scrolled to the retreat Facebook page. 'He gave five stars obviously and oh yes, here we go. *A truly unforgettable stay. The yurt was surprisingly comfortable, the host incredibly attentive, and I left feeling... well, deeply satisfied on every level. Would absolutely come again. And again.*'

Rita reddened; Zenya smirked. 'I told you that you were the hostess with the mostest.'

'I'm saying nothing.' Rita sighed.

'You don't need to... and Madam Satisfaction.' Zenya reached into her pocket and pulled out a folded paper, a sketched floor plan. 'You remember your idea of converting the outhouse into a fancier toilet and shower area? Well, we can do this quite easily. Keep the outside rustic; there is basic plumbing in there with the old utilities. And to keep in line with your sustainability thoughts, we can swap to a solar-powered water heater on the roof.'

Rita opened the paper, eyes scanning the notes, the little drawings. 'I love it,' she said quietly. 'Really love it.'

Zenya tried to hide her delight. 'Good. So I suggest we get this next shorter retreat out of the way, then we can start implementing changes for the next one. Jude's friend from an eco-build co-op said he could take a quick look for free. It may be worth him looking at solar for the farmhouse too. I am pretty handy, and I know that Teo would get stuck in too.' Zenya paused. 'I hope you don't think I'm interfering.'

'I love your enthusiasm when mine is waning slightly.' Rita smiled. 'This place really *is* becoming something, isn't it?'

'It's already something,' Zenya said gently. 'You made it that way.'

Rita took a sip of coffee. 'I just wanted to create a space where people could relax and exhale.'

Zenya spontaneously kissed Rita's cheek, then, shocked by her own reaction, pulled away embarrassed. 'You did. And you will, yourself, be able to do both again. I know it.'

There was a brief silence and then Zenya ventured, 'I saw Jago kiss you.'

Rita plucked at a loose thread on her shorts, heart thudding.

Zenya held up a finger. 'Hang on one sec.'

She vanished back to her tent again and returned moments later clutching a small silver tin, chipped and scuffed.

'I'm not taking any kind of love potion.' Rita raised a brow.

Zenya opened it to pull out a deck of cards and a little booklet.

'Better.' Zenya grinned. 'Guardian angels. Just pick one. Don't think. Put your hand in and the right one will find you.'

Rita rolled her eyes but reached in. Her fingers brushed past a few smooth cards before settling on one. She pulled it free. *Clarity*.

She stared at the word. The letters were embossed in gold, surrounded by clouds and light beams. Zenya took it from her gently and reached for her accompanying guide. Reading aloud, her voice lilted with delight.

'*You are being shown the truth of a situation. Trust that the fog is lifting. What was hidden is now revealed. Clarity will bring peace, not chaos. You already know what to do.*'

'That's a bit on the nose,' Rita said eventually.

'Truth always is,' Zenya replied softly. 'But this card... clarity... isn't about fixing everything. It's about seeing things as they really are... and deciding if you want to go with them anyway.'

Rita's throat tightened. 'I don't know if I'm brave enough for that.'

Zenya smiled and tucked the tin back under her arm. 'You don't have to be brave all at once. Just honest. With yourself, first.'

With a lighter heart, Rita walked slowly back to the farmhouse. She so appreciated Zenya and what they had, a blossoming true friendship built on trust, support, and the quiet knowing that love, in its purest form, can take many shapes.

FORTY-SIX

Rita had spent the entire day trying *not* to think about the angel card. Which, of course, meant she'd thought of little else.

By six o'clock, the sky had started to blush with the promise of sunset, and she could no longer sit still. She waxed, bathed, and styled her hair the way Kelly had shown her. Dressing like she might be heading to something casual-but-significant: not full glam, but enough to say 'I like you'. High-waisted jeans that did good things for her arse. A tucked-in white linen blouse. Diamond ear studs and coral lipstick. Smart white pumps to finish.

By the time she stood in front of the bathroom mirror, dabbing perfume onto her wrists, her stomach was doing cartwheels.

'Clarity,' she whispered to her reflection. 'Peace, not chaos.'

Outside, the old Suzuki Jimny sat waiting, blue and battered, not quite matching her smartened-up appearance.

As she set off down the drive, Rita drummed her fingers on the steering wheel and let the windows down. She needed air. Air and answers, that was all. And now she was going to ask. Now she was going to *know*.

Rounding the bend, she caught sight of Hawthorn Acre and nearly turned around. But she didn't. She took a deep breath, flicked the indicator, and turned in slowly, tyres crunching over gravel.

Jago was feeding his goats. Cedric, father to Billy and Vince, was bleating theatrically before Rita had even stepped out of the car.

Jago looked up. His eyes narrowed, the crease between his brows flickering as if unsure how to read her arrival. He straightened, shifting his weight from one foot to the other like a wary animal himself.

'You came,' he said.

Rita nodded, taking a steadying breath. 'I did.' She smiled, despite the somersaults inside her.

'Do you come in peace?' he questioned with a lopsided dimpled smile.

'I do.' Rita felt her breath quicken slightly

Jago looked right at her. 'You look good.'

'Thank you.'

They weren't aware they were speaking in staccato, but both knew that the big fat Jenken–Jory elephant of a will was about to stomp into the room and start the slow, inevitable legato song of truth.

Jago's gaze flicked toward the farmhouse, then back to her. 'Shall we talk?'

He led her down the garden to a wooden bench tucked beside a sprawling buddleia bush, its long purple spires swaying gently, butterflies hovering in the warm air. The view unfolded in quiet splendour, revealing the same vast, shimmering stretch of ocean she could see from the High Meadow.

'Not a bad spot for a chat,' Jago said, lowering himself onto the bench.

'*Nearly* as good as my view,' Rita replied dryly.

She settled beside him, eyes scanning the distant horizon. Seabirds wheeled and cried overhead, their calls catching the breeze.

'Noisy buggers,' she muttered.

Jago nodded, still facing forward. 'There's been a lot of noise lately.'

'There has.' Rita half smiled. 'Funny, though. All that noise... and it's the silence that's been driving everything.'

Jago didn't speak for a second and then put his hand on her knee. 'I'm so sorry I ran out on you the other night, after the birth, you know.'

'I didn't understand what was going on.' Rita sighed deeply.

'I... I... panicked,' Jago groaned. 'Are they doing OK, the kids, I mean?'

'Fine, thanks to you, Vincent van Goat and Billy Idol are doing just great.'

'Bloody brilliant!' He removed his hand and sighed deeply to himself.

Another slightly awkward silence, until Rita turned towards him, her jaw set. 'I'm so sorry I touched a nerve the other day, about you being single. You're right, I know nothing about your past.'

'My wife left me five years ago,' Jago stuttered. 'Ran off with my best mate because she was pregnant with his kid.' Rita felt another surge of guilt at her meanness. 'So, with Mum in a home and Dad's dying wish that the farm was not to fall into the hands of a stranger, and me unable to watch the whole sorry cheating saga unfold in front of my eyes, I came back. I decided to continue with what Dad had taught me in scraps and slivers growing up and do the best I could.' He paused, his gaze distant. 'So here I am. Living in a bay in Cornwall, with mainly cows and sheep for friends, trying to earn an honest living and bring back my sanity.'

There was something in his tone now. Something cracked and raw.

'Shit,' was all Rita could muster.

'Yes, shit.' Jago managed a smile. 'My vision was to move back here, heal, find a partner, start a family, and maybe one day retire here by the sea.'

'And live happily ever after.' Rita let out a little laugh. 'But we know that rarely happens, right.'

He suddenly was serious. 'And when I said I liked you, Rita, I meant it... more than I've liked anyone in a long time. You're the first woman I've trusted since my wife did the dirty.'

Her hand flew to her heart. The words tumbled out of her before she could think. 'Teo... is... Archie's son.'

Jago's voice cracked slightly. 'I know.'

'Of course you do.' Her voice was cool now, sharp with exhausted emotion. 'You know everything, don't you?'

He swallowed. 'Quite a lot, yes.'

Rita ran her hands through her hair. 'It's OK. You have to tell me. Every single detail. Warts and all.'

Jago stretched his long legs out in front of him. 'Where to begin?'

'How about the *very* beginning.' Rita blew out a huge breath as Jago began his sorrowful soliloquy.

'OK... My mother... had an affair. My dad, God bless him, wasn't the life and soul of the party, but he was kind. Steady. A good farmer. A good man. Her lover, my biological father, was full of banter. A good man, too, just with a wandering eye.'

He paused. 'When I was eighteen years old, my mother told me everything. I couldn't believe it at first. But she said she'd had a crisis of conscience, then made me promise not to tell my dad. I've never known pain like it. Holding that secret. Because my dad... he was *my* dad. The man who raised me. Loved me. He was there for me until the day he died last year. I was so grateful for him.' He looked down at his hands. 'The affair, it wasn't love. I know it. It was distraction for my mother. She hated the farm, but she'd never have left. Too easy being with a man who provided. She liked the rebellion, the thrill. And when I came along, well, that cemented it. Precious Isobel, a single mum? She could barely look after herself and was never going anywhere after that.'

He gave a hollow laugh. 'I don't think he was her only lover, either. And now she's burning through his savings in the care home up at Seahaven Point, three gourmet meals a day and her arse wiped for eternity. Where's the fairness in that?'

Rita exhaled slowly. 'So, you *do* know who your real father is, then?'

Jago nodded once, then closed his eyes. 'I know of him, but I didn't know him, not really. He died when I was just seven.' His bottom lip wobbled. Rita felt her heart thud. A knot tightened inside. And then it came, the words she now knew were true, words she hadn't wanted to believe till now.

'Mum told me Hilda never knew for certain, but I reckon she did. She does,' Jago said quietly. Rita gasped and went to speak. He put his hand up to stop her. 'I don't remember much but what I do remember is that my dad and Ralph used to work together on the farm sometimes. And that my mum was really sad for a while when I was younger; she was grieving for Ralph, too, I expect. Who knows? But knowing her, like I do... it was probably because her plaything had been taken away.'

Rita shook her head. 'So, you are the mystery brother. You're Archie's brother.' She gave a small tut. 'Wow.'

'Please don't hate me,' Jago said, offering a small, cautious smile.

'It's a lot,' Rita admitted with a half laugh, half groan. She closed her eyes, trying to process it. 'With you and Teo.'

'I'm sorry.' Jago's eyes met hers.

'So, now it all makes sense – the rift. Hilda's actions.'

'Yes, the rift was between the women,' Jago said.

'And Hilda being Hilda,' Rita added, 'would've known how to control the situation, cut the Jenkens off completely. Keep Ralph and my Archie at a distance from her. It makes sense now. It's so sad, though.'

'It really is.' Jago looked out over the ocean.

'She adored Ralph; it must've broken her. That's why she's so bitter. And why she's trying to keep me away from you, too.'

Jago nodded. 'I'd kind of hoped that now Archie and my father have passed, she might be able to forgive.'

'Yes.' Rita's voice was gentle. 'You were the innocent party in all of this.'

'And we both share a certain disdain for my mother.' Jago managed a smile.

Rita looked out to the horizon, where the sky was deepening to a bruised mauve and the sun hung low like a deep orange yolk, slipping slowly into the sea. She spoke, her voice barely above a whisper. '"*Hope' is the thing with feathers that perches in the soul.*" I love that poem. Emily Dickinson. Clung to it, after Archie died. I don't know why... it just... stayed with me. It's a powerful reflection on the quiet, enduring nature of hope, even through life's darkest and most turbulent moments.'

Jago said quietly, 'That's beautiful.'

There was a long pause. The silence between them felt heavier until she took a minute to look right at Jago's face, like really look at it. Archie hadn't been lucky enough to be in the queue where dimples were given out, but he'd had the same lopsided smile as the striking man in front of her.

'Your colouring, your eyes...' she let slip. 'No wonder I...' Rita paused. They held their gaze for a second until Jago suddenly jumped up and stretched, a tired smile tugging at his lips.

'I don't know about you, but I'm starving. Let's go inside before we get bitten to death by mosquitos.'

He led her into the kitchen of the old farmhouse, where rustic met modern in a way that felt effortlessly cool. Reclaimed wood shelves were lined with artisan jars and sleek black matte cookware, while industrial pendant lights hung low over a polished marble island. A smart coffee machine sat ready beside a neat stack of vinyl records leaning casually against the wall. The walls were painted a calming slate grey, softened by a few pots of fresh herbs on the windowsill.

Jago looked around the space proudly. 'Since Mum moved into the care home, I've been doing a bit of sprucing up. Thought it was time this place felt like mine, you know? Got rid of the clutter, added a few bits and pieces here and there. Figured if I'm going to be cooking for myself, might as well do it somewhere I actually like.'

'It's really funky, I love it. I need to get round to doing our... I mean, my place now the money is coming in.'

'Pizza and garlic bread OK?' He grinned. 'Only the best for Mrs Jory.'

'Ah. The classic modern man's cordon bleu kitchen with a take-out menu.'

Forgetting the enormity of what she had come here for, Rita laughed. Jago walked over to the fridge and pulled out a bottle of Sauvignon. 'A white wine for the lady?'

'Yes, I'm going to need a drink for this next bit, aren't I?'

Jago opened a second bottle of wine, poured and took a huge slurp of his. 'We got close. Quietly. Behind Hilda's back. Archie and I... we had a bond. Stronger than most would expect, given what had happened. Or maybe because of it... who knows? If ever you didn't know where Archie was, Rita, you could be sure he was with me. Always in secret, though. We kept it quiet, too many eyes, too many questions. We fished a lot, on the beach. Stupidly early and late into some evenings mostly so as not to encroach on farming time. We used to chat about everything and nothing.' His voice cracked slightly. He looked across the table, a faint, bitter-sweet smile tugging at his lips. 'We trusted each other. More than anyone else. And when things got messy, when Teo came on the scene, well, that's when Archie asked me to do something that I'm now so sorry for, as it has caused you so much pain.'

'The will.' Rita took a drink and leaned in, heart pounding.

The wine had loosened Jago's tongue. 'It was so strange that we had the conversation just weeks before he died about me taking it. It all seems so ridiculous now. He said jokingly that if ever anything happened to him before he had told you about Teo that I must take the will and destroy it. He was going to tell you. He really was. But he wanted to meet the lad and his mother first. I'm not sure why. Maybe to suss them out, maybe to see if he thought they would fit into the Jory fold. I don't know.'

He swallowed hard, the weight of that secret pressing down. 'I've carried that secret, too, alongside all the others. But there was one part of this wish that I didn't do...'

Her heart thudded, a knot twisting deep inside.

'I took it. But I didn't destroy it, and now I know that you know about Teo, I'm so glad I didn't. As there will be no secrets now and Thom will be able to rest and hopefully stop being so damn nasty to you. Teo told me.'

'Shit, so you're in cahoots with Teo too?'

'Rita, please believe there's not a huge conspiracy against you. We love you.' Startled at his own comment, Jago suddenly sat upright. 'Oh, bugger, I forgot to put the pizza and garlic bread in.'

Rita gave a tipsy laugh. 'Well, that explains why I'm feeling the way I am. All this wine on an empty stomach. We'll be legless before the mozzarella even melts. I'm not feeling that hungry now to be honest; I just need to know everything. So, what about the electronic copy? How on earth did you manage that?'

Jago gave a dry laugh. 'You know what those Brimbles are like. Chloe being one, I knew she'd take a cash bribe. She was new, green as spring grass. I told her to say she hadn't got her head around the system yet and had deleted it in complete error. Poor thing looked like she was going to faint, but I made sure she knew exactly how to get rid of it.'

Rita stared at the ground. 'Is that illegal?'

'Immoral, too,' Jago agreed. 'I hear she has lost her job now which I do feel a bit guilty about. But I did it for you, Rita. You and Archie. All of it. And I'd do it again.'

Jago scooped her into his arms without asking, the wine making everything feel soft edged and slow. Rita didn't resist. He lifted her as if she were a feather and carried her through to the lounge, her head resting lightly against his chest.

The room opened out into a wide, warm space, golden lamplight making for a cosy feel. A huge bay window looked down over his garden, where fairy lights glowed in tangled hedges and wound around the old apple tree. Beyond, the sea shimmered under an almost full moon so bright it looked painted onto the darkened sky.

He laid her down gently on the vast, soft cream sofa that faced the view. For a moment, he just looked at her, then he kissed her again. Tenderly at first, then deeper. Hungrier. He tugged her shirt free from her jeans with urgent hands, kissing along her jaw, her neck, as if he couldn't bear another second without her. She kissed him back with the same heat, her fingers in his hair, pulling him closer. Wanting.

But then, suddenly, 'No! Stop!' she gasped. Pushing at his chest, she sat bolt upright, heart hammering. 'I can't. I can't do this. You're Archie's brother.' Tears welled in her eyes as her breath came fast and panicked. 'It doesn't make sense. None of this makes any sense. I have to go.'

She staggered to her feet, but Jago caught her gently by the wrist. 'Rita, wait, please. You're not thinking straight.'

'Don't tell me what I am thinking!' She pulled away from him. 'How dare you? How dare you keep something like that from me and then try to make love to me?'

She wiped angrily at her face, swaying slightly. 'I haven't drunk like this in so long and now I'm here, and I don't know what I'm doing, and...'

She leaped up and turned for the door.

'You're not driving.' Jago stood in front of her. 'Look what happened to Archie.'

Her face crumpled. 'How could you be so heartless' – her tears spilling over – 'to say that. To use that. After everything.'

Jago looked stricken, as if she'd just winded him. His voice cracked. 'I'm not heartless. I'm... I'm sorry... I just... I can't lose you, too, Rita. I just can't.' His voice lowered and slowed. 'I can't lose you because... I think I'm falling in love with you.'

Rita stared at him as though he'd slapped her. 'Don't be so bloody ridiculous!' And then, without another word, she rushed past him, through the hallway and out into the darkness, the front door swinging wide behind her.

When she finally got back to the farmhouse, she was too distraught to notice Hilda standing at the annexe window, watching with a look of quiet heartbreak, sadness etched deep into her face, worry clouding her eyes.

FORTY-SEVEN

It was early evening on a Friday, and the harbour buzzed with tourists and locals grabbing a cheeky drink or bite to eat to make the most of the mid-August sunshine. Rita arrived at the Winking Pilchard where the low hum of chatter and clinking glasses immediately relaxed her. Jilly was already there, perched on a bench outside, a cheeky grin spreading across her face the moment she spotted her friend.

'Well, well, look what the tide dragged in.'

Rita smiled tiredly and slid onto the bench seat beside her. 'I know, I look rough. I've had a lot going on.'

'Sorry, girl, you look boss, I was only messin' with youse.'

'Thanks for meeting at such short notice; I needed human contact. And chips. But definitely not alcohol.' Rita sighed.

'Oh, Lordy, I feel a story coming on.' Jilly signalled to Pete the Pilchard, who ambled over with a roguish sparkle in his eye.

'So,' Pete said, raising his eyebrows at Rita. 'How's my favourite buxom blonde these days? Still making the poor lads work for it?'

'If you mean Kelly, she's still happily married, but dreaming of you regardless, I'm sure.' Rita didn't dare confess that that really was the case.

Pete grinned. 'That's what I like to hear. You send her my way next time she's down, she'll be dreaming all right.'

Rita chuckled, shaking her head. 'You're a bad man, Pete Perkins.'

'Nah, just a man. Now, can I get you two lovely ladies a drink to save you getting off your sweet derrieres?'

As Pete took their order and wandered off, Rita leaned closer to Jilly, lowering her voice.

'It's all been kicking off.'

Jilly's expression softened. 'Is it on top of you telling me about the will and that Jago is Archie's brother? I mean, that alone is enough to tip you.'

'Erm... yes.'

'It's OK, girl. I've got you.'

Rita took a drink of her sparkling water. 'The other night, at Jago's place, it was... intense. We were both a bit drunk; well, I was more than a bit drunk. He kissed me, and it felt like everything cracked open. He picked me up, literally carried me through to the lounge. It was like all the grief, tension and guilt and longing just spilled out. He started to, well you know... and I let him. I *wanted* him. God, I really did.' Jilly raised her already raised eyebrows but stayed quiet. 'But then I just snapped. I pushed him off, started crying, said awful things. That he'd betrayed me. That I couldn't do it. I ran out.' Rita's face fell. 'I'm so mixed up, Jilly. Aside from this, my body's all over the place, my periods have started vanishing, coming back, then stopping again, so my hormones are like the bloody shipping forecast. I think menopause is creeping up on me too. I'm certainly not ready for that. Everything is just so messy!'

Jilly placed a steadying hand on her arm. 'You're grieving. You're trying to move forward. And your mind and now body are throwing curveballs. Of *course* it's messy.'

Rita shook her head. 'But it's Archie's *brother*, Jilly. Isn't that wrong?'

Jilly leaned back, took a sip of her drink and was thoughtful for a moment. 'No. You loved Archie. Deeply. And it didn't end because you stopped loving him; it ended because life stole him. Jago's not a replacement. He's not a carbon copy. But he shares something with the man you loved, and maybe that's not such a terrible thing.'

Rita blinked, her eyes beginning to sting.

'Follow your heart,' Jilly added softly. 'Not what you think your heart *should* be doing. There's no rulebook here. We all deserve a slice of happiness, Rita. And after what you've been through, especially you.'

A young bar man placed two bowls of chips in front of them and winked at Jilly.

Rita laughed through the lump in her throat. 'Oh my God, did you see the way he looked at you? He can only be twenty.'

'Twenty-two, actually. And I have to say, after our chat with Annie the other day about men, I found myself wanting to sprint towards the floppy-haired ones who know what they're doing in bed. Who cares if they're confused about their careers? It's some good sex I'm interested in whilst I look for the grown-up with a huge pension and no emotional baggage.'

'Whatever floats your boat, I guess. And yeah... he *is* hot.'

Jilly leaned in, eyes twinkling. 'Talking of hot, one of my clients pointed him out to me the other day. Jago, I mean. He was down at the harbour, chatting to some bloke with a speedboat. Said he was the talk of the Seahaven Bay Facebook Gossip Group under "eligible bachelors".'

Rita raised an eyebrow.

'I'm telling you, girlfriend' – Jilly grinned and took a sip of her vodka and tonic – 'that man is *hot*. Total catnip. I mean, come on... broad shoulders, brooding expression, bit of mystery? That's the jackpot. But more than that... from what you told me, he's not a bad man. And he's yours for the taking if you want him.'

Rita looked down, stirring the ice in her glass. 'Not sure I like other women lusting over him.'

Jilly smirked. 'Well, that's a good start.'

Rita gave her a look. 'Don't push it.'

'I'm just saying' – Jilly leaned back, smug now – 'you said it yourself. He wasn't trying to trick you or twist things with the will. He was trying to protect you. There's a difference. And deep down, I think you know that.'

Rita sighed, but a small smile tugged at her lips. 'Maybe.'

'Maybe,' Jilly echoed. 'That's a hell of a lot closer to "yes" than "no".'

And with that the Pilates instructor raised her glass. 'To hot men, good instincts, and not letting fear get in the way.'

FORTY-EIGHT

The next morning, Rita sat on the sofa in the den, the will spread out on her lap. The room was stuffy with late-summer heat and outside, bees buzzed lazily around the lavender bushes, but inside, everything was still.

The sudden sound of a voice approaching made her jump so high that Henry barked.

'Honestly, if you frown at that paper any harder, it'll catch fire.'

Rita's heart leaped into her throat. 'Bloody hell, Hilda!'

Hilda stood in the doorway, one eyebrow cocked and a pink trainer tapping lightly against the wooden floor.

'The back door was open,' Hilda tutted. 'I could've been anyone.'

Rita let out a shaky laugh and wiped tea off her shorts with a tissue. 'You scared the life out of me.'

'Good. You needed a jolt.' Hilda's tone softened as her eyes dropped to the paper in Rita's lap. 'You found it, then.'

Rita paused, fingers tracing a crease in the corner of the document.

'He left everything to me. The house. A few savings he'd hidden. Even cited that ridiculous stone gnome he stuck by the pond that I hated. He knew that would make me laugh.' Rita's eyes glistened.

'Sir Cedric,' Hilda said fondly.

'He named his brother as executor.' Rita smiled weakly.

With a slow shake of her head, Hilda plonked herself down on the window seat.

'And there was a provision for one Mateo Serrano, but that's OK. I get it. It's a token amount but will make a difference to him. An amount to show that Teo was loved by him, despite all, I guess.'

Hilda sighed. 'Finding Carmen and bringing her here, I thought it may help you move on, you know. My Archie was a good boy and we mothers protect, don't we? Do what we think is best for our kids. He didn't cheat on you, Rita. He was doing what Archie did best, trying to keep everyone happy.'

'I realise that now.' Rita swallowed hard, the back of her throat tight. 'It just feels so final now. Like he's... properly gone. And there will always be a space that won't ever be filled and what do you do with that?'

Hilda didn't speak for a moment. Then she covered Rita's hand with her own.

'You live in it. You plant something in it. You scream into it if you need to. And it's OK to fill it. And bit by bit the space gets less, but that doesn't mean the memory has to.'

Rita blinked rapidly, tears threatening. 'I hate that you always say the right thing.'

Hilda gave her hand a squeeze and stood. 'Now. Come on. Enough wallowing. Rumour has it you are having a little birthday-come-thank-your-team get-together and I'm sure it's not organising itself.'

'Yes, I'd better get in the Snack Shack and give Zenya a hand.'

'Have you spoken to Thomas?' Hilda added gently.

Rita's voice wobbled. 'I've left him a couple of messages, but I can't get hold of him.' With a sigh, Rita stood, folding the will and tucking it between the pages of her now dog-eared copy of *Wild*, the book that had nudged her toward starting the retreat.

'Thank you, Hilda. And I mean that truly. I can't even imagine the pain you've been through yourself.' Rita paused, her voice barely steady. 'With everything.'

Hilda gave the smallest nod, her eyes shining. She didn't speak. She didn't need to. She knew Rita knew and that was enough. The old woman then uncharacteristically looped her arm through Rita's. 'But before we head outside, there's somewhere else I think we both need to go.'

Rita looked up, instantly wary. 'Hilda?'

'Just keep walking.'

They crossed the hallway slowly, side by side, their footsteps soft on the wooden boards. The big lounge door was ajar, light spilling out in ribbons of warmth and colour from its huge bay window with the view of the sea.

Rita paused in the doorway. Her breath caught. The room was just as it had been. The sofa, the chairs, the photos, the piano. Nothing had changed and yet everything had. This was the room where Archie used to sit in the mornings, reading the paper aloud like it was a radio broadcast. This was the room where they danced, badly, after too much wine. The room that had held him, and her, and all the ordinary days that had quietly meant everything. Now dusty and a bit musty, but still her favourite room in the house.

Her throat tightened. 'I haven't been in here since he died,' Rita whispered.

'Love doesn't live in the dust, Rita. It's in the people who stay, and the life you keep choosing.'

Rita's tears welled, unbidden. 'As mothers-in-law go, I'm not sure what I did to deserve you.'

Hilda smirked. 'Oh, probably something terrible in a past life.'

Hilda walked over to the bay window, took a moment to drink in the wide coastal view, then turned to face her son's wife. 'And for the record, I'm OK with whomever you choose to share your heart with in this one.'

Rita's lip wobbled. Hilda sniffed loudly, then shook herself.

'Now stop all this maudlin nonsense. I need a cigarette.'

FORTY-NINE

Rita had thought of nothing else but Jago since the night she'd run out on him. Not properly. Not clearly. But like a song stuck in the background of her thoughts, looping and unresolved. She didn't know what to do, not yet. She was waiting. Waiting for the moment to feel right, for her heart to stop racing every time his name entered her mind. To be a grown-up and work out exactly the best way to deal with a situation that was so huge, so scary, and so out of control.

If you don't know what to do, do nothing. Let the answer come to you.

So, she had done nothing, except check her phone more times than she could admit, hoping he might come to her first. Hoping he'd open the conversation, close the distance, make it easy. But he hadn't. And now the silence between them felt heavy. Awkward. Like a thread they'd both let go of at the same time.

She felt awkward, too. Off-balance. Because if she did open herself to him, really open herself, what would that mean? Was it too soon? Would it be disrespecting Archie? What would the twins think? And were her feelings duping her, was Jago truly who she wanted, or was he just a shelter in the storm of her grief?

The questions had no shape. No voice. Just a constant churn beneath the surface.

The smell of roast potatoes and thyme filled the Snack Shack, curling around the bunting Kelly had taped to the ceiling in a slightly wonky zigzag. A paper crown was sliding off the back of Sennen's head as she grinned over her third helping of Zenya's chicken traybake.

'How can anyone make anything so delicious with their own fair hands?' Sennen mumbled, mouth full and slightly inebriated on the flowing fizz.

'Because I use love,' Zenya said, taking a slurp from her flute. 'And three whole bulbs of garlic on this occasion.'

'As long as you didn't use Mavis, Vera, Blanche or Deirdre,' Kelly hooted.

'Says the cockerel killer!' Sennen guffawed.

'I thought I could smell it from the annexe.' Jude laughed, leaning back, his face flushed, as Teo looked at him adoringly.

The birthday energy was buzzing, and the table was crowded with food and people Rita loved. She looked around and smiled at Kelly fanning herself with a huge flamenco-type fan that Hilda had lent her, and announcing, 'I swear if one more person says "peri-menopause" to me, I'm moving to Iceland and taking them with me.'

'Not you as well,' Rita added.

Hilda, meanwhile, had commandeered the end of the table and was now giving Zenya a detailed description of how Eric had enticed her into his hot tub naked. Laughter rippled between them, cracker gifts were strewn everywhere, and someone had stuck a cherry tomato onto the top of a bottle of Prosecco like it was a party hat.

It was all joy, all colour, all that Rita had hoped for. All that was missing was her number one son. For it was his birthday too.

'So, when are your next retreat guests arriving?' Kelly wiped her mouth on a napkin.

'Last week of August, so we've got a bit of time,' Rita said, starting to clear some plates to make way for the cake.

'I still think we should get a mobile sauna in one of the outhouses,' Teo suggested.

'Maybe. Once that group has paid their way, I'll take a look.' Rita sat back down.

Hilda took a slug of her drink. 'Because nothing says relaxation like boiling to death in a shed.'

Rita raised her glass. 'Before we all get too wasted, I just want to say thank you. To Zenya and Teo, for keeping everything afloat, feeding us, and somehow making this place feel like home and a healthy retreat at the same time.'

Teo stood and took a small bow. Zenya waved her fork like a queen.

'Oh, and let's raise a glass for Stan,' Rita added quickly. 'His wife's got a bad cold, and he didn't want to leave her. But I said we'd save him some cake.'

'Two bits,' said Teo. 'One for his wife and one for him being the biggest sweetheart of a man.'

Zenya nodded. 'Done. I'll label them. FOR STAN: DO NOT TOUCH, EVEN IF YOU'RE DRUNK.'

She then slipped out the back without a word, and a moment later returned, carrying the birthday cake in both hands. A glorious, slightly lopsided Victoria sponge crowned with candles, the last strawberries from the garden and oodles of clotted cream.

'We ready?' She grinned.

Everyone leaned in, the flickering flames dancing on Sennen's face. She blinked quickly, trying to hold it together, but her eyes were already welling.

'Oi,' said Rita gently, nudging her side. 'It's unlucky to cry on your birthday.'

'It's not just my birthday, though, is it?' Sennen whispered, eyes on the candles. 'It's *our* birthday. Mine and Thom's.'

And then, just as the first notes of 'Happy Birthday' filled the room, the flap of the Snack Shack marquee flew open. And to Rita's joy, Thomas Jory stood there, all six foot two of him, auburn hair catching the light, looking more like Archie with every passing day. His eyes immediately searched for his sister. 'Happy birthday, Thomas and Sennen!' he sang out, not missing a note as his voice joined the chorus.

Sennen laughed. Rita felt her heart skip a beat.

The song ended in a ragged cheer. Teo clapped. Jude blew an invisible trumpet. Zenya set the cake down triumphantly, then handed Sennen a knife.

'Make a wish,' Kelly shouted.

Sennen glanced at her brother. 'Already did.'

Later, when the cake was half eaten, the sun slipping into the horizon, and the Prosecco bottles mostly empty, Rita found Thom standing at the edge of the orchard, facing the fields and the wide shimmering stretch of sea beyond.

She walked towards him quietly. 'Did you get some cake?'

He nodded, not turning. Just stared out over the trees now promising their crops of apples, pears and plums. A lone gull passed overhead, reminding them they were very much in the moment.

'I'm sorry,' Thom said eventually, his voice low. 'I've been a bit of a mess since... everything. And I can't even imagine how much I've hurt you.'

Rita breathed in slowly. 'Let's sit.'

They sat on the bench seat at the end of the orchard. Thom took a visible breath. 'I've avoided the farm because it reminded me too much of Dad.'

'I understand.' Rita reached for his hands across the table, and he let her hold them.

'I didn't know how to talk about him or Jago. The will. Any of it. And then after me sending that letter to you... and Sennen letting me know about Teo... well, even with your message to come today... it was just... easier not to call.'

Rita looked at him, properly looked, and saw the little boy he used to be, wild-haired, fiercely loyal, and now pouring out a heart that had always seemed too big for his chest. Her Thomas was back.

'Thom, it's OK,' Rita soothed.

'No. It's not, Mum, let me finish. I knew too much. A few years ago, I overheard a conversation between Dad and another man. Dad had his phone on speaker... he was in the barn... he didn't know I was outside... and I listened... and I wish I hadn't. And I didn't really understand what it was about, until Dad died and then I realised that someone else may be getting some of our share – mine and Sennen's, and I didn't think it fair. And I so appreciate you emailing me the will, to put it straight and...'

Rita sighed deeply. This wasn't the time to tell Thomas that he had another uncle in Jago and that he had been the other man at the end of the phone. 'And when you saw Jago that time I spotted you... was it really that the sheep had escaped?'

'Yes, yes, that was all true. Jago didn't say a word to me. Nobody is planning to take the farm from under you. I've ended all the solicitor representation. I'm such a twat!'

'It broke me.' Rita couldn't help it. 'To know my son was trying to oust me out of my own house.'

'Please don't,' Thom begged. 'I realise now I didn't really want the money, or for you to sell. I just didn't want a complete stranger getting something, especially as I realised that you probably knew nothing about it. I just want to know that you're OK. That we're OK. I love you, Mum, and I'm going to come and see you more. I promise.'

'I'll believe that when I see it.' Rita was more measured now.

'I haven't been the best son, I know that. I'm driven, my job is important and when Dad went... I couldn't face it here. I miss him so much, so I can't even imagine what it's like for you.'

Rita thought of not being able to walk into the big lounge for nine months. 'I get it. I really do. And we're OK. Even when we're messy. You're my son, for God's sake.'

Thomas hesitated, then reached into his pocket and pulled out a small jewellery box. He held it out to her, voice thick. 'I... I know it's silly, but I wanted you to have this.'

Rita blinked, confused. He opened it, revealing a delicate necklace sparkling in the fading light, an exact replica of the one Archie had given her for her thirtieth birthday, lost in the mud months ago. Her throat tightened.

'Dad would have done the same,' Thom said, voice breaking, eyes glistening. 'I just... I wanted you to have it.'

Rita felt tears sting, warm and sudden. She took the box and pressed it to her chest. 'Oh, Thom... We will never forget him, love. He will always be part of us.'

Thom got up, lifted his mum off the bench seat, then surprised them both by pulling her into a tight bear hug. A hug that didn't ask for anything other than his mother's love.

FIFTY

It was just after ten the next day when Stan turned up at the farm, unannounced as ever, in his usual uniform of sun-faded cords and an old jumper, despite it being twenty-five degrees. He stood in the kitchen doorway with a paper bag in hand. Everyone else was still in bed, he assumed, since the celebrations hadn't finished until the early hours.

'Mrs Jory. I've brought you a slice of Mrs Bodkin's bread and butter pudding and a nudge, as I'm thinking you might need both this morning.'

Rita stopped loading the dishwasher and laughed. 'You're so right. Far too much fun was had by all. And what do you mean by a nudge?'

He stepped inside and set the bag on the table. 'Might be worth taking a walk up to the Singing Tree, that's all I'm saying.'

Her heart did a tiny somersault. 'Why?'

He just shrugged. 'Call it a hunch. Or maybe a whisper from someone who's not quite done saying what they wanted to say.'

Rita's mouth fell open. 'Stan, was it you who's been leaving messages for me in the Singing Tree?'

The friendly farmhand winked. 'All I'm going to say to that question, Mrs Jory, is ask no questions and I'll tell you no lies.'

Rita sped up to the High Meadow in the Jimny. The breeze was up. The sea in the distance looked like a shaken sheet, glinting in the morning light. She felt absurdly nervous.

The note was tucked into the crevice where the others had been. Folded neatly. Her name written on the outside, this time in handwriting she recognised.

She opened it slowly, hardly daring to breathe, and began to read.

> Dear Rita,
> 'Hope' is the thing with feathers
> That perches in the soul –
> And sings the tune without the words –
> And never stops – at all –
> If you still feel what I think you feel, meet me here at sunrise on Sunday.
> Here's hoping.
> Jago X

She stared at the words, her throat catching. Then, as she ran her fingers across the etching on Archie's bench, the tears came. The wind whispered through the branches, like the tree was urging her to believe it would all be OK. She folded the note carefully, held it to her chest for a minute and then, slowly, reached for her wedding ring. With trembling fingers, she turned it once, twice, then slid it from her finger. For a moment, she simply stared at it in her palm, so small, and yet it had held so much. Then, reaching into the tree's natural cubby hole, she placed the ring inside. Her voice cracked as she whispered to the wind, 'I will always love you, Archie Jory.'

FIFTY-ONE

Later that day, Rita insisted Sennen and Thomas come with her in the Jimny to their favourite beach. As the little blue car rattled and bounced along the coast road, the three of them were jostled, laughter bubbling out, at each bend that was taken.

'Is this thing even road legal?' Thomas grunted, bracing a hand on the dashboard as they hit another dip and managing to stop his head from bashing the roof. 'Why don't you use Dad's... the Land Rover, I mean, it must be a lot safer.'

'Because Jimmy and I have a very close relationship,' Rita announced, deftly parking up as near to the beach as she could. Thomas turned in his seat and exchanged a cheeky wink with his sister, quietly amused by their mother's declaration.

The morning was humid and close. A blanket of low grey cloud hung over the bay, threatening a summer storm. The tide was far out, leaving behind a vast expanse of damp, rippled sand streaked with glistening seaweed and pools that reflected the dull sky. The air smelled faintly of the earlier rain.

'Now I don't want you to think your mother is going mad, although she clearly has recently, but we did this at our moonlight mantras session during the first retreat.'

Sennen glanced at Thomas, amused. 'What is it? Cold-water swimming? I really don't want to go in there on a day like this.'

'Worse.' Rita grinned, pulling a drawstring pouch from her coat pocket. 'Woo-woo stuff.'

'Woo-woo, what?' Thomas frowned.

The beach was surprisingly quiet apart from a few dog walkers in the distance. Rita led them down towards the tideline.

'Everyone picks a stone,' she explained, handing the pouch to Sennen. 'Then you hold it, and you say, or think, something you want to leave behind. Or something you're ready to welcome in. Then you lob it into the sea.'

Thomas gave a dry smile. 'And the sea magically fixes our lives?'

'No, love,' she said gently. 'But it helps to say it aloud. To let it go.'

'Can you imagine what Dad would have said about this?' Sennen laughed.

'Yes...' Rita smiled, eyes misting as she clutched her pebble. 'He'd probably tell us we were a bunch of sentimental fools and ask if he could go to the Winking Pilchard instead.'

They each took a pebble. For a moment, the three stood in silence, staring out at the endless horizon.

'I'll go first.' Sennen turned the stone over in her hand, then closed her eyes. 'I want to stop pretending everything's fine all the time. I want to be allowed to feel things and talk to either of you about it when I can't process it myself.'

She threw the stone with a firm, clean arc. Rita looked up to quell her tears.

Thomas looked down at his. He swallowed. 'I want to forgive myself and be forgiven fully for the way I treated my mother. I was angry, and I didn't say the right things. I want to do better as a son from now on.'

He sent the pebble skipping.

Rita smiled at them both. 'I want to believe I can still make good choices. To be always ready for open and honest conversation with my children and believe in myself that it's OK to let other people in.'

Her stone made a soft plop as it disappeared beneath the surface.

They stood together for a moment longer, the wind tugging at their jackets.

'Right then.' Rita brushed her hands together. 'Tea and cake in Betty's Tearoom?'

'Always,' Sennen shouted.

'Can we listen to *my* music on the way there?' Thomas asked.

FIFTY-TWO

Rita slipped quietly out of the farmhouse, the door clicking shut behind her. The world outside was hushed, suspended in that soft grey stillness of civil twilight, the fleeting time when night had loosened its grip, but day had yet to take hold. Even at this unearthly hour, she'd put on mascara and lipstick, a summery floral dress, and her old denim jacket.

As she crested the hill, a slow bloom of colour began to stretch across the horizon.

Jago was already there, sitting on Archie's bench beneath the Singing Tree. Hands clasped between his knees, head bowed like a man in prayer. When he looked up, his eyes met hers, full of that complicated warmth that had begun to rise between them in recent weeks.

She walked the last few steps toward him, slow and cautious.

'I wasn't sure you'd come,' Jago said, smiling softly.

'I wasn't sure either,' she replied. 'But I needed to know what this is. Whether it's real... or just grief playing tricks on us.'

He tapped the bench beside him. 'You timed it perfectly. Look.'

Slowly, the sun began to rise, inching up from the edge of the sea like a great golden coin being pushed through the surface of the world.

'I'll never tire of this,' Rita murmured.

'And I'll never tire of you.' He took her hand and kissed it gently. 'A new start. A new day, Rita Jory.' The dimple appeared. 'And whenever you've got a spare second, minute, hour, month, year... I want to spend it with you.' He looked at her through his impossible lashes. 'I meant what I said the other night. My love for you is real. I didn't plan any of this. But you're just so damn beautiful, how could I not?'

Rita gave a sad smile, folding her arms against the morning chill. 'You should've just told me everything.'

'I know,' he said quietly. 'I was scared. Scared it would end *this* before it even began.'

She let out a long breath. 'I loved him, you know. With everything I had. And he loved me. He really did.'

'I know.' Jago's voice was barely a whisper. 'I saw it. I envied it.'

Rita brushed her fingers along the edge of the bench.

'He's gone, but he's still everywhere. In the sea. In this tree. In Thomas's stubbornness. In Sennen's laugh. But he's not here, not in this moment. Not in this... ache I feel when I see you and don't know what to do with it.'

Jago reached out and tipped her chin up, kissing her softly on the lips. 'I'll never replace him, Rita.'

'I know that.' She nodded. 'But I want you to know this isn't just because you remind me of him. You've shown me who you are. Helping with the yurts, paying for Stan's time, the marquee, delivering Vince and Billy, the flowers to wish me well... You're a good man, Jago Jenken.'

He stood and helped her to her feet. 'So... what do we do with it?'

She looked up at him, eyes glassy but calm. 'I think... we stop running. From this. From ourselves.'

When he leaned in and kissed her, she didn't think, she just melted. Warm lips, and the sexy feeling of a night's stubble against her cheek. Her fingers curled into the fabric of his hoodie.

Somewhere behind them, a blackbird startled into flight.

Rita pulled away, breathless. 'The yurts are unlocked,' she whispered. 'You know if we wanted to... talk more. Or maybe not talk.'

'Oh very much not talk,' he replied, his expression smouldering.

They ran. Giggling like teenagers, hand in hand across the field. The grass was damp underfoot, the air crisp and clear. Rita's laugh echoed across the High Meadow far louder than she meant it to be. Jago ducked through the flap, holding it open for her like a gentleman, even though his eyes said something far less chivalrous. The yurt was dim inside. The air cool, but neither of them noticed. Rita tugged his top off. He pulled her dress over her head. Clothes were strewn across the rug. For a moment they just stared at each other, half naked, breathless, vulnerable. It was clumsy at first, arms knocking, knees bumping, a low laugh here, a whispered 'hang on' there, but it was real, raw, breathless sex that came not from lust alone but a measured understanding of each other and what was to come.

Afterwards, they lay tangled together, her head on his chest, both of them staring up at the lantern swaying gently above them.

'That was unexpected.' Rita snuggled into him further.

'Speak for yourself.' Jago smiled. 'I've been planning that for days.'

She thwacked him with a pillow. 'You absolute...'

'... gentleman,' he finished, grinning, the dimple oh so evident.

Eventually, they dressed slowly, shyly. Rita's hair was a mess. Jago's socks inside out. They opened the yurt flap and peered out, checking the coast was clear.

Hand in hand, they headed towards Jago's Defender. Once inside, Rita took a breath.

'You'll need to be patient with me.' She searched his face. 'I can't promise I'm fully ready for whatever this is. But what I can promise is that I want to be.'

'Then I'll wait.' He beamed. 'For as many sunrises as it takes.'

And as the sun rose quietly over High Meadow, Rita Jory smiled to herself. Letting it be was its own kind of wild, and for once, she truly understood what that meant.

A LETTER FROM THE AUTHOR

Don't miss out on all my news!
A huge thank you for taking the time to read the first of my series, set in Seahaven Bay. I hope you love my new characters' journeys as much as I enjoyed writing them.

If you want to join other readers in hearing all about my new releases with Storm, please do sign up to my mailing list.

www.stormpublishing.co/nicola-may

And if you want to keep up to date with all my other publications and other writerly goings on, you can sign up to my mailing list:

www.nicolamay.com

Your review is like gold dust!
If you could also spare a few moments to leave a review that would be hugely appreciated. Even a brief review can make all the difference in encouraging a reader to discover my books for the first time. Thank you so much!

www.nicolamay.com

facebook.com/NicolaMayAuthor

x.com/nicolamay1

instagram.com/author_nicola

WHY I WROTE THIS STORY

I've been asked many times over the years if I'd ever go back to Cockleberry Bay. While Seahaven Bay isn't quite the same, I think it's the closest I've come to capturing a similar spirit.

Cornwall has always held a special place in my heart: the salty air, the wild coastline, and that wonderful sense of community that makes small coastal towns so magical. It felt like the perfect backdrop for a whole new set of stories.

This time, I wanted to introduce you to a cast of characters who are funny, flawed, and hopefully feel just as real to you as they do to me. There's love and friendship at the core, but also a little dash of mystery.

Writing *Escape to Seahaven Bay* has felt like coming home in many ways, and I hope when you read it, you'll feel the same

Thanks again for being part of this amazing journey with me and I hope you'll stay in touch – I have so many more stories and ideas to entertain you with!

Nicola May

www.ingramcontent.com/pod-product-compliance
Lightning Source LLC
Chambersburg PA
CBHW011554190726
48287CB00010B/2887